ROSANNA
OF THE
AMISH

Rosanna of the Amish tells the unusual story of an Irish orphan, Rosanna McGonegal, who was reared by Elizabeth Yoder, an unmarried Amish woman.

The author, Rosanna's youngest son, reveals how she was initiated into Amish ways and adopted their customs and practices.

You will enjoy reading about—

- Rosanna's first husking bee and singing.
- German preaching services and choosing ministers.
- Amish weddings and funerals.
- Simple dress, hard work, and good food.
- Wrestling matches between farm boys.
- The Amish taking care of their own.
- Warm family and community relationships.

This book portrays simply and honestly the religious, social, and economic traditions the Amish have followed for three centuries and still follow.

ROSANNA QUILTING

ROSANNA
OF THE
AMISH

JOSEPH W. YODER

ILLUSTRATIONS BY
JOY DUNN KEENAN

CENTENNIAL EDITION

HERALD PRESS
Scottdale, Pennsylvania
Waterloo, Ontario

Library of Congress Cataloging-in-Publication Data
Yoder, Joseph Warren, 1872-1956.
    Rosanna of the Amish / by Joseph W. Yoder. — Centennial ed.
      p. cm.
    Includes bibliographical references (p.).
    ISBN 0-8361-9018-1
    1. Yoder, Rosanna McGonegal. 2. Amish—Pennsylvania—
      Biography.
  I. Title.
  F160.M45Y62 1995
  974.8'041'088287—dc20
  [B]
                                                        95-10113
                                                                  CIP

The paper used in this publication is recycled and meets the minimum requirements of American National Standard for Information Sciences—Permanence of Paper for Printed Library Materials, ANSI Z39.48-1984.

Library of Congress Catalog Card Number: 95-10113
International Standard Book Number: 0-8361-9018-1
Printed in the United States of America
Book design by Paula M. Johnson

04 03 02 01 00 99 98 97 96 95 10 9 8 7 6 5 4 3 2 1

377,500 copies in print in all editions

*Dedicated to
my mother,
Rosanna McGonegal Yoder*

Editor's Note

Special thanks to Rosanna McGonegal Yoder Hostetler, great-granddaughter of this storied Rosanna, and John E. Sharp, director of the Mennonite Church Historical Committee and Archives. Both are Big Valley natives. They read this Centennial Edition and gave valuable counsel for improving the text and ensuring authenticity. Hostetler also wrote a new foreword, and Sharp supplied map information.

Contents

Foreword

I T C O U L D H A V E B E E N a balmy spring day in 1930. My father and expectant mother were visiting Dad's childhood home near Belleville, Pennsylvania. They took a respectful walk through the Locust Grove Cemetery and checked gravestones for family names. This was customary in those times, particularly if folks were from a different community, as was my mother.

Mother and Dad stood by his grandmother Rosanna's gravestone, reading the inscription: "Born 1838, daughter of Patrick and Bridget O'Connor McGonegal. Died 1895, wife of Christian Yoder, Belleville." Perhaps then and there they decided to name me Rosanna, if I were a girl. On June 9, 1930, I did become Rosanna's namesake.

My great-uncle J. W. Yoder, singer, lecturer, and compiler of Amish hymns and other music, came to our home many times during the 1930s. Often on his visits, he told us about his project, writing a book to tell the story of his mother who was born Irish Catholic, orphaned at the age of five days, and raised by a devout Amish woman.

On those visits, J. W. spoke with deep feeling about ways the American public misunderstood the Amish people. I recall his mention of Helen Martin's *Tillie, A Mennonite Maid* (1904), which he felt was a slur on plain people. "I want to write a book which shows the true picture of Amish customs and practices in religion, industry, and social life," he would say. What better way to do this than through a narrative of his mother's life? She herself was a faithful Amish woman, thanks to the unusual turn of events in her early life.

As a ten-year-old listening to this dramatic author and singer, I was awed and felt honored by the attention I received for being his mother's namesake. That changed when I arrived home from school one day to encounter a special request. Great-uncle J. W. had come and wanted me to dress up as an Amish girl to be portrayed in his book!

What was I to do? I made a hard decision on the spot, shook my head, and protested, "Please, no!" Then I disappeared upstairs into my room. Inside myself, I said "I'm sorry" to my great-grandmother, Rosanna. Fifth-grader that I was, how could I stand the ridicule of my peers? This was a disappointment to my family, especially to my esteemed great-uncle.

Fifty-five years later, I am honored that I could preview the third edition of *Rosanna of the Amish*. I was moved. I feel that I have been inside another culture and in touch again with one of the generations before me. "To be in touch with the past, we receive more than we can ever give" (Edwin Muir).

While reading, I paid attention to the mention of Rosanna and Little Crist's firstborn son, my grand-father Yost McGonegal Yoder. My dad spoke of him as a horse trainer and farmer, and I saw those interests emerge in the family story.

Currently *Rosanna* is among many books written about the Amish. Differing from many others, however, *Rosanna* is not fiction. It is notable for its documented settings, names, and happenings. This new edition appears in 1995, exactly a hundred years after Rosanna's death.

I commend this story to you. Although the events happened more than a century ago, the book was written with sensitivity and care. *Rosanna of the Amish* has thus become a monument to my great-uncle J. W. Yoder, who set out to share about the Amish and their deep commitment to a way of life through the story of his mother.

—Rosanna McGonegal Yoder Hostetler
Scottdale, Pennsylvania

Preface

THE AUTHOR WAS inspired to write *Rosanna of the Amish* because several writers with vivid imaginations and little regard for facts have published books about the Amish and missed almost entirely the cardinal virtues of this people. Some authors have exaggerated a certain characteristic out of all proportion and have made even an Amish virtue look ridiculous. Apparently their goal was to write an unusual story rather than to adhere to the truth.

Joseph W. Yoder was born of Amish parents and grew to manhood as one of the Amish. He knows his people intimately. Thus he can explain their customs in minute detail, including social, economic, and religious practices.

All the episodes in *Rosanna of the Amish* are based on fact. All but one name in the book is the real name of the person mentioned, and the story is the actual life story of Rosanna. Instead of making fun of the Amish, as some writers apparently delight in doing, the author desires to tell the truth about this devout people. He does so by setting forth their sincere efforts to live by the Bible, as well as their peculiarities. What seems odd to the outsider becomes a virtue when experience enables one to understand the underlying motives and principles.

The author personally knew every principal character in the book except Simeon Riehl, whose name is fictitious. The O'Connor boys and Rosanna's parents were the author's ancestors, and he has portrayed them in accord with family lore. Every Amish ceremony and service is described exactly as it takes place and as it has been carried out practically unchanged for three centuries.

—*Joseph Warren Yoder*

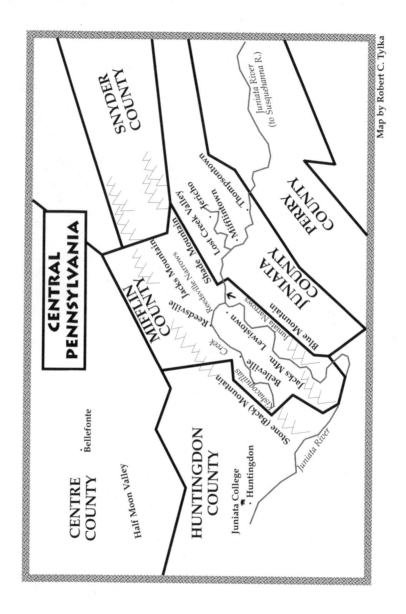

CENTRAL PENNSYLVANIA

SNYDER COUNTY

PERRY COUNTY

JUNIATA COUNTY

Juniata River
(to Susquehanna R.)

Thompsontown

Mifflintown

Jericho

Lost Creek Valley

Shade Mountain

Reedsville Narrows

Jacks Mountain

Reedsville

Blue Mountain

Juniata Narrows

Lewistown

Jacks Mtn.

Belleville

Kishacoquillas Creek

MIFFLIN COUNTY

Stone (Back) Mountain

Juniata River

HUNTINGDON COUNTY

Juniata College

Huntingdon

CENTRE COUNTY

Bellefonte

Half Moon Valley

Map by Robert C. Tylka

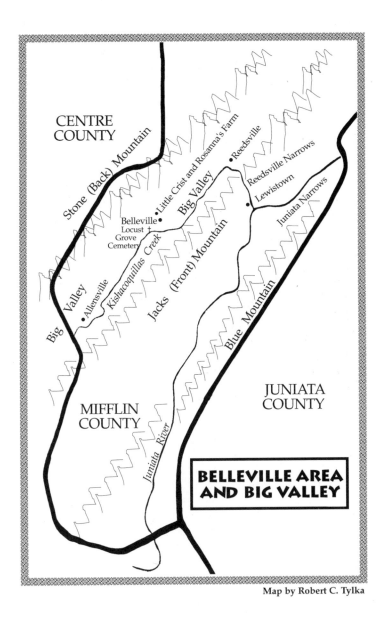

CENTRE
COUNTY

Stone (Back) Mountain

Little Crist and Rosanna's Farm

Reedsville

Big Valley

Reedsville Narrows

Belleville
Locust †
Grove
Cemetery

Lewistown

Juniata Narrows

Kishacoquillas Creek

Jacks (Front) Mountain

Big
Valley

Allensville

Blue Mountain

JUNIATA
COUNTY

MIFFLIN
COUNTY

Juniata River

**BELLEVILLE AREA
AND BIG VALLEY**

Map by Robert C. Tylka

CHAPTER 1

The Voyage

THE POTATO FIELDS of Ireland were already waving their luxurious growth of green on that hot afternoon in June early in the 1800s. Big John O'Connor leaned on his spade in deep meditation. He had been to the village tavern the evening before and heard Tim O'Tool tell of wonderful opportunities in America. Tim had just returned from a three-year sojourn in the new country. With many a flourish of head and hand, he told of the easy jobs to be found in merica.

"Why, could you believe it, biys?" cried Tim. "All I iver did was carry bricks up three stories, and a man up there, sure, he did all the work."

It was the freedom and the opportunities that John O'Connor was thinking about. He had been to the village just yesterday to see Sandy McGinnis about learning the blacksmith trade and was sent away. "You're a farmer's son, ain't ye? Then why do you come here wantin' to be a blacksmith? Home wid ye, and do your faither's bidding—a farmer's what the likes o' you is calculated to be."

Those words were still ringing in his ears and burning in his heart: "A farmer's what the likes o' you is calculated to be." As he hilled the potatoes, he muttered to himself, "I guess it's true, if I stay in these parts. But America! What did Tim O'Tool say about America? 'Why,' sez 'e, 'in America a man can be whativer he has a mind to.' Why should I wear out my young life settin' potatoes in Ireland when I might be ownin' a business in America?"

As he resumed his work, speeding up a bit to make up for his meditations, he overtook his younger brother William and called out to him, "Step aside, me biy. You're interferin' with the progress of a prosperous American businessman."

"American businessman, me eye!" exclaimed William in wide-eyed wonder.

Then William doffed his hat and made a mock bow. "Well, may the saints be blessin' ye. Might you be having a job for your humble servant and kinsman, also of Irish descent, Mr. Prosperous Business American Man, or whativer it is ye aire?"

That evening at the supper table, when the meal was well under way, John O'Connor addressed his father thoughtfully. "Faither, is it not the rule o' Ireland that a son must engage in the same business as his faither? Sandy McGinnis told me as much yisterday when I asked him if he would be good enough to teach me to be a blacksmith. 'A farmer is what the likes o' you is calculated to be,' he snarled, as though I was a blockhead and he was teachin' me the rule o' three.

"But at the tavern last night, Tim O'Tool, who has just returned from America, said that there are no family rules nor trade rules over there. A young man may choose any work he fancies.

"Faither, I've been thinkin' all day that if you and Mither are willing, I'll be sailin' for America the last o' the month. Tim says the harvest will be on then, and they'll be needin' a lot of cradlers. By workin' in the harvest field, I could earn enough to tide me over while I look for a trade that suits me fancy."

As John spoke, his mother rose from the table and busied herself about the stove to hide the tears that were beginning to trickle down her cheeks.

The father listened in silence to all John said, and it was not surprising to him. John was an excellent worker, always taking the heaviest tasks cheerfully. But he knew that John did his work as a dutiful son, that he never wanted to be a farmer, and that his heart was in learning a trade or business. These words kindled fires of love and admiration in the father's eyes as he looked at his broad-shouldered son, so much like himself.

"Me biy, it would be no light matter for me and

your mither to see you breakin' the family circle like that, but what you say is the truth, and we would not be standin' in your way. You're a likely lad, and in great free America, you'll have a chance to rise to the top. Someday your mither and me will be proud of our son, a prosperous American businessman. May the saints bless you."

As the father spoke these words of seeming finality, Bridget, the only daughter in the family and next to John in age, could no longer conceal her emotions. She wept audibly as she hid her face in her apron.

"Don't be screechin' the likes o' that, Bridget, for someday you'll be comin' to America to see me," John promised. There was more truth in those words than he suspected.

John had scarcely finished when William spoke up. He was just three years younger than John and possessed a fine sense of Irish wit and humor. "Faither, don't you think that the elder brother will be needin' a bodyguard among those fierce American Indians, and don't you think it advisable for me to join the colonies with him?"

The father looked at William with a slight twinkle in his eye, trying to keep back a tear rising in sympathy with Bridget and her mother. "A bodyguard for John would no be a bad idea. If John is willin' to have ye clutterin' after him, I suppose we might as well let you go now as later. It'll be hard for you to conform to the customs of Ireland and be a farmer when there are so many opportunities in America for work and so much liberty in choosing what pleases you."

"You see," boasted William, "I have much experience as a bodyguard. Have I not driven that varmit of a Pat McGonegal off the place when he came here a-courtin' Bridget? Come on, Bridget. Stop your blubberin' and tell your faither that you're willing to give me a recommendation as a first-class bodyguard."

At the thought of giving William a good word for being a bodyguard, Bridget could not help smiling through her tears. "You may be pokin' fun at me, William, but it's no small affair to have your big brother crossin' that awful ocean. As for Pat McGonegal, I think I can take care of him myself without any bodyguard from you."

"Aye, Bridget," said John, "there's entirely too much truth in what you say. If you iver marry that Pat McGonegal, you'll be having to take care o' him, for I don't believe that lazy spalpeen will iver be able to take care o' you."

When the family circle had agreed that John and William should sail for America, the news of their going spread rapidly. They worked hard in the field to help father all they could before leaving. Passersby frequently hailed them with "Safe journey! Good luck in America!" The older men would always add, "And may the saints bless you."

Time passed almost too rapidly. There was much washing and mending and many preparations to make for the great journey. Finally, the last day of June arrived. Bidding their parents good-bye, the two brothers made their way to the harbor where the great steamship *Normandy* lay at anchor. They soon booked passage for New York and were off to America, the land of opportunity.

Tim O'Tool had told them about the great coal mining interests at Scranton. During the weary voyage, they had plenty of time to decide that Scranton should be their destination. On the boat they met other young men from Ireland, England, and Scotland who were out to seek their fortunes. Luckily for John and William, they met James MacDonald from Scotland, also on his way to Scranton. He had been there before and offered to pilot the boys to their destination.

Scranton was in the heart of Pennsylvania's hard-coal fields, and the boys had no trouble finding work. There were houses to build, streets to grade, water systems to lay, and coal to mine, to say nothing of job opportunities in stores and factories and hotels.

John O'Connor was a big man, six feet, two inches tall, weighing 210 pounds, all muscle and sinew. In the White Horse Hotel one night, he helped the landlord throw out three husky and unruly sons of Hungary, whereupon the landlord hired John to tend the bar. The wages were good. In comparison to Ireland, John felt that he was rapidly becoming a prosperous American businessman.

    🙢   🙢   🙢

William O'Connor was somewhat slighter than John but wittier, with the sunshine of Killarney always embellishing his smile. After mass one Sunday morning, he happened to meet Patrick O'Harra, who operated a large store in Scranton. In the flow of conversation, Mr. O'Harra was so delighted with the ready wit and Irish brogue of William that he was moved to say,

"And what are you doin' here, me biy?"

William replied that he was looking for work but that he was not much interested in mining coal.

"Well," responded Mr. O'Harra, "I have a general store down on Main Street. Come down in the mornin' and look the place over. If you like the setup, I might be findin' something for you to do. It's the Irish, you know, that have the will to work and advance."

William showed some interest in the idea but not too much. He didn't want to give the idea that he was anxious for a job in a good store. But he lost no time in seeing John at the hotel and telling him with uncontrollable joy that he too was on the rapid road to becoming a "prosperous American businessman."

The next morning William appeared at the store early enough to show punctuality and late enough not to appear too anxious for the job. He greeted the proprietor with, "The top o' the mornin' to ye, Mr. O'Harra. It's a fine place you're havin' here."

The lilt of his Irish brogue and the sunshine of Killarney in his smile caught Mr. O'Harra's admiration and confidence. The hiring of William O'Connor as a clerk in his large store was merely a matter of pleasant conversation. William worked hard and was conscientious about the smallest details, so it was no wonder that he was promoted rapidly until he was head clerk.

He was even sent to New York by himself to buy goods for the growing store. He welcomed these opportunities of broadening his knowledge of merchandising, for he had resolved deep in his heart that he would not always be a clerk. Much as he liked Mr. O'Harra, someday he would have a store of his own.

Then, what a glorious thought: "Maybe Faither and Mither and Bridget would be comin' over to join the prosperous sons in America."

John and William had already talked about this joyous prospect. While William was going forward in merchandising, John was making strides in the hotel business. John was not satisfied to tend the bar and be the master bouncer when some poor addict became uncontrollable. He decided to lease a hotel he had heard about and go into business for himself. But John needed a woman to take general charge of the house. Why couldn't Bridget come over and do that for him?

It was three years since he and William had left home, and Bridget was now a full-grown woman. Had not mother written from time to time that Pat Mc-Gonegal was more insistent upon marrying her than ever? Here would be a good chance to get her away from Pat.

So John wrote to Bridget, enclosed a check for more than her fare, and begged her to come. In that letter, he did not mention this strategy against Pat Mc-Gonegal, but he wrote to his mother secretly and pushed his scheme. He explained that in America, there were many up-and-coming young men who would admire Bridget's beauty and Irish charm, and one would make a fine husband for her.

Eventually the letter arrived with the check, urging Bridget to come to America, and painting in glowing colors the possibilities of a fine home and a prosperous husband. The family agreed that America was her great opportunity, too. In due time, Bridget O'Connor with a few other girls from Killarney came to America to seek their homes, their husbands, and their fortunes.

To make the journey a little easier, John met Bridget in New York as the great steamship docked in the harbor. He recognized Bridget as he met her and her companions and reached out his hand in welcome. "Hello, Bridget, my dear! How beautiful you have grown! Why, the rose of Killarney is on your cheeks, the music of her birds is in your voice, and the blue of her skies is in your eyes. Bridget O'Connor, if ye weren't me own sister, I'd be fallin' in love wid ye meself."

"Go along wid ye, John O'Connor. It's just Irish blarney you're givin' me, and I don't believe a word of it."

John was introduced to Bridget's companions, and all of the jolly Irish group boarded a train for Scranton. On the way John managed to find out from Bridget everything about Father and Mother and whether they would consider coming to America.

That evening William, dressed in the latest style, came over to Hotel Killdare to see his sister and find out all he could about Father and Mother and his good friends in Ireland. The evening was a joy to the rising O'Connor boys. They delighted in luring Bridget far away from Pat McGonegal and having her with them, and they reveled in the presence of the other Irish girls, and their brogue and wit and humor.

CHAPTER 2

The Birth of Rosanna

BRIDGET, WHO HAD always helped her mother at home, sharing the responsibility, found no trouble in managing the household duties of her brother John's Hotel Killdare. This hostelry soon built up a reputation for good food, clean beds, and an orderly barroom. John O'Connor's business began to thrive far beyond his fondest dreams. Bridget was doing the work well. But imagine John's surprise and consternation, while walking down the street one day, to see Pat McGonegal coming toward him.

"Why, hello, Pat," greeted John, greatly surprised. "What brings you to America?"

"Well, it's a foin question you're askin' me, and a foin answer it is that I have for ye. I've come to America to marry Bridget O'Connor. You may know the lady. I believe she's related to you by rather close family ties, you broad-shouldered son of St. Patrick.

"You thought you'd separate us by that little stream called the Atlantic Ocean, but it might do you good to know that I was thinkin' o' comin' to America on me own accord. And when Bridget came, all the king's horses and all the king's men could not a-kept me from comin'.

"John O'Connor, you know that I've always been deeply in love with Bridget. She's the only girl in the world I'd be livin' for, and by the holy cross of St. Michaels, I'll die for her if called upon to do it."

John stood amazed as he heard these unequivocal words from Patrick McGonegal, whom he had not seen for three years or more. By now Pat had grown into rugged manhood. Though not as tall as John O'Connor, he was solidly built from the ground up. John sized him up and decided he would not force Pat to fight for her, not if John was to be the other contestant. Bridget's brother could hardly believe what he saw and heard in Pat—a man of resolution, determination, self-control, and confidence.

At last John found his voice. "Pat, you'll be rememberin' that in the auld country I was against ye. But as I see you and hear you now here in free America with all its opportunities, I've changed me mind. Since you've shown gumption enough to cross the ocean for Bridget, you'll have gumption enough to be a good husband for her. That's all I am interested in."

"Sure, it's a good husband I'll be to her. Who could be less for a girl like Bridget—the beauty o' Killarney written all over her face, and the blessed St. Cecilia herself putting music into her voice. John, she's the only perfect woman I've iver seen."

John extended his powerful right hand and took Pat by the hand. "You and Bridget it shall be, Pat. You have my consent and my blessing. I'm running Hotel Killdare on the next block. You'll find Bridget there, and you're welcome at any time."

"John O'Connor, it's a great favor and blessin' that you're conferrin' on me this day. By all the saints in Ireland, I swear you shall never regret what you have just said."

Pat hurried off to Hotel Killdare, where Bridget was supervising the evening meal. He stepped into the parlor and asked a waitress to call Bridget. When Bridget came and saw Pat, better dressed than she had ever seen him before, she flushed with surprise and delight.

"Why, Pat McGonegal, where in the world did you come from? How did you ever get here?"

Pat reached out his hand and took hers. "Bridget O'Connor, I've just come from me native country, beautiful Ireland. I waded the Atlantic Ocean by the aid of a steamship. I shipped from New York on the fastest train I iver saw, and I came to Scranton, Hotel Killdare, to see the most beautiful girl in the world, Mistress Bridget O'Connor by name. Is me explanation clear?"

The love-light in Bridget's eyes assured Pat that he was treading on safe ground. That together with

John's consent and blessing filled him with an inward happiness that almost ruined his studied control.

During the past few years, Pat had worked in the iron-ore mines of Cornwall, England. Thus it was not surprising that he soon heard of the iron-ore mines in Centre County, Pennsylvania, in the Half Moon Valley not far from Bellefonte, and headed in that direction. He was reluctant to leave Bridget after seeing her for only a few minutes. But he wanted to prove to John O'Connor that he, too, came to America to take advantage of the many opportunities for work. He would not let himself look like a slacker now.

᪐ ᪐ ᪐

When Pat arrived in Bellefonte, he went first to see the priest, Father O'Day, to get instruction in American ways of living and directions on how to get to the ore mines. When he arrived in Half Moon Valley, he had no trouble obtaining work, but he did have some difficulty finding room and board. The settlement was rather small, and the Irish Catholic families had their rooms all filled. The Irish foreman, Sandy McGuire, came to his rescue.

"Me biy, there's no room among our own folk, but there's another class of people livin' hereabouts that are mighty foin—the Amish farmers. They're a bit peculiar lookin'. The men have long hair, big beards, and broad-brimmed hats. The women wear black kerchiefs around their heads, and long capes instid o' coats. But they set a good table, and they put their religion into their everyday lives. You'll not be needin' to hide valuables in their homes."

Pat started out to find a boarding place among the Amish. The first Amishman he met was Reuben Kauffman, a sturdy young man with a slight chin beard and long hair. Pat was amused at the peculiar costume, but he concealed his curiosity. "Neighbor, I'm a stranger in this country, and I'm looking for a boardin' place. Could you tell me of one?"

"Yes, sir," replied Reuben. "Miss Elizabeth Yoder, who lives near the mines, sometimes takes boarders."

Soon Pat found the place. Elizabeth Yoder was an unmarried woman, large of stature, and quite capable. When Pat asked her whether she could accommodate him with board and room, she paused a moment and then said in a low, well-modulated voice, "I sometimes take a roomer, and if you think it will be good enough for you, I believe I could give you board and room."

Pat quickly discovered that the work in this mine was easier than in the Cornwall mine and the pay considerably better. His happiness grew as he learned more about American ways of living. Soon he took account of the low rents in Half Moon Valley and the reasonable cost of food bought from Amish farmers. It would not be long till he could marry Bridget, rent a house, and have a home of his own. He quickly learned to confide in Elizabeth Yoder, and it was a pleasure to tell her about their plans for marriage. Her counsel always seemed so sound and sensible.

After working at the mines a little less than a year, he told Elizabeth one evening, "Elizabeth, I'm thinkin' a bit of marrying in June and bringing Bridget here. There's nothing in the world I want so much as to have Bridget near me. Work is good, and the Half Moon

Valley is almost as beautiful as Killarney. What do you think?"

"Other men no better off than you get married. Why can't you? Where there's a will, there's a way."

To Pat, that was approval. Knowing that houses were scarce, Elizabeth offered, "If you want to get married in June, you may bring your wife here for a while, till you can find a house." That welcome inducement settled it.

Pat and Bridget were exchanging many letters, getting ready for the wedding in June. They would be married in the church. John, who was fond of his sister, would invite a score of friends to his hotel for the wedding dinner. The dining room would be decorated with orange blossoms and June roses, and it would be a real wedding. A few days before the wedding was to take place, Pat came to Scranton. He purchased a fine black suit for the wedding and bought Bridget a beautiful dress of white silk and a long white veil.

On the chosen day they gathered at the church. The priest said the solemn rites and pronounced them husband and wife. The dinner party was resplendent with choice foods, a beautiful bouquet of flowers, a drap o' wine, and much celebrating. The brothers, John and William, tried to be happy with all their friends, but they could not quite conceal a bit of sadness in having their beautiful sister taken away from them.

The newlyweds took the afternoon train for Philadelphia to visit some friends. After a few happy days, they went to Bellefonte and on southwest to their new home in Half Moon Valley. For a few months, they lived with Elizabeth Yoder, accepting her offer that Pat bring his new wife to her home until he found a house in which to live.

These two women, so different, became fast friends. Bridget was a buxom Irish girl with quick wit and fluent speech. Elizabeth was tall and rugged, plain of dress and slow of speech. She always wore a white cap with strings tied beneath her chin, a kerchief folded tightly about her waist and breast, a plain dress, and an apron. She generally spoke in short sentences, but her words always seemed to say something that stimulated Bridget's courage or deepened her confidence. Bridget was happy in this quaint, unadorned home where simplicity and sincerity were natural forms of religion.

Often these two women sat of an afternoon planning Bridget's new home. Elizabeth would tell how to plant and care for a garden, how to can fruits and vegetables, how to dry corn and tomatoes for the winter, how to raise chickens and have her own eggs, how to make tallow candles and soap, and many other things that would save an outlay of money.

With Elizabeth, as with other Amish, thrift was not religion, but it was a next-door neighbor to faith. She was able and glad to give Bridget many ideas that would make her housekeeping less expensive and enable them to save some of Pat's earnings every month. Elizabeth passed on to Bridget one of the Amish mottoes: "Spend less than you earn, and you'll never be in debt."

After several months of boarding, a house was vacated, and Pat immediately put in his application for it.

Late in October, with trees on the mountainsides turning from green to gold and brown, the McGonegals with the aid of Elizabeth moved into their little home. It was not far away. These two women, whose friendship grew with the passing days, frequently visited back and forth.

Pat, too, was not forgetful of Elizabeth's kindness to him. Many times when wintry snows were filling the air, he could be seen at her woodpile, sawing and splitting firewood and carrying it in for her. Sometimes Elizabeth walked over to see Bridget, with a basket on her arm filled with doughnuts and half-moon (dried apple) pies and maybe a jar of tomatoes or a head of cabbage. The two women seemed to complement each other. Bridget's Irish sunshine shed a ray of joy into Elizabeth's somber life, while Elizabeth's calm reserve gave Bridget poise and assurance.

ë ë ë

Time sped rapidly in Half Moon Valley. By day the song of industry cheered the inhabitants, and by night the whippoorwill and the katydid filled the air with bedtime melodies. As the years slipped by, Pat and Bridget became the parents of a growing family. How Elizabeth rejoiced at each new arrival! First came Margaret, a year later William, and two years after that John. So deep was Bridget's love and respect for her two fine brothers that she named her sons after them.

Two years after John was born came another girl, Rosanna. How glad Bridget was for this second baby girl! But, alas, she was not privileged to enjoy Rosanna for long. Complications set in. Elizabeth cared for the baby and for Bridget during her illness, but five days after the birth of Rosanna, Bridget died.

It was a terrible blow to Pat to be left with four little motherless children, and one only five days old. Again Elizabeth came to his rescue. With the aid of a few of the Catholic women, Elizabeth made all the preparations for the funeral. Elizabeth at once took the little baby, Rosanna, over to her own home, where she could care for her and let her rest in quiet surroundings.

After the funeral, Pat came to see the baby and decide with Elizabeth what seemed best to do. After considering first one plan and then another, Pat declared, "Elizabeth, I believe I can take the three older children to Philadelphia, where my friends will give them homes, but how in the world can I take a nine-day-old baby so far?"

"You're right, Pat. Rosanna is too young to take that far. If you want me to, I'll keep her for you till you find a place for the other children. Then when she is a little older, you can come and get her."

"The saints be praised," responded Pat. "Nothing in the world would suit me better."

As soon as Pat could, he disposed of his household goods. Reuben Kauffman offered to take Pat and the three children to Bellefonte, where they could catch a train to Philadelphia. Just a little over seven years ago, Pat remembered, he had hired a liveryman to bring him and his new bride to Half Moon Valley. What unspeakable joy had filled their hearts! But today he was leaving the broad peaceful valley, and his heart was heavy.

As the horses trotted along light-footed and spirited, they neared the entrance to the valley where the road leads between the mountains. Pat knew that when he passed the next turn in the road, the valley would be lost from his view, maybe forever. As they neared the turn, Pat looked back once more to the little cemetery on the hillside which now held the most priceless person he had ever known. In spite of the presence of Reuben and the children, tears rolled down his cheeks.

With a voice as steady as possible, he turned to Reuben. "You'll be excusin' me, Reuben, but me heart is terribly pained to leave her there on the hillside alone. She was so young and beautiful. I'm glad Elizabeth is keepin' Rosanna. If iver there was a woman who had the qualities of the blessed Virgin Mary, it is Elizabeth Yoder. Reuben, ye'll be takin' a little interest in Rosanna, too, won't you?"

By now they had passed Beaver's Gap and were rapidly approaching Bellefonte, nestled among the foothills of the Alleghenies. When they had taken the children and the few little bundles from the spring wagon, Pat turned to Reuben and asked, "Now, what do I owe you, Reuben, for bringing us out?"

"Nothing at all," replied Reuben. "We Amish folks are always glad to help our neighbors when they're in need, but not for money."

Pat insisted on paying, but Reuben was adamant. "Well, Reuben, if you won't take any pay, accept my everlasting gratitude. Believe me, I'll always be praying that the Holy Virgin will be blessin' ye with peace and prosperity."

Reuben did not know much about the blessings of the Holy Virgin. But from the way Pat said it, and from the gratitude in Pat's eyes, Reuben knew Pat wished him well. These two men, so different, had become fast friends. The one was a plain Amishman faithful to the rules of his church, simplicity of attire, and unworldliness. The other was a Roman Catholic, faithful to his church, the rosary, and the confessional.

What a compliment to both these groups, differing so widely in religion, that they lived in perfect peace and mutual respect in the fair Half Moon Valley. The Amish farmers supplied the Catholic miners with food. The Catholic iron-ore miners provided the Amish farmers with a market for what they produced. Each complemented the other. Were Pat and Reuben different? Yes, but much alike in one thing: each was faithful to his own church.

Reuben stood on the station platform, watching the passenger car bearing Pat and his three children away. As the train glided down along the winding stream and out into the great Penn's Valley, it was finally lost to view. Reuben, turning to untie his horses for the journey home, said half aloud and half to himself, "Sorry to see Pat McGonegal go away. He's a good man."

CHAPTER 3

Lost Creek Valley

T O E A R N A L I T T L E spending money, Elizabeth Yoder frequently cooked for Amish threshing crews. Sometimes when farmers were short of men in the harvest field, she would even help to bind sheaves. It was well known that it took a good man to bind more wheat or oats in a day than Elizabeth could. Generally it took two men to "take up" after a cradle. On a few occasions, Elizabeth volunteered to do it by herself, and to the amazement of the men, she did not lose a single sheaf.

It was not unusual among the Amish farmers to have the women who could be spared from household chores do the lighter work in the hayfield, the harvest field, and cornhusking. But when it came to unpleasant farm work like spreading lime, loading manure, or threshing, the women were never asked to help. One of the crowning virtues among the Amish, however, is to be able to do hard work rapidly, skillfully, and without complaint. A slow, lazy worker is regarded as a weakling either in mind or body, and is never held in high esteem among them.

Besides these cooking and farming tasks, Elizabeth often helped Amish women when they gave birth. She knew well how to care for new babies. Thus she did not hesitate to volunteer to keep five-day-old Rosanna McGonegal until her father could find a place for her among relatives in Philadelphia. In her quiet home, it was no wonder that Rosanna grew rapidly. There was always an abundance of fresh cow's milk, vegetable juices, meat broth, and so much else that could contribute to a baby's health and comfort.

One day Mary Riehl, the wife of one of the ministers, came to see Elizabeth. Rosanna was lying in the cradle, prattling as healthy babies often do. Mary Riehl went to the cradle to see the little Catholic baby. When Rosanna saw her, she kicked and cooed happily.

Mary was so pleased that she commented to Elizabeth, "Why, Lisabet, this baby cackles chust like a little Amish *Buppeli.*"

Elizabeth answered in a voice of mixed joy and sadness, "Yes, sometimes I think I can hear Bridget McGonegal's voice as she prattles away, trying to tell me something. I had a letter from her father the other day. He told me he has found good places for the other children and that he is working in a gravel pit near Philadelphia. As soon as he can afford it, he will come for Rosanna.

"My goodness, Mary, I don't know how in the world I could give her up now. At first I thought she would be a good bit of work and bother, but instead of bother, she's such company for me. I never get lonesome any more at all. When Pat left, he said, 'Ye've been so good to me and Rosanna. May the blessed Virgin Mary comfort you and bless you every day of your life.' Mary, do you know who this Virgin Mary is?"

"*Ach* (oh), them Catholics always talk about her, but I don't know who she is."

Then Mary changed the subject. "Lisabet, I heard the other day that Cristal (Christian) Kauffman comes sneakin' over here sometimes. Is it so?"

Elizabeth lost just a little of her poise for a moment and then said as casually as possible, "*Ach*, why would he want to come over here anyhow now, since I have this little baby to take care of?" She said no more about that, for no Amish woman or girl of advanced years discusses her love affairs with someone else. She keeps such thoughts to herself.

Mary, however, was not willing to drop the matter. "Well, I believe Cristal would make any woman a good man." Cristal Kauffman was Reuben's bachelor uncle, with a quiet disposition and gentle manners.

As the women went on talking, Elizabeth asked, "Mary, is it true that you and Jacob are thinking of moving to Lost Creek Valley with your family?"

"Yes, Lisabet, we've been thinking about it a little. You see, Jacob and John Yoder are the only preachers here anymore, and neither one of them is a bishop. One of the bishops from Lost Creek Valley or Big Valley must come here whenever young people are to be baptized or married or when we have communion.

"Here the congregation is getting pretty small, with so many moving away. Our children would like to move someplace where there are more Amish young folks. These Catholic people around us are all nice people and I like them, but they are not for our young people to run with. So maybe we'll go too, sometime."

❧ ❧ ❧

About nine o'clock one evening, Rosanna was sleeping in the cradle and Elizabeth had just read a chapter in the New Testament and an evening prayer in the prayer book. She heard someone on the porch. Just then the door opened softly, and who should enter but Cristal Kauffman.

Elizabeth was not surprised nor was she annoyed, for Cristal always came without previous arrangement. She invited him to sit down, and they began to visit. When Rosanna tossed a bit in her sleep, Elizabeth went to the cradle to fix the covers. To her surprise, Cristal came over to the cradle to see the baby.

As Rosanna lay there, peacefully asleep with her black curls and chubby red cheeks, Cristal said, "*Mei, des is aver en schee Buppeli* (my, isn't she a pretty baby)? *Ich deht so suhr gleiche es ruhm draage selwer* (I'd like to carry her around myself)."

At that moment, for the first time, Elizabeth noticed that her heart was strangely warmed toward Cristal. Her motherly feelings were awakened more and more, and her love for baby Rosanna grew even deeper.

When the long winter was over, Elizabeth was a little disturbed. At preaching service at John Yoder's, it was reported that seven or eight families were moving to larger Amish settlements elsewhere in central Pennsylvania—some to Big Valley (Kishacoquillas), some to Buffalo Valley, and some to Lost Creek Valley. With hardly enough people left to have preaching services, she felt lonely and sensed the need for some outside help.

Elizabeth remembered Mary Riehl's comment about Cristal Kauffman: "He would make any woman a good man." Mary's opinion together with Cristal's growing fondness for little Rosanna made her feel that Cristal would indeed be a great comfort.

Not long after this, Cristal came to visit her again about nine o'clock in the evening. They talked about so many families leaving Half Moon Valley, the congregation getting too small for preaching services, and the feeling of loneliness it brought. Finally Cristal got up his courage and gently proposed, "Lisabet, if we would get married, maybe I could help you to raise Rosanna, and maybe we could get along better than we do now."

Elizabeth did not speak for some time. Then with a little smile, she replied, "I think maybe you're right." For them, that was engagement.

Since Elizabeth had no near relatives in the valley, they decided just to be married at the close of a regular preaching service, and not have a regular wedding. They set the date for spring, when a bishop would have to be present anyway to officiate at the communion service. That would be a convenient time to be married.

ಶಿ ಶಿ ಶಿ

The next spring Cristal and Elizabeth found themselves among the few still left in the Half Moon Valley congregation. So they began planning to sell the home and move to Lost Creek Valley where so many of their friends had gone.

To avoid imposing on neighbors to help haul their household goods so far, they held a sale. They kept only the essentials of housekeeping and a few articles they treasured highly. Cristal would be able to put everything they still owned on his two-horse wagon, which for years he had used to haul wood and coal for the people who lived near the mines.

Although Rosanna was now nearly three years old, they thought it wise not to make the trip as long as stormy spring weather continued. It was a long journey, and early in the spring there might be considerable exposure.

When the May sun began to warm the earth and farmers were busy plowing in the fields, they decided to set out for their new home, Jericho, in Lost Creek Valley of Juniata County, Pennsylvania. Early on the morning of the chosen day, several of the Amishmen still remaining in Half Moon Valley came with their wives to help load the flittin' (moving wagon).

The large cookstove was heavy, and the kitchen cupboard was awkward to handle. Except for these articles, Cristal and Elizabeth could have loaded everything themselves. But among the Amish, it was customary to gather for friendly helpfulness, especially when people were leaving the community or when they had some unusual task to perform where "many hands make light work" (John Heywood).

When the last article was loaded, Cristal brought out his two sorrel horses and hitched them to the wagon. Elizabeth took her place on the wagon seat, held Rosanna till Cristal took his place, then tucked Rosanna cozily between them. They waved good-bye to the friends and were off. The horses felt the crispness in the spring air. Prancing and dancing, their nimble feet sped along the smooth road just a bit too fast for comfort.

Elizabeth felt a pang of sadness as she left her beloved Half Moon Valley home behind. She could not help thinking about the little party Reuben Kauffman took down this same road almost four years before. As she mused, she finally said to Cristal, "Pat has never returned for the baby. I wonder why. I'm sure something has happened. Will we ever know?"

Cristal responded confidently, "All things work together for good to those who love the Lord [Rom. 8:28]."

They drove on in thoughtful silence, except when Rosanna would point to some beautiful bird, or flock of sheep, or herd of cattle. Elizabeth and Cristal generally spoke to each other in Pennsylvania German. While Rosanna could prattle away in that language, Elizabeth was careful to teach her English also.

As she explained to Cristal, "It would be a great disappointment if her father should come for her and she could not talk what he could understand."

At Bellefonte they turned right, to go southeast. By noon they were crossing the Seven Mountains. Here they stopped to feed their horses, eat their lunch, and take the noon hour off. Cristal always said, "If you want fine horses, you must take care of them."

When they resumed their trip after lunch, the horses had worn the edge off their high spirits and were content to walk instead of prance. By the time twilight shadows began to fall, they had reached Reedsville, where they rested for the night.

Since there was no loading to do the second morning, by the time the sun was well up, they were passing through the Reedsville Narrows. By noon they arrived at Lewistown. They headed on into the Juniata Narrows, where the river's blue water winds down between the mountain ranges.

Progress through the Narrows was slow. All they saw were huge oak and chestnut trees on either side of the road, mingling their branches overhead, and an occasional rabbit scampering along the road or a deer bounding up from the river bank where it had gone to drink. It was twelve miles further to Mifflintown, where they had to go to begin the trek up through Lost Creek Valley.

By the time they reached Mifflintown, horses and people were nearly exhausted. But Cristal knew an Amish family, Jacob Hartzlers, just two miles beyond, and the road was good. On the smooth valley road, the horses seemed to forget their fatigue. Soon they were turning into Jacob Hartzler's barnyard for the night. When Jacob saw that they were Amish people on the move, he gave them a warm welcome, called the boys to unhitch the horses, and graciously escorted the tired travelers to the house.

How good the cooking supper smelled to these hungry travelers! The long table in the spacious kitchen assured them that there would be room for all. With a good night's rest, they were ready to finish their journey before noon the next day.

Joseph Yoder, distantly related to Cristal, lived on a large farm near Jericho. He had arranged for the house where Cristal and his family would live. When they arrived, he was on hand with a few other Amishmen and their wives. In a short time, the flittin' was unloaded, everything was in its place, and dinner for all was cooking on Elizabeth's own stove.

When dinner was ready, they all sat down together and bowed their heads in silent grace, thanking the Lord for food and friends and a safe journey. Even little Rosanna seemed to bow her head longer than usual. She was taught always to bow her head and be quiet at the table before she ate.

As a young man, Cristal had visited Lost Creek Valley. Elizabeth had been here twice before—once to attend a funeral, and once for a wedding. However, now that they were beginning their new home here, they agreed they never knew it was such a good place. The land was fertile, just rolling enough not to be swampy. The seasons were early. Best of all, many Amish people lived here, with a bishop and three preachers.

Surely Lost Creek Valley was a good place to live. They were content.

CHAPTER 4

Early Education

A S M A Y D A Y S warmed into June, they were all busy fixing up the new home. Fortunately the former owners had taken considerable pride in the place and beautified it in many ways. Fine grass covered the front lawn. Morning glories twined about the trellis near the front porch. Rose bushes, lilacs, and hollyhocks grew in profusion in the yard and in the garden, and the very atmosphere seemed to be scented with happiness and thrift.

Elizabeth rejoiced in all these things. Rosanna was old enough now to learn to work a little. Elizabeth was beginning to assign her some small responsibilities. As

Elizabeth worked in the garden, Rosanna was always with her, eager to help, asking which plant was a weed and was a flower. When Elizabeth set out tomato or cabbage plants, she would show Rosanna how and then let her try to plant one. They would remember which one Rosanna had set.

Through the summer, Elizabeth often called attention to how well Rosanna's plant was developing. She complimented Rosanna for being able at her age to plant something that would grow. When Elizabeth praised her for what she had done so well, Rosanna was always so pleased that she would say "Momli." That was Rosanna's affectionate childhood name for Elizabeth, meaning "Little Mother" or "Dear Mother." All through Rosanna's life she called Elizabeth "Momli." There was no other name that represented so much respect and esteem and love as that name did.

Because Elizabeth was so kind to all the young people and considerate of their wants and wishes, many of them called her Momli, too. As they walked or worked in the garden, Rosanna would often say, in her childish love for Elizabeth, "Momli, someday I can take care of the whole garden for you, and you can just sit on the porch in the rocking chair and rest yourself."

When Elizabeth was baking bread, she would always give Rosanna a little dough to knead and shape into a small loaf. Other times Momli would parcel out some pie dough and a little plate and have her make a tiny pie. In that way, Rosanna learned to do the things that Amish people think are worthwhile. Elizabeth could not have qualified as a schoolteacher, but she intuitively knew child psychology. Elizabeth was always

ROSANNA'S FIRST LESSON
IN GARDENING

able to inspire the best in Rosanna.

In Jericho, many people had horses of their own, so Cristal did not have as much hauling to do as he did in Half Moon Valley. He gave more of his time to carpentering, but he still kept his two beautiful sorrels.

While Rosanna was small, they continued to use Cristal's buggy to go to preaching and to go visiting. Single men drove buggies, but married men, especially after they had families, used carriages with two seats. Amish carriages were built to order and not bought on the general market. The local Amish church required that carriages have a square stationary top and be covered with white muslin or yellow oilcloth.

One evening when Cristal came home from carpentering and they were eating supper, Cristal said, "Elizabeth, what would you think of us getting a new carriage to drive to preaching instead of using our buggy? Rosanna is getting a little too big for you to hold on your lap when we go anywhere."

"I think that would be nice," responded Elizabeth. "Then we could take somebody with us sometimes, too. Can we afford it?"

"Oh, I reckon so. Do you think people would consider us proud if we put a tongue onto it and drove both our horses?" Cristal had a look of uncertainty.

"It might look a little stuck-up, but the people know that our horses do not like to be separated, since we have only two. I don't believe they would say much about it. Besides, everybody knows that a carriage rides much better when drawn by two horses."

The couple knew that among their people, *Hochmut* (pride) was the cardinal sin to avoid. Like other

Amish, they always guarded against the possibility of being regarded as proud.

Cristal went to Mifflintown, where there was a good carriage maker who built carriages for the Amish as far away as Big Valley. Cristal placed his order for a regular Amish carriage, yellow top, brown body, with black running gear and a tongue instead of shafts—a regular two-horse carriage.

The Saturday it was finally finished, Cristal took the two sorrels to bring it home. As he drove into the little barnyard, Rosanna was overjoyed to see how pretty the new carriage was. Even Elizabeth could not quite conceal her pleasure at its bright appearance. How the wheels glistened in the sunshine. As Cristal stopped the horses, he asked, "Well, what do you think?"

Elizabeth tried to look serious. "It looks a little big feelin' for us, I'm afraid. But it isn't against the rules of the church to drive two horses, and everybody knows we needed a new carriage."

That evening Cristal said, "Now, you womenfolks get everything ready this evening for us to go to preaching in the morning. Church is over at Benjamin Byler's, and it's close to ten miles, so we must start a little before seven in the morning."

They were off good and early in the morning. The full-grown corn along the way seemed to cool the air, and the horses were in fine fettle. The new carriage ran so quietly and the horses were so spirited that Cristal and Elizabeth began to search their own feelings to see if they were truly humble, or if there might be a little pride within. It was just eight-thirty when they drove into Benjamin Byler's well-kept lane.

They were not the first to arrive. Already many white carriages and yellow carriages stood in straight rows in the sod field just outside the barnyard. Mixed in with these were the buggies driven by the young unmarried men. Elizabeth and Rosanna alighted from the carriage and went into the house. One of the Byler boys came quickly to unhitch the horses and put them in the stable.

Cristal joined a good-sized group of men gathered under the barn's overshot (forebay, overhang), waiting until it was time to go into the house and begin the services. He shook hands all around, whether he knew the men or not. Then, seeing Joseph Yoder, his relative, Cristal approached him, shook hands, and joined in the conversation. Just then Bishop Shem arrived. Two of the ministers and the deacon were already there. The bishop greeted the ministers and deacon with the holy kiss and shook hands with all the others.

Soon after these greetings, the bishop remarked, "Well, I guess it's about time to go into the house," meaning it was time to begin the preaching services. As Bishop Shem started for the house, most of the old men followed. Soon one of the middle-aged men said, "I guess it's about time to go in," and that group went to the house. Shortly afterward, the younger men and boys followed, and the house was full. While the men were taking their places, the women and girls came in and occupied seats reserved for them.

ﭼ ﭼ ﭼ

As customary, the Amish would hold their preaching services in a house, or in the barn if the house was not large enough to accommodate the congregation. They never held services under trees or out in the open. Members shared in turn at "taking preaching," which usually came around to each family about once a year. To accommodate these preaching services, the Amish built their houses with movable partitions on the first floor. For preaching day, all partitions could be removed, to make the lower part of the house into one big room. This made it possible for almost everybody in the house to see and hear the preacher.

In this area, each family provided itself with a set of benches that fit the house exactly. On preaching day, these were arranged to provide seats for the whole congregation. In one corner of this large room, a table was placed, and on it the *Ausbund* hymnbooks were stacked. The hymns were all in German, and the hymnals were called *die dücke schnalle Bücher* (the thick buckle books), because they were held shut by a buckle or clasp. These books contained about four hundred pages and were bound in leather.

Around this table, the men singers were seated. Other men filled the benches next to the table and running parallel the full length of the room. Opposite this table, in center at the same end of the room, a bench or a row of chairs was reserved for the bishop and the ministers. The ministers faced the singers' table. About two rows behind the ministers were three or four benches for the young unmarried women. Back of them sat the middle-aged and older women, and farthest away the mothers with babies and small children.

While the congregation was gathering, not a word was spoken. The men sat in silence with their hats on. When the house was well filled and the proper time arrived, about eight-thirty or a quarter of nine, the deacon rose, took some of the hymnals, and passed them to the unmarried young women sitting just back of the men. One of the *Vorsinger* (song leaders) then announced the number of a hymn, and the men removed their hats.

As the *Vorsinger* began singing and others joined in, the ministers rose and withdrew to a prepared upstairs room for *Abrot* (*Abrat*, counsel). Here they prayed, attended to any church business, and determined who would *der Anfang mache* (make the beginning, preach first) and who would preach the main sermon (*Gemeh halde*). If there was any business relating to the church or any member, they would discuss it here and agree upon a course of action. Sometimes a decision would be reached to bring the matter before the whole membership.

While the bishop and the ministers were in the *Abrot*, the congregation continued singing hymns. The second hymn, by tradition, was always the "*Lob Sang* (Praise hymn)." It was never announced. Amish hymns, sung in one part only, were difficult to sing. There was no written music for these hymns. Young men had to learn them by rote from older singers, and it frequently took a long time. For that reason a young singer usually tried to lead the "*Lob Sang*" as his first attempt. He had the assurance, however, that if he slipped off the tune, older men sitting at his elbow would take up the melody and help him along.

A third hymn was announced, but if the ministers returned from the upstairs room before it was finished, the song period concluded with whatever stanza was being sung. It was not considered appropriate to sing long after the ministers returned. As the ministers took their places again, they shook hands with all within reach who may have come in since the service began.

When the hymn was finished, the minister "making the beginning" rose and preached for about thirty minutes. At the close of his talk, the congregation knelt in silent prayer. After a while, the bishop stood up to indicate the close of the prayer period, and the congregation rose with him. Then the members stood while the deacon read a chapter from the New Testament (never from the Old Testament).

After the reading, the congregation was seated, and the minister who was to give the main sermon stood up. Frequently this second preacher would hold forth for an hour and a half or on special occasions for two hours. All this time the people were seated on backless benches, demonstrating endurance as well as devotion.

Soon after this speaker had begun his exhortation, the hostess came in quietly, carrying a platter filled with good-sized pieces of half-moon (dried-apple) pies. She gave a piece to each child in the room, for by this time the children were getting a little hungry and restless.

When the second preacher finished the main sermon, he sat down. Then he called on each minister and deacon present for any *Zeugnis* (testimony) or additional thought they wished to give. If a respected visiting Amishman were present, the speaker might call on him for a response whether he was a minister or not.

After the testimonies, the main speaker rose again and expressed gratitude that his discourse was considered as God's message. After a few brief remarks, the congregation again knelt in prayer while the preacher read aloud from the prayer book. The same prayer was always used (the Amish never offer original prayers aloud). When this prayer was ended, they all stood again while the minister pronounced the benediction. As he ended with the words, *"Durch Jesum Christum, Amen* (through Jesus Christ, Amen)," the whole congregation bowed perceptibly at the knee and then was seated.

At this point the deacon made all the announcements and published the names of any intending to marry soon. If there was any church business, he requested *members* to remain seated while others were excused. Following other announcements, he named the home where preaching would be held in two weeks. When he was through, a man at the singers' table announced the number of a hymn. After the last note of the hymn had died away, the men rose slowly, put on their hats, and passed out of the house without rushing. As the men filed out, the young women began leaving, and then the older ones. The women either went outside or to some other part of the house.

As soon as the room was empty, the man of the house and his helpers removed all the benches except a few retained for tables and seats. Then at the most convenient place, usually through the longest part of the house, they set up one table for men and one for women. Each table was made of two benches set side by side, with longer legs unfolded to hold them at table height.

Girls who had volunteered to help the hostess came quickly, spread white tablecloths over these bench tables, and set them. First a knife, a spoon, a cup and saucer, and a drinking glass were placed along each side of the table about two feet apart. Then on the table they placed large plates of bread, half-moon pies, green-apple pies, butter, apple butter, cream, red beets, and pickles. To this were added large bowls of hot bean soup. This was the standard preaching meal, and it never varied.

When all was ready, the man of the house went to the door and announced, "Dinner is ready." The bishop, the ministers, the deacon, and the old men went in first until the table was full. While the men were taking their places, the old and middle-aged women were being seated at their table. When both tables were filled, the host stated, "The tables are full," whereupon the bishop said, "Let us pray." All bowed their heads and engaged in silent prayer. (No audible blessing is ever uttered.) When grace was over, the girls who had set the tables came with large pots of hot coffee, offering it to all. These girls waited on the tables, replenishing bread plates and pie plates, and serving second helpings of coffee as desired.

When everyone had finished eating, a brief pause was observed. Then the bishop said, "If we are all through, let us give thanks," and a silent prayer of thanksgiving followed. When this prayer was over, both men and women arose from the tables and left the room. The waitresses came and resupplied the tables with food, but they did not wash the dishes.

When the tables were ready the second time, the man of the house again went to the door and announced that dinner was ready. The older men who had not yet eaten and the middle-aged men sat around one table, and the older women and the middle-aged women filled the table for the women. When the places were all taken, the man of the house again stated that the tables were full, and without any word from the bishop or anyone else, they all bowed their heads in silent grace.

In the same way, table after table was served and replenished, being filled each time with younger persons. Finally Rosanna and the other little boys and girls who could care for themselves filled the tables. Younger children had already gone to the tables with their parents. Finally, when all had eaten, everything was cleared away.

The housewife never needed to worry about what she would serve for dinner; the meal was always the same. There was also a regular form of preparation. On the Wednesday prior to preaching services, a half dozen women of the same church had come to help polish the tinware. On Friday three or four had come to help bake the bread, as many as forty big loaves. On Saturday a dozen women had arrived to help bake about sixty green-apple pies and four or five hundred half-moon pies.

The half-moon pies were made of dried apples cooked to about the consistency of applesauce. A piece of pie dough was rolled out to the thickness of pie crust, circular in shape. The dried apples were spread on one half of it, and the other half was brought over the apples and pinched tight at the edges, making a pie the form of a half circle. These were laid on tin pie plates and baked. Since they were all of one piece with the edges sealed together, they could easily be held by hand for eating.

It usually took from about one o'clock to three to serve a Sunday dinner. While one group was eating, the other men stood around the barn or in the yard and visited. The topic of conversation was usually crops, weather, markets, cattle, and sometimes religion.

While the men chatted outside, the women visited in the house. They generally talked about gardens, housecleaning, chickens, butter making, or some moral question. Sometimes a little gossip slipped in. In this way, Amish preaching served two purposes, religious guidance and a social occasion.

About three o'clock, or earlier, if the family had all had dinner, the husband went to the house or sent a little boy to see whether the mother was ready to go home. From about two-thirty on, long rows of white carriages and yellow ones moved quietly out the lane, until the field where they were parked was again empty, and preaching was over.

🙢 🙢 🙢

On this particular Sunday, as Cristal drove his two prancing sorrels up to the gate for Elizabeth and Rosanna, the bishop happened to be there, too. He looked over Cristal's shiny carriage and high-spirited horses and commented good-naturedly, "Be a little careful, Cristal. This looks pretty high toned."

Cristal laughed. "Well, a carriage has to be new *once,* you know."

"*Jah, well* (okay)," responded Bishop Shem.

On the drive home, Elizabeth sighed with relief as she told Cristal, "Well, if the bishop didn't scold about our two-horse carriage, I guess it's all right."

Just then little Rosanna spoke up. "Cristal, did you notice? We had the nicest carriage at preaching today."

Elizabeth felt it her duty to say, "Tut, tut, Rosanna, you must not talk that way. We must not be proud."

🖋 🖋 🖋

A little later in the fall when the chestnut burrs began to crack open, Rosanna was old enough to start to school. Fortunately, the schoolhouse was not far away, and there was a good lady teacher, all of which relieved Elizabeth greatly. She had been talking to Rosanna about school and how nice it would be to learn new things with the other children.

Rosanna's eyes shone with the idea of going to school. Her wavy hair had a glossy luster, her bright eyes sparkled more and more, and her cheeks took on a rosy red that assured Elizabeth that Rosanna was in perfect health.

When Rosanna left for school that first morning, Elizabeth stood watching until she had almost reached the schoolhouse. Elizabeth was not emotional, but this morning she had great trouble in restraining her tears. In her heart she prayed, "O Lord, let nothing happen to this dear little motherless girl whom you have given

HOME FROM FIRST DAY
AT SCHOOL

me to raise. Guard Rosanna from all harm, that she may grow up and glorify your name."

It was the first day in over six years that Rosanna was away from Elizabeth. All day Elizabeth felt that there was a dreadful emptiness in the house and a painful fullness in her heart. It was also a long day for Rosanna, sitting there on a bench and not being able to talk to Momli. So when school was out, she took her little dinner pail and hurried home as fast as she could go.

As the afternoon wore on, Elizabeth could not help but keep looking down the road to see whether Rosanna was coming. When she finally saw her skipping up the road in her little blue dress, long black apron, and little white cap, her heart swelled with joy. Never before had she realized just how much Rosanna meant to her.

That evening at the supper table, Rosanna told Cristal and Elizabeth all that had happened at school that day. The teacher, Mary McLaughlin, had called her a smart little girl. Rosanna liked her for that, for she did want to be smart. She was glad that she could say almost all of the ABCs the very first day. Before going to bed, she had Cristal go over them once more with her.

Mary McLaughlin liked Rosanna, and Rosanna liked Mary McLaughlin. Occasionally Elizabeth would send a rose or an apple or a cookie to school with Rosanna for the teacher. Elizabeth wanted Mary McLaughlin to know that she had a high regard for her. Besides, it was a good way to teach Rosanna to be thoughtful and considerate of others. On the way home from school, Mary McLaughlin would sometimes stop and talk to Elizabeth, mentioning how well Rosanna was getting along with her studies and how well-behaved she was. And all this seemed to fulfill Elizabeth's prayers.

✍ ✍ ✍

Year after year followed pleasantly. However, Cristal eventually developed a bad heart condition. Gradually he became worse, and finally he died.

One evening when they were by themselves and feeling lonely, Elizabeth said, "Rosanna, we never know what will happen. Someday you may have to make your own living. You get along so well in school that I have been thinking it might be wise for you to get ready to teach school. That pays better than lots of other jobs. Besides, it's much nicer work. Do you think you would like to be a schoolteacher, Rosanna?"

"Oh, yes, Momli. That way I could earn money for you, too, if you ever need it."

As a rule, the Amish people were opposed to education beyond the "three R's." They quoted the Bible (1 Cor. 3:19), *"Die Weisheit dieser Welt ist Torheit bei Gott* (the wisdom of this world is foolishness with God)." For Elizabeth to decide deliberately to train her little orphan girl to be a teacher took genuine courage.

CHAPTER 5

Finding Little Sister

ROSANNA'S OLDER sister, Margaret, and her brothers, John and William, were taken to Philadelphia, as mentioned before, and good homes were found for them among friends and relatives. Being considerably older than Rosanna, they had by this time almost grown up.

Margaret favored the O'Connors and became a tall, stately woman. William, the older of the boys, was ambitious. As soon as he was old enough, he secured a position in a store in Philadelphia. He and John Wanamaker, of later department-store fame, clerked together as young men in the same store. John, the younger brother, was smaller and less rugged. John learned to be a typesetter and worked for the *Philadelphia Public Ledger* all his life.

William, the older of the boys, assumed responsibility for the family after his father, Pat, was killed in an accident. He was old enough to remember how Reuben Kauffman, the young Amishman, had brought them to Bellefonte to the railroad station. William could still hear Reuben refusing to accept any pay for this service: "We Amish like to help our neighbors, but not for pay."

He distinctly recalled that Reuben had long hair, wore a broad-brimmed hat, and had hooks and eyes on his coat and vest. William knew that other plain sects wear long hair and broad hats, but the Amish are the only ones with hooks and eyes on their coats and vests. This knowledge was useful to William as he clerked in the general store. He had no trouble recognizing Amishmen as they came to buy and trade. Big brother also remembered that somewhere among the Amish, his little sister Rosanna was being brought up.

In those days farmers from Centre, Mifflin, and Juniata counties hauled their grain to Philadelphia in large Conestoga wagons drawn by four or six horses or mules. After marketing their grain, they would enter the stores to buy groceries and dry goods for the year. William McGonegal decided that he would try to find his sister, Rosanna. He felt sure that someday an Amish farmer would come into the store who knew Rosanna.

Whenever a man came into the store wearing hooks and eyes on his coat and vest, William would step up to him and say, "Pardon me, neighbor, but do you by any chance know a little girl named Rosanna McGonegal?" He asked this question of scores of Amishmen for two or three years. They all looked at him soberly for a moment and then replied, "No, I never saw her." It was discouraging when so many said no, but he felt confident that someday he would find the right man.

One day Joseph Yoder of Lost Creek Valley took a load of grain to Philadelphia and went into this store to buy groceries. Joseph Yoder was a short, stocky man with long hair, a well-kept beard, an honest face, and a pleasant disposition. When there was a good opportunity, William stepped up to Joseph and said, "Pardon me, neighbor, but do you by chance know a little girl named Rosanna McGonegal?"

Joseph looked at him and smiled. "Yes, I know her well."

"I'm William McGonegal, her oldest brother," William informed him excitedly. "Would you be kind enough to tell me how I could find her?"

"She lives in Jericho and is being raised by Elizabeth Kauffman."

William was overjoyed. He remembered that Elizabeth Yoder, an unmarried woman, had agreed to keep Rosanna till his father could come for her. Surely this was the woman and this was his little sister.

"How can I go there?" wondered William.

"Take a train to Thompsontown. Then take a stagecoach to Jericho, and ask for Mrs. Cristal Kauffman. Anybody there can tell you where she lives."

When Joseph returned from his long journey to

Philadelphia, he went over and told Elizabeth how he had seen William McGonegal, and how William had asked about Rosanna and the way to come and visit. "So," Joseph predicted, "I suppose this young man will come to see you someday. He's a fine looking young fellow, and he's very polite."

"*Jah, well,*" said Elizabeth resignedly, sensing a little danger of losing Rosanna, "if he comes, I guess we can keep him."

That evening after the store closed, William hurried over to see his sister Margaret and tell her about the glorious discovery. William threw his arms about her, kissed her, and exclaimed, "Oh, Margaret, I have the most wonderful news. I have found Rosanna. For years I've been asking Amishmen whether they ever saw Rosanna, and they all said no. But today a fine-looking Amishman came into the store, and when I asked him whether he knew a little girl named Rosanna McGonegal, he replied, 'Yes, I know her well.' I learned that she's now living in Jericho, and he told me how to get there."

Margaret could hardly find words to express her joy. Then she suggested to William, "Perhaps you can bring her here, and we can have her baptized and confirmed in the Catholic Church."

"I'll go as soon as the spring rush is over, and I'll bring her here if it's at all possible. Of course, Margaret, the Amish are a mighty fine religious people, and I can't help but believe that she's all right with them. But it would be so nice to have her here, going to church with us. I'm anxious to see how she looks. Do you think the lady who took her is dressing her Amish?"

One morning early in July, William McGonegal bought a ticket on the Pennsylvania Railroad for Thompsontown. William had never traveled far from the city before, but he felt equal to the occasion.

He left the Atlantic plain about Philadelphia and approached the foothills of the Alleghenies, with their mountains, ravines, and river valleys. On the way, his memory brought back vividly the scenes of his boyhood in Half Moon Valley. He remembered again the railroad station at Bellefonte and half wished his journey was taking him there.

When the train finally stopped at Thompsontown, about four o'clock in the afternoon, he got off and began looking for a stagecoach. Presently he saw what he supposed was one—two horses hitched to a good-sized covered wagon. William saw the driver approaching, a big husky fellow, and asked, "Is this the stagecoach for Jericho?"

"Yes sir, my boy," replied the driver accommodatingly.

"Could you take me there and let me off near the house of Mrs. Cristal Kauffman?"

"Yes sir, my boy. Step right in."

"Do you know whether a little girl lives there named Rosanna McGonegal?"

"Yes sir, my boy. And she's just about the smartest little girl in the community. She's a friend to everybody, and everybody is her friend," responded the driver in a reassuring way.

The stagecoach jolted William every time it hit a rough spot in the road, but in his anxiety to see Rosanna, it did not go half fast enough.

Elizabeth did not know what day William was coming, so she had not made any special preparation. But there always was plenty of good fresh milk in the cellar, eggs in the basket, hams in the smokehouse, and a supply of bread and pies in the cupboard. She could set a good meal at a moment's notice, any time.

When William arrived, he knocked on the front door and heard a pleasant voice say, "Come in." He had expected someone to come to the door. Since no one did, he opened the door softly and found Elizabeth and Rosanna in the living room.

As William looked at this tall muscular woman, he thought he recalled Elizabeth Yoder of Half Moon Valley and asked, "Are you Elizabeth Kauffman?" William remembered that Amish people are not much for titles, so he didn't address her as Mrs. Kauffman.

"Yes," answered Elizabeth quietly.

"I am William McGonegal. And is this little girl my sister Rosanna?"

"Yes, that is Rosanna McGonegal. I have never changed her name because your father said he would come for her sometime, and I thought he could find her easier if I didn't change her name. Is your father still living?"

"No, he was killed. After taking us children to Philadelphia, he worked in a gravel pit to earn money to clothe us children and someday come for Rosanna. While at work one day, the pit caved in. Three men were killed, just covered up with tons and tons of rock and gravel, and father was one of them. He was so anxious to come for Rosanna so he could have us all together."

Elizabeth was silent for a moment, then continued in a voice filled with deep sympathy. "I knew something had happened. When we moved out of Half Moon Valley, I told Cristal, my husband, 'I know something has happened to Patrick McGonegal.' He had written me a letter not long before, saying that he was working in a gravel pit. As soon as he could earn enough money to make the trip, he hoped to come for Rosanna. Now I know why he never came."

Although Rosanna was nine years old, she was somewhat wary of this stranger. He did not have long hair and a beard like Cristal had, and he did not wear hooks and eyes on his coat and vest. His hands were softer and whiter than Momli's hands, and his clothes were so smooth. *Such a different looking man,* thought Rosanna as she stood close to Elizabeth's chair.

After they had talked a few minutes, Momli asked, "You haven't had any supper yet, have you?"

"No. I'm not usually a heavy eater, but I must confess that stagecoach ride has made me rather hungry."

Momli left the room. In a surprisingly short time, she announced, "Supper is ready. Just come out here to the kitchen. It's only a light meal. Would you like to wash before you eat?"

When William said he would, Momli filled the basin with warm water, placed it on a nearby bench, laid a piece of soap beside it, and hung a fresh towel on a nail. "You can wash here."

William was not accustomed to washing in the kitchen. But since he knew that Amish people do not have bathrooms, he conformed gracefully, with Rosanna watching his every move.

When William sat down to the table, he was amazed at what Momli had prepared in so short a time: luscious thick slices of chestnut-brown fried ham, three fried eggs with golden yellow yolks, fried potatoes flavored with onion, stewed tomatoes, red beets and pickles, homemade bread, butter yellow as gold, apple butter and quince jelly, and for a final course, a piece of cherry pie cut from the largest pie William had ever seen.

"Will you drink coffee or milk? You're welcome to both if you care for them."

"This supper is so good," responded William, "that I think I can't refuse either of them, so I'll take both."

When he had eaten all he could hold, Momli urged, "Take some more. You've had a long ride."

"I've already eaten more than I usually do, but everything is so good and I was so hungry, I just couldn't quit, Momli." William had heard Rosanna call Elizabeth 'Momli,' so to make her feel free with him, he also called her Momli. "If this is just a light meal, I would like to be here sometime when you prepare a regular meal. I don't believe it could be better than this one was."

Momli never responded to anything that sounded like flattery, so she simply said, "I hope you had enough to eat."

William tried to make friends with Rosanna, but his smart clothes and his unusual interest in her seemed to put her on her guard. Trying to explain to her that he was her brother and that his name was McGonegal, too, didn't seem to help. How could he be her brother? He was not Momli's son, and she certainly was Momli's little girl. Not until Rosanna was thirteen years old did she come to understand that Momli was not her real mother. When she did, she wept brokenheartedly for two days.

When William went to bed that night, he noticed that there was no carpet on the floor, no pictures on the walls, no curtains on the windows, and no washbowl in the room. Everything was severely plain, but immaculate. The bed was high, and the mattress was filled with finely cut straw. When once his tired body nestled down into that crude mattress, he thought he had never rested more comfortably.

Before he drifted off to sleep, he pondered the simple, efficient life of this plain woman. Again and again, the words "quiet simplicity, peace, and contentment" floated through his mind. What a supper! What cleanliness! What piety! What freedom from strife and rivalry! And what joy and gladness Rosanna showed in obeying Elizabeth's every wish!

As sleep approached, his mind drifted back to Half Moon Valley. Once more he heard his father say to Elizabeth, as he left his newborn Rosanna with her, "Elizabeth, it's bin mighty fine and good o' ye to help me so, and I'll never stop askin' the Virgin Mary to bless you and the baby and shield you from harm and want." Surely that prayer was answered. As the mountain shadows of Lost Creek Valley closed in upon him and shut out the light, he slowly fell into a restful sleep.

The next day, Rosanna agreed to take William out to the garden to see the flowers and to inspect the vegetables she had planted. She also took him down to the schoolhouse where Mary McLaughlin had taught her for the last four winters. Forgetting her reserve for a moment, Rosanna confided, "When I get big, Momli wants me to be a schoolteacher, and I want to be one too. Then I can earn lots of money and help Momli, if she needs anything."

William had hoped to take Rosanna back to Philadelphia with him. Yet he could not help but appreciate the loyalty she showed toward Elizabeth.

That afternoon, William mentioned the matter that had been weighing heavily on his mind. "Elizabeth, will you let me take Rosanna back to Philadelphia with me and make a little Catholic girl out of her?"

Elizabeth had sensed from the beginning that this was why William had come. She was silent for a long moment. Then in a voice almost breaking with sadness, she said, "No, Rosanna is the only little girl I have. I have taken care of her ever since she was born, and I could not give her up now."

At this Rosanna spoke up with her usual Irish quickness. "And I would not go with you, either. I would not leave my mother."

When William saw that he could not persuade Elizabeth to give her up, he proposed, "Well, then just let her go along with me to the station on the stagecoach tomorrow."

Elizabeth's quick intuition warned her of his intentions. "Oh, no, it is too far for such a little girl to go on the stage."

William kept insisting that she go along. As the Amish people practice the biblical injunction to be easily entreated (James 3:17), Elizabeth felt she had no other choice but to let Rosanna go with him to the train station. However, she took a precaution that she felt would work. She knew that everyone took an interest in Rosanna as a little orphan girl, and that they all loved her for her witty sayings and her friendship for everybody. Elizabeth was confident that if she confided in big John Young, the stage driver, she could arrange things all right.

That evening after supper, while Rosanna and William, were washing the dishes, she walked over to see big John. He was busily greasing the axles of the stagecoach and looked up from his work. "Why, good evening, Elizabeth. What can I do for you this evening?"

"Much," replied Elizabeth.

Then she told him that Rosanna's brother was visiting there, and how he had pleaded for permission to take Rosanna back to Philadelphia with him and make a little Catholic girl out of her, and how she had refused to give Rosanna up. She explained that William was begging her to allow Rosanna to go along to the station with him in the morning, and that she had grave misgivings, suspecting that he intended to take her with him by force.

"You see, John, I almost had to allow her to go to the station with him because he insisted so hard. But when I gave my consent, I felt that I could depend on you to look after her and see that he does not take her."

Big John straightened up to his full height and took off his hat. "Elizabeth, go home and don't worry a minute. If he takes her, he'll do it over my dead body.

We'll never let anyone steal our little girl."

Next morning when the stage arrived, William and Rosanna were ready to go. When they were safely seated, big John gave Elizabeth a knowing look, cracked the whip, and the two slick-coated black horses whisked them away in a cloud of dust.

When they arrived at the station in Thompsontown, big John tied his horses to the nearest hitching pole. Then he came over to where Rosanna stood, took her hand in his, and looked at the slick, slender city boy as much as to say, "Now, smarty, just you touch this little girl to take her with you by force, and I'll tie your scrawny body into knots."

William saw through it all in a moment. He did not even ask Rosanna to get on the train with him to say good-bye.

Big John and Rosanna stood watching the train speed away till it was lost around the curve in the river, then walked to the stagecoach. Big John lifted Rosanna into the coach and said, "Little girl, you do not know what I did for you today."

On the way back to Jericho, the thought of that young fellow kidnapping Rosanna made big John so angry that he clenched his huge fist and exclaimed, "By the eternals, if that smarty had touched this little girl, I'd a punched the daylights out of him." He swelled with pride as he thought of the confidence Elizabeth had placed in him.

When Rosanna came running into the house, Elizabeth asked, "Was it a nice ride?"

"Oh, yes, and at the station, big John stood beside me and held my hand. Momli, why did he do that?"

"Maybe he thought William might take you along, if he didn't take care of you."

"I thought of that, too. But when big John held my hand in his, I wasn't a bit afraid."

❧ ❧ ❧

William went back to Philadelphia with a glowing report of Rosanna's brilliancy and beauty. "Does Elizabeth dress her in Amish clothes?" Margaret wondered.

"Yes, she does, and with her little black apron and her little black bonnet, she looks as pretty as a little nun. Why, the beauty of the shamrock is in her grace, the roses of Killarney shine in her cheeks, its waters sparkle in her eyes, and Saint Cecilia's own music tinkles in her voice."

These were almost the very words their father had used about their mother many years before. But William's scheme to bring Rosanna back with him had not worked. It was thwarted by an untrained woman with a keen mind and a simple faith in God.

CHAPTER 6

The Kishacoquillas

As THE SEASONS came and went, the people around Jericho became more and more friendly with the quiet widow and her little Irish charge. Everyone seemed to take an interest in Rosanna, as though they too had been appointed by Providence to help bring her up.

When Elizabeth took her along to the village store, Mr. Banks would ask her questions about the garden or about school just to enjoy her enthusiasm. To see her black eyes sparkle, one only needed to say something disparaging about Mary McLaughlin, the schoolteacher, and Rosanna defended her staunchly.

Elizabeth and Rosanna lived happily in Lost Creek Valley, where the orchards, gardens, fields, and cattle all suggested peace and plenty. However, they did miss Cristal, and the two beautiful sorrel horses they had to sell after he died.

As they discussed their loneliness for Cristal, they talked more and more about Rosanna studying to be a teacher. If she continued to make such fine progress in school, it would be only a few years until she could take the county examination, get a certificate, and teach.

"But what will we do about your dress?" wondered Elizabeth. "There are no Amish girls who teach school. Maybe they'll laugh at your plain dress and cap." (The Amish did not found their own schools until the next century.)

"Well," declared Rosanna, "I'll be such a good teacher that they will not think about my clothes. Besides, I might be able to get the Renno School, and there the pupils are nearly all Amish."

It was a fine idea. Together they looked forward to the day when Rosanna would be a teacher.

❧ ❧ ❧

As harvesttime approached, Rosanna said, "Momli, would you let me go over to Joseph Yoder's to help in the harvest field, if they need me? I could earn some money, and then I could buy some of my own clothes. That would save some for you."

"Do you think you are strong enough to work in the field?"

"Well, I'm not very big, but I believe I can do more

work than Joseph's girls can, and they help sometimes."

"*Jah, well,*" Elizabeth reluctantly agreed.

The next time Rosanna saw Joseph Yoder in the village, she greeted him, "Good morning, Joseph. I'd like to help you in the harvest. Do you need any help?"

"Well, now, let me see," parried Joseph. "Do you think you could carry sheaves or heap hay?"

"Of course I can. And I can bind wheat sheaves too, I believe."

"Well, you're pretty spunky. I'll let you try. I'll send for you when the hay is ready to haul."

Rosanna could hardly wait till she reached home to tell Momli that she was going to help Joseph Yoder make hay and harvest. For the first time, she would have some money that she had earned herself, and that would be something to look forward to.

When haymaking time came, she found that she could heap hay almost as fast as the men. She could tie up sheaves for the man who cradled the grain with a scythe. Some of the other jobs she could not handle as well as the men, but she worked hard. When she had helped ten days in all, and Joseph paid her thirty-five cents per day, she was delighted.

"Momli, just think. I have three dollars and a half, and I'm going to save it, too."

Like all Amish children, Rosanna was learning to earn money as soon as possible and save it for a useful purpose. To the credit of the Amish people, none of them accept welfare payments of any kind. They may not make much money, but they try to save part of all they earn.

A year or so before Cristal Kauffman passed away, Sarah, the wife of Bishop Shem Yoder, died. Shem had two sons, Sam and Yost, and one daughter, Leah. Yost, the oldest of the children, was already married and had a home of his own. The bishop got along reasonably well in managing the house by hiring someone to do most of the work and letting relatives come in to help sometimes. But it was not real housekeeping, Shem observed.

He was also concerned that Leah was not being taught to work as a young girl should be. A bishop had to set a good example for the congregation. Till now, Shem Yoder had showed no outward signs that he was interested in finding another wife. According to the Scriptures, however, a bishop should have a wife and a family of well-instructed, obedient children (1 Tim. 3).

Since Sarah had been gone for almost three years now, Shem felt that no one could criticize him if he decided to marry again. Not many women were available. It would not look right for him to marry a young woman. He knew a few middle-aged women who had never married. Because of the very fact that they had stayed unmarried, he did not care to consider them.

As Shem pondered the problem, he found that the most suitable woman in the congregation to become a bishop's wife was Elizabeth Kauffman, Cristal Kauffman's widow. She was a good worker, had a quiet disposition, was devout, and dressed strictly according to the rules of the church.

There was only one slight drawback—the half-grown Irish girl she was raising. How would Leah and Sam get along with her? He knew that Rosanna was smart in school, a good worker, and quick-witted, while his own Leah was much less gifted. He had trouble keeping Sam in school till he mastered the three Rs. He knew, too, that Elizabeth simply adored Rosanna. If he married Elizabeth, it would take some fine diplomacy to keep things running smoothly.

One day when he had some business in the village, the bishop stopped to see Elizabeth on the pretext of finding out whether Rosanna wasn't about old enough to join the church. He found Elizabeth cordial and rather quiet. As for the little Irish girl, she was so pleasant to the bishop that he could not help but like her. Rosanna seemed quite helpful and friendly. She was already taking over some of the responsibilities of the house so Elizabeth would have fewer cares. Nothing could please the bishop more. Here was the good fruit of Christian education, and he did not even try to conceal his pleasure.

As he mused on the way home, a new concern arose: Why, Rosanna is much more considerate of Elizabeth than Leah and Sam are of me. If Elizabeth and I should marry, and Rosanna were as kind to me as she is to Elizabeth, I am afraid I would like her better than my own children. "*Immer Druwwel aeryetz* (always trouble somewhere)," he muttered.

The bishop felt that his visit had gone well. He had inquired about Rosanna joining the church, whether Elizabeth had plenty of firewood for the winter, and whether she had much trouble in finding a way to go to preaching. But he was uncertain whether he showed too much approval of Rosanna and whether he had entirely concealed his admiration for Elizabeth. *"Well, was machts aus* (well, what does it matter)?" If people talk, let them talk. He would pray over the matter and try to follow God's leading.

The next Sunday at preaching, his full round cheeks became a little redder when Rosanna came to him. "Bishop Shem, Momli and I have been talking about my joining church this summer. Momli thinks I'm still a little too young. So I will wait a year or two yet."

"Jah, well," responded Shem, just a little embarrassed, "but you will not put it off too long, will you?"

"Oh, no. I'll join just as soon as I am big enough."

Shem noticed that a few men overheard what Rosanna had said. From the conversation, they could easily conclude that he had been over to Elizabeth's house. He was aware, too, how little it takes to start rumors flying about a widower and a widow. Shem tried hard to make it appear that he was simply attending to his duties as bishop.

☙ ☙ ☙

As autumn approached, Shem saw clearly that his household was not being well run. Leah was young. Although she tried hard, she did not accomplish everything that needed to be done. There was little canned fruit in the cellar, few dried apples and tomatoes, and no dried corn. It was time to cook apple butter and soap, and there was nobody to go ahead with it.

As he prayed for guidance, the leading seemed clearly toward Elizabeth Kauffman. But he must not be hasty. Whenever he could think of a reason to talk to Elizabeth, he never lost an opportunity. The more he saw of her and Rosanna, the better he liked both of them.

When the autumn days were deepening into winter and the young Amish folks were being "published" (having their intended marriages announced in church), Shem felt that the time was right. He went over to David Renno, one of the ministers under him, confidentially laid the matter before him, and asked his advice. After thinking through the situation, David expressed entire approval.

Shem was happy with this confirmation of his proposal. "If you approve, Brother David, then I choose you to be my *Schtecklimann* (go-between). Do your duty."

According to Amish custom, David's duty then was to go by night without anyone knowing it, call on Elizabeth, mention Shem's desire to marry her, and receive her reply.

David waited until he was sure Rosanna would be asleep. When he was seated in Elizabeth's house, he confided, "I have come at the request of Bishop Shem to ask you to consider being his wife." He gently called attention to her widowhood and her need of both moral and financial support. Shem Yoder was the bishop of the church, well-thought-of by both local congregations, and even by other denominations, and was well-to-do.

Since Sarah passed away, David explained, Bishop Shem needed someone with character and experience, in good standing in the church, to help him raise his family. "And," David concluded modestly, "I think, Sister Elizabeth, that you would suit the place better than anybody else in the church. What answer may I take back to Shem?"

This visit from David Renno was not entirely unexpected to Elizabeth. She had been noticing the bishop's friendliness to Rosanna and her. Intuition told her unmistakably that Shem Yoder was interested in her. She remained silent for a few moments. Then she stated, "If the bishop wishes it that way, I will try to do my part."

The next day David Renno went over to see the bishop, who was obviously anxious to know the answer. David told Shem that he had fulfilled the duties of his office, but he teased just a little by withholding the answer for a moment. Then he reported, "Elizabeth agrees that if marriage is your wish, she will try to do her part."

"Thank God!" exclaimed the bishop. "And thank you, Brother David, for interceding for me."

After a brief wedding ceremony, Elizabeth and Rosanna moved to Shem Yoder's big house to become part of his family. Elizabeth's experienced eye saw many things for the women of the house to do. Her own house, although plainly furnished, had been kept immaculate. Here windows needed washing, floors needed scrubbing, the tinware was unpolished, the stove had lost its luster, and there were no flowers in the house or in the yard.

Rosanna settled into a faithful routine of helping to milk, looking after the chickens and eggs, and carrying skimmed milk to the pigs. She found that the round of chores gave her more to do than when they lived in the village. But when there was work to be done, she did it uncomplainingly.

✍ ✍ ✍

Bishop Shem had just returned from Big Valley, where he had gone to help hold a communion service. Besides being interested in the growing congregation there, he was greatly impressed with the fertility of the land and the unmistakable signs of prosperity. He explained this to Elizabeth and asked whether she would be willing to move to Big (Kishacoquillas) Valley if he could buy a good farm there.

When Elizabeth saw his enthusiasm, she simply said in her quiet way, "*Jah, well,*" meaning, I am not greatly interested, but I am willing to do as you wish.

What Shem did not tell her at once was that he had already spotted a farm for sale that appealed to him. This farm lay just north of Belleville, a thriving little town in the heart of the Kishacoquillas Valley.

It was part of a tract of two thousand acres granted by the William Penn Estate to Captain John Armstrong for his services in the French and Indian War. While most Amish are not greatly interested in historic facts, Bishop Shem nevertheless liked the idea of owning a farm so closely connected with the history of the country.

He made it a point to go to the valley soon to see whether he could buy the farm. Bishop Shem had no trouble arranging the purchase and getting a clear title and deed. When he returned to Lost Creek Valley this time, anybody could see that there was a new joy and inspiration in his heart. He was moving to Big Valley soon, to live in the midst of large congregations of Amish people.

Early the next spring, Bishop Shem asked a few of his members to bring their teams and help him move to the valley. They loaded all the wagons in the evening so that the bishop and his family could get an early start the next day. The bishop had a two-horse team and a four-horse team of his own. With the help of a few of the members, they had no trouble getting all the household goods and the farm implements on the wagons.

Next morning before daybreak, a caravan of five horse-drawn wagons started on the long journey to Kishacoquillas Valley. More than half the trip was over the same road that Cristal, Elizabeth, and Rosanna had come some ten years before. But at Reedsville, where they stayed overnight on their first journey, they turned to the left. A new road led southwest into the beautiful Kishacoquillas Valley, to new friends and a new home.

Rosanna was pleased at the prospect of a larger church, more young folks, and greater prosperity. But the pleasure was slightly dimmed by the thought of leaving her good friends in Lost Creek Valley. However, the farm which the bishop bought could not have been better chosen so far as Rosanna's future joy and happiness were concerned.

CHAPTER 7

New Friends

THE WOMEN BUSILY arranged the furniture in the new home while the men parked the farming implements in the barn. Elizabeth and Rosanna were pleased with the new house. It was large, with a high porch running all the way along the front. On the ground floor was a cool basement, to be used as kitchen in hot weather, with two small rooms for storing canned fruits and vegetables. Large bins of apples would make winter months a delight.

On the second floor was a large kitchen, a dining room (although most of the eating would be done in the kitchen), a large living room, and a bedroom. Here the walls were movable so when they had preaching, the first floor could be converted into one large room, and everyone could see and hear the preacher. Upstairs were five large bedrooms, assuring them adequate room to house visitors.

Accompanying a large bank barn were all the necessary outbuildings. This farm was complete in every detail. There was plenty of stable room for Bishop Shem's six horses, eight or ten cows, a dozen steers, and a flock of sheep. The upper part of the barn was divided into four large mows, two of which were used as threshing floors. These floors were so well laid that, if occasion demanded, they could be swept and used for preaching services or for a "barn-party" when the young folks gathered for an evening of party games and singing.

Being rather large, the farm required lots of work and long hours. During the summer months, everybody arose at five o'clock. Since Amish bishops and ministers do not receive any pay for their services, Bishop Shem rose with the rest. He usually fed the horses and the cows while Sam, his son, curried the horses and harnessed them for the field.

While the men were doing their morning chores, Elizabeth built the fire in the kitchen stove and prepared breakfast. Rosanna and Leah went to the barn and milked the cows. By the time Shem had the horses and cows fed, Sam had the horses harnessed and ready for the field, the girls had the milking done, and Elizabeth had breakfast ready.

Then they all gathered in the kitchen at the table and bowed their heads in silent grace. Amish people

ROSANNA'S BIG VALLEY
HOME WITH BISHOP SHEM

never engaged in audible grace. In this area, they rarely had family worship, but at the close of each meal they observed a silent prayer of thanksgiving. In an Amish family, everybody had to be at the table on time and remain at the table till the silent prayer of thanksgiving was over. To leave the table before the last silent thanks was observed would be a violation of a religious observance.

Elizabeth had been a good mother to Rosanna, and now she wanted to be a good mother to Leah, too. Elizabeth would let one of the girls wash the dishes while she and the other one made the beds, did the sweeping, cleaned the yard, or worked in the garden. Shem could easily see that Rosanna was much better trained to work than Leah was, so he urged Elizabeth, *"Nau, mach sie schaffe* (now, make her work)." The bishop's own daughter certainly did not dare stigmatize the family by being a poor worker.

Elizabeth spent a lot of time with Leah, trying to teach her better working habits. When Rosanna showed some impatience with Leah and complained to Elizabeth that Leah was so slow, Elizabeth would say in her kind, patient way, "You see, Rosanna, Leah did not have an Irish mother who was quick, like you had, so you must just be glad and patient. She'll learn someday."

"Yes, Momli. You're right, I know."

One of Rosanna's great concerns was the kind of school they had at Belleville. One day at the dinner table, she mentioned that she could hardly wait for school to start. Turning to Sam, Rosanna asked, "Are you going to school the first day, Sam?"

"Oh, no! I'm done going to school. I don't like it."

"Why, I just loved to go to school and learn from Mary McLaughlin," responded Rosanna. "I hope they have a good teacher here, for I want to be a teacher too someday."

Bishop Shem looked up in surprise but merely said, "So?"

Rosanna did not like the upward inflection of his voice that seemed to mean, "We'll see about that." She knew that the Amish were not favorable to education beyond the eighth grade, but she had never talked to her new foster father about it.

Nothing more was said at the table, but Elizabeth sensed trouble ahead. She knew how determined Rosanna was to become a teacher, and she also knew the bishop's awkward position. As the head of a church opposed to education, he could hardly allow a member of his own household to become a teacher.

That evening in the privacy of their room, Elizabeth told Shem about Rosanna's great desire to become a teacher. "I guess I'm to blame," she admitted, "but you see, she was really an orphan girl. I thought maybe someday she would have to make her own living, and she could do that a little easier by teaching than in any other way. Besides, she learns very easy."

"I can't have anybody in my house studying to be a schoolteacher," stated Shem, feeling the weight of the church on his shoulders. How could he preach against "worldly wisdom" and allow a member of his own household to get all of it she could? It would put him in an embarrassing position and undermine his authority in the church. He could not permit that.

Elizabeth understood the situation. But how could she tell Rosanna? Next day Elizabeth sent Leah to the garden to weed the onions. She asked Rosanna to sit in the kitchen with her and sew rags together to make a rug.

When they had worked quietly for a while, Elizabeth began, "Rosanna, I must tell you something that hurts me very much because I know it will hurt you, too. Shem asked me whether you really intend to become a schoolteacher. I told him what we had planned. He said that since the church is against worldly wisdom and education, he could not allow anybody in his house to study to be a teacher. If he did, the people would blame him for not upholding the rules of the church.

"I can see, Rosanna, the position it puts him in. I guess you'll have to give up being a teacher. I am so sorry, but I believe things will work out all right some other way. God never lets us suffer long if we trust his leadings."

"Oh, Momli, how can I ever give up being a teacher? I had my whole heart set on that work." Rosanna began to cry, but when she saw tears in Momli's eyes, she realized she was not bearing this disappointment alone. Her heart welled up with great love for Momli, unlimited confidence in her, and a firm desire never to hurt her in any way. These thoughts somehow gave Rosanna strength to dry her tears. All that the other family members ever knew of this great struggle was that the Irish lilt in Rosanna's laugh was missing for several days.

Shem sensed this. While he felt he had to be firm,

he could still be sympathetic. For several days he tried to show Rosanna every consideration he could. He did one thing that proved to Rosanna that he was trying to be as nice to her as his position allowed.

Every year traveling circuses came to Belleville. It was not against the rules of the church for Amish people to go to a circus if there were animals on exhibition. So Shem said to Elizabeth at the supper table, "There's a circus coming to town in a few days. There will be some tigers and lions and elephants and other animals to see. How would you like to take Leah and Rosanna to the circus to see the animals?"

The local Amish consensus was that if you paid to see the animals, you were right there anyway. So there was no reason not to go in and see the rest of the performance. The rationale was that God made the animals, and surely it could not be wrong to go and see them. About the rest of the show, there was no argument to support it, but nothing was said about it.

How Rosanna and Leah enjoyed the circus! They had never seen an elephant before and were greatly amused to see one swing his great trunk around to ward off flies. When they had looked at the tigers and the lions and the giraffe, they stood in front of a cage for a long time, watching the monkeys leap from one perch to another and swing by their tails. Finally Leah said, "*Sie gooke schier wie Mensche* (they look almost like people)."

In the big tent, they were hardly seated before a parade began, led by the band. How that band music thrilled Rosanna! "*Wann ich danze keent, deht ich* (if I could dance, I would)."

Elizabeth was pleased to hear the ring in Rosanna's laugh again, for now she felt sure that Shem's gesture of peace was having its effect.

Rosanna was living down her greatest disappointment. While she was still heavyhearted, she consoled herself with the thought of Cristal's comforting words, "All things work together for good to those who love the Lord."

At the supper table that evening, Shem saw that his peace plan was working, and he was inwardly relieved, for it hurt him to sadden Rosanna. As she told them about the animals and the band and the clowns, he could hear the familiar lilt in her laugh which he had missed so much during the last few days.

🙠 🙠 🙠

Rosanna learned to know a lot of girls her age at the preaching services. And what preaching services they had in Big Valley! Why, in summertime the houses were filled, and sometimes they even had to put benches on the porch for some of the men. And the singing, what volume! Rosanna began to study German so she could sing, too. She loved music.

When preaching was at Reuben Kauffman's one Sunday, she was surprised to have Reuben come to her and say, "Why, Rosanna, how you have grown! I knew you when you were a little Irish baby. Baby Rosanna, we called you. I'm glad you came to Big Valley. Long ago your father asked me to look after you a little, and I told him I would." Then he told her how he had moved to Big Valley from Half Moon Valley just about the time his Uncle Cristal and Elizabeth had moved to Lost Creek Valley.

Rosanna was delighted to have such a fine-looking man come to her and tell her that he knew her when she was a baby in Half Moon Valley, and had known her father, Patrick McGonegal. She learned that Reuben had taken her father and the three older children to the railroad station at Bellefonte when they departed for Philadelphia long ago.

She had heard Reuben lead one of the hymns at preaching that day. Now she said to herself, "Just as soon as I can learn to read German, I am going to ask Reuben to teach me the '*Lob Sang* (Praise hymn).' " Because it was always used as the second hymn of every preaching service, young folks tried to learn that hymn first. If they could not learn to sing the "*Lob Sang*," they might just as well give up trying to learn any of the slow tunes, or hymns.

At preaching that day, Rosanna got acquainted with two sisters about her own age. They were Sarah and Franey (Frances) Yoder, who lived just a field's breadth away, in the big stone house. They were Lame Yost Yoder's daughters. Rosanna heard these girls talking to some others about beginning to join church in two weeks.

In each congregation, preaching service was only held every other Sunday. Rosanna listened attentively to the girls' plans to take instruction for membership. Two years ago in Lost Creek Valley, she had promised Bishop Shem that she would join church as soon as she was old enough. Maybe now was the time.

When they had returned from preaching that Sunday and Rosanna was alone with Momli, she said,

"Momli, today at preaching I heard Lame Yost's girls, Sarah and Franey, saying that about twenty boys and girls will begin joining church in two weeks. Do you think I'm old enough to join now?"

Momli thought for a moment and then replied, "I can hardly believe you're sixteen years old already. How quickly you've grown up! If you feel like joining church now, I would be glad."

Thus two weeks later, Rosanna was one of those who began the process of joining church. What a joy it was to belong to a group of twenty young folks who were bound together by a common purpose! She liked the girls, who were all dressed the same style.

Each girl wore a black *Kapp* (head cap), a white *Halsduch* (cape) bound at the waist front and back and crossed over the bosom, and a white apron. In these details they were all alike, but some had blue dresses, and others brown, dark red, or black. Yet no matter what the color was, they were all perfectly plain with no figures or flowers, and every dress was cut from the same pattern.

The skirt was long and full, the bodice tight-fitting, the sleeves long and rather close-fitting, and each dress had a little tuck in the center of the back at the waistline called a *Lapplein*. Each girl wore an apron almost as long as her skirt, fastened around the waist with a single apron string about an inch wide, and pinned at the side.

The boys wore a *Mutze* (MUHT-sa), a frock coat with a split tail, and broadfall pants. Their hair reached an inch below the ear lobe, and each boy had to begin letting his beard grow. Any young person unwilling to comply with these requirements would not be considered for membership.

Rosanna and the others were required to come to the next six or seven regular preaching services for definite religious instruction. They went into the house each Sunday before church services began and were seated on benches reserved for them. The fellows sat on the bench just back of the one reserved for the ministers, and the girls sat just back of the boys. The first hymn was announced, all the men removed their hats, and the singing began. Then the ministers withdrew to an upstairs room prepared for them, and the group joining church followed.

There, for twenty minutes or a half hour, the bishop instructed them on the plan of salvation, baptism, foot washing, communion, nonresistance, nonswearing, nonconformity, separation from the world, and the godly life in general.

After six or seven Sundays of instruction, the members of the group were asked one by one if they were willing to conform to the rules of the church and whether they still wished to become a member of the church. Those who answered yes, as they always did, were considered eligible for baptism on the following church Sunday.

On the day the young folks were to be taken into the church, preaching services were held at Lame Yost Yoder's home, just across the field from Rosanna's home. Bishop Shem and his family walked to preaching that day. Lame Yost Yoder lived in the large stone house built by Captain John Armstrong on the two-thousand-acre tract received from the William Penn

Estate for his services in the French and Indian War. This house was built about 1770 and was purchased from Captain Armstrong in 1796 by Joseph Yoder of Earl Township, Lancaster County, Pennsylvania. It has remained in the Joseph Yoder family for more than a century and a half.

When they arrived at preaching about half past eight on that special Sunday morning, the August sun was already hot. Rosanna opened her cap strings as she walked, hoping she might be a little cooler. The large barnyard was already almost filled with white-top and yellow-top carriages. Yost had seen to it that his two boys, Christian and Eli, had everything in tip-top shape. The barnyard was raked and swept, the stables cleaned, the entries swept, the manure pile built up straight on every side, and all farm machinery strictly in its place.

As the boys were busy unhitching horses and taking them to the stables, Eli called out, "Oh my, Cristli, what will we do? The stables are almost full already, and just look at that string of carriages coming in the lane!"

"When the stables are full, put the horses onto the barn floor, and when that is full, tie them to the barnyard fence and give them hay. That's the best we can do," said "Little" Crist (Christian), oldest son of Lame Yost Yoder. By nine o'clock everything was full and many of the carriages had to be placed in the field adjoining the barnyard.

Christian called to Eli, "You boys will have to take care of the horses now. I must go in. They're beginning to sing." Crist belonged to the group that was joining church, so he had to be there when the ministers withdrew to the upstairs room for instruction.

In a few minutes the great stone house was filled to overflowing, and Reuben Kauffman announced the first hymn. All hats were removed, and men's and women's voices singing in unison filled the house. The ministers rose and led the way to the upstairs room, followed by the twenty young folks who were to be baptized and taken into the church that day. Rosanna thought she had never heard such wonderful singing.

This was the last meeting with the ministers in private counsel and instruction. "Dress plainly, according to the rules of the church," Bishop Shem reminded them. "Abstain from all worldly amusements—entertainments, festivals, ball games, and dances. Avoid profanity, vulgarity, boasting, and gossip. Abstain from drinking and carousing, and above all, do not yield to the lust of the flesh.

"Let your conversation be mild and modest, your conduct kind and gentle, and all your actions dominated by the Golden Rule. Tell the truth. Your word must never be questioned. Walk soberly, and let your light shine before the world so that they may see your good works and glorify your heavenly Father."

Every young man and young woman felt the weight of the bishop's words and the solemn gravity of the step they were about to take. The young folks were given a final opportunity to express their willingness to obey the rules of the church. Then they were dismissed to go downstairs and take the places reserved for them, the two benches just back of the ministers' bench.

The order of services on this baptismal day was the same as usual. Christian L. Yoder preached first. This was followed by silent prayer. The Scripture was read by deacon John Hostetler, with the congregation standing. The main sermon was delivered by Bishop Shem, who spoke mostly on the duties of young people entering the Christian life, quoting freely from the Bible and especially the New Testament.

After he had preached a little over an hour, Bishop Shem stated, "Today we solemnize the rite of baptism. Twenty young folks have expressed their faith in God, have promised to obey the rules of the church, have requested baptism, and have asked to be taken into the church.

"We are convinced that they are sincere. But if any member knows a good reason why any one of these applicants should not be received into the church, let us hear it now, for after this no complaint will be heard." After a brief pause, he declared, "There seems to be no objection from any member. We will now prepare for baptism."

The deacon went out and returned with a pitcher of water. The applicants stood up, the benches were pushed aside, and they all knelt in a line before Bishop Shem, who remained standing. When all was ready, the bishop asked, "Do you believe that Jesus Christ is the Son of God?" Each applicant replied in turn, "I believe that Jesus Christ is the Son of God."

"Do you promise by the help of God to renounce the world, the flesh, and the devil, to obey the rules of the church, and to live faithfully according to the Scriptures?" In turn again, each one answered, "I do."

The bishop then stepped up to the first young man in line, and held his hands funnel-like above the young man's head while the deacon poured water through the bishop's hands three times as the bishop said, "Daniel (using only the first name of the applicant), I baptize you in the name of the Father, and of the Son, and of the Holy Spirit." The deacon timed the three pourings to coincide with the mention of the three names of the Godhead.

The bishop then took the young man by the hand and said, "In the name of the Father, arise." Then he greeted the young man with the holy kiss and invoked God's blessing upon him. He repeated the same ceremony with each of the other young men.

When the bishop came to the young women, his wife, Elizabeth, came forward to assist him. She removed the young woman's cap, and the bishop placed his hands above the young woman's head. The deacon poured water three times, and the bishop said, "Mary, I baptize you . . . ," as before. The bishop's wife then replaced the young woman's cap, took her by the right hand, and said softly, "In the name of the Father, arise." She kissed the young woman and invoked God's blessing upon her. They repeated the ceremony with each young woman in turn.

Elizabeth did her part with grace and poise till she came to Rosanna. When she removed Rosanna's cap, her eyes filled with tears. Even Bishop Shem, who had baptized scores of young folks, could scarcely control his own voice and emotions as he intoned, "Rosanna, I baptize you in the name of the Father, and of the Son, and of the Holy Spirit."

As Elizabeth replaced Rosanna's cap and took her by the right hand, saying, "In the name of the Father, arise," her voice broke. She kissed Rosanna, put her strong arm about Rosanna for just a moment, and whispered brokenly, "God bless you."

As the people looked on, there was hardly a dry eye in the house. Some of the older women said softly through their tears, *"Wie die Lisbet doch des Meedli liebt* (how dearly Elizabeth loves that little girl)."

When the baptismal service was finished, the benches were put back in place, the young folks seated, and the sermon continued for some time. Then all knelt while the bishop read the prayer from the prayer book. After the prayer, everyone stood up. The benediction was pronounced. Then all the worshipers bowed deeply, bending the knee, and were seated. The deacon announced the home where preaching would be held in two weeks.

The closing hymn was sung, and when the last sound had died away, the men arose slowly, put on their hats, and methodically moved out of the house, into the yard, and out to the barn. The women adjourned to the porches and to the summerhouse to make room for those whose duty it was to set the tables and serve the dinner. Preaching was "out," and twenty young members had been added to the congregation.

As the people finished their dinners, the white-top and yellow-top carriages began to move out the lane in long rows. Bishop Shem stood in the houseyard talking to some of the older men. When he saw Elizabeth and the girls, Rosanna and Leah, coming through the yard, he joined them, and they headed toward home, across the field.

As they walked through Lame Yost Yoder's outer barnyard, Rosanna could not help observing Little Crist. He had resumed his duties—going for horses, hitching them up, and helping people get on their way. While he was not tall, he was well-built, with light wavy hair, blue eyes, and red cheeks.

Rosanna had noticed Little Crist before. Today, as she saw him move about his work with such ease and enthusiasm, she thought that he was about the nicest young man she had seen in the Kishacoquillas Valley. But what of it? It was not yet time for her to think about the boys.

🙠 🙠 🙠

In the evening, when the church benches (*Gemeh Benk*) had been stored away and all the furniture put back in its place, the tired family sat in the living room. Sarah commented, "Franey, didn't you think Rosanna McGonegal looked pretty nice today with her black wavy hair and red cheeks?"

"Yes, I think she's a beauty," replied Franey.

"What did you think of her, Crist?"

"None of your business," retorted Little Crist, blushing.

The girls tittered as though they knew a secret.

"Don't mind the girls," his mother soothed him. "*Sie sin glene Babbelmeiler* (they're little babblers)."

Christian said nothing more, but he knew what he was thinking.

CHAPTER 8

New Joys

A S THE HOT September days began to shorten and the evenings became longer, Momli planned some fall projects. "Girls, there's a saying that when the wind blows over the oat stubble, the women must begin working in the evening. The oat stubble has already been plowed under. Rosanna, you may do the patching and the darning. Leah, you may get your knitting. I want you to knit your father a pair of woolen stockings for Christmas. I will show you how to make the stitches."

Rosanna had already learned to knit stockings. So as soon as her mending was finished, she began a pair of stockings for herself. The autumn nights were becoming more chilly, and Rosanna knew that it would not be long now until the big frost. Chestnut burrs would crack open. Chestnuts would fall, and there surely would be some chestnut parties.

Long rows of corn shocks waited in the field. Maybe Bishop Shem would pay her a little for each shock she husked, and that would give her some money for Christmas and winter. Then, too, there might be some cornhuskings, and maybe Momli would let her go to one.

Rosanna was thrilled with the thought of the good times just ahead. Soon she would ask Momli to let her and Leah go to a Sunday evening singing. She had never been to one yet, and how she did love to sing with a large group of people. At a singing she could talk to more people than at preaching. She would learn to know more of the young folks and to sing new tunes.

However, Rosanna had one disappointment to live down. When the school bell rang in the morning, it seemed to say, "Rosanna, come to school." How she did want to go! But Momli said it would be wrong to go now that she had joined church. She certainly did not want to do anything that was wrong, and certainly Momli knew what was best. With that, she began to sing and think of the singings and the cornhuskings that she knew Momli would soon let her attend. It was a joyous world after all.

One day Rosanna received a letter from Philadelphia. It was from her brother William. Now that she understood Momli was not her real mother, she accepted the fact that William and John were her real brothers and that Margaret was her sister. As she grew older, she began to feel a longing, a sort of secret tie, binding her to them.

Knowing that they really belonged to each other, she wanted to see them all. She would write to William—to all of them—and tell them what a happy home she had, with nice clothes, so many good friends, joy in her church life, and Momli, what a mother Momli was!

❧ ❧ ❧

When the men had gotten the cornhusking well under way, Shem said at the dinner table one day, "Girls, if you will help husk corn, I will pay you two cents for each shock you husk. We will tear down the shocks and then bind the fodder after the ears are taken off."

The girls were delighted. Every day, just as soon as Momli could spare them, the girls went to the cornfield. Rosanna had nimble hands, and when the men prepared the shocks for her, she could husk twenty-five shocks per day. "Why," Rosanna rejoiced, "that's fifty cents each day. I'll soon have plenty to buy a new dress and new shoes, with money left over."

Shem knew that he would have to buy clothes for the girls anyway. He was willing to pay them for helping with the corn to give them a feeling of independence and self-respect.

At the breakfast table one morning, Sam reported, "I was in town yesterday evening, and young Crist Yoder told me there's going to be a cornhusking at

Reuben Kauffman's on Thursday evening."

The girls could hardly hide their excitement, but they did not want to appear too eager.

When the morning work was done, the girls went to Momli with their request before leaving for the cornfield. "Momli, may we go to the cornhusking at Reuben Kauffman's on Thursday evening?"

"Will you stay out of trouble?"

"Oh, yes, indeed we will."

"*Jah, well.*" Momli's eyes glowed approval.

"Oh, good!" The girls laughed and could contain their joy no longer.

As they scampered out to the cornfield, they plotted how they could persuade Sam to take them to the cornhusking. They agreed to ask him, "Will you take us to the cornhusking, if Momli lets us go?" The girls told each other, "He'll say yes to that because he'll think Momli won't let us go, so he won't need to take us."

When they arrived in the cornfield, Leah sprang the trap. "Sam, if Momli lets us go, will you take us to the cornhusking Thursday evening?"

"Yes, if Momli lets you go."

The girls giggled, and Bishop Shem advised Sam, "*Nau hen sie dich* (now they've got you)!"

Sam looked a little sheepish, but he couldn't back down after he'd promised them.

When Thursday evening came, the girls quickly washed the supper dishes, ran upstairs, and put on their brown dresses, white caps, black kerchiefs, and aprons. For social occasions, they reversed the colors of their caps and aprons. For church, it was always black caps and white kerchiefs and aprons.

When they arrived at Reuben's, a number of fellows and girls were already in the field. It was a beautiful October evening with a bright full moon. The boys tore down the shocks, and then each one asked a girl to help him husk. In that way, each boy chose a partner.

If girls were not immediately chosen, they began to husk anyway. Soon a boy would come along. When he saw an attractive girl not yet chosen, he would say, "Need any help?" If the girl liked him, she would say, "Sure I do." If she didn't, she would say, "My helper is coming soon." That meant, "Pass on, buddy. I'm not interested."

Reuben Kauffman, being the man of the house, was out in the field directing the work somewhat. When he saw Rosanna and Leah coming into the field, he welcomed them and chatted pleasantly. He knew this was Rosanna's first party, and he was anxious that she have a good time and get started right. "Do you have a partner, Rosanna?" he asked.

"No, we just arrived," she replied.

"I know a fine partner for you. He just came and is not husking yet." Reuben felt a great interest in Rosanna because he knew her when she was a baby in Half Moon Valley. He recalled Patrick McGonegal's parting words to him at the Bellefonte railroad station: "Reuben, ye'll be lookin' after baby Rosanna a bit too, won't you?"

Reuben walked over close to where some boys were standing and called, "Come here, Cristli. I want to have a word with you."

Christian Yoder came at once, and Reuben sug-

CRISTLI AND ROSANNA
HUSKING CORN

gested, "Cristli, why don't you husk with Rosanna McGonegal?"

Cristli was obviously pleased. He walked over to where the girls were standing and said to Rosanna, "I need a partner. Will you help me?"

"Yes," agreed Rosanna. "Could you find a partner for Leah, too?"

Cristli soon found a partner for Leah, and they were off—Cristli and Rosanna at one shock, and Leah and her partner at another. Cristli soon saw that Rosanna knew how to husk corn. As they talked about Lost Creek Valley and the different members of the group who had joined church with them, and raced to finish first, they had a wonderful time.

Many young folks came to the husking, and there was much laughing everywhere. Whenever a red ear of corn was found, the boy had to kiss his partner. Cristli wished he could find a red ear in his shock but, unfortunately, none appeared. He would gladly have done his duty. To him, Rosanna with her bright eyes and red cheeks was a beautiful girl.

While the young people were husking corn, Lydia, Reuben's wife, and a number of helpers were preparing supper. About ten o'clock she sent word out to Reuben that supper was ready. Reuben shouted out, "Everybody in for supper."

A cheer of joy went up, and each couple hurried to finish their shock of corn. Then each boy escorted his partner to the supper. Tables were set up in every available space so that the entire group could be seated at once. When all were settled, Reuben said, "Let us give thanks," and heads were bowed in silent grace.

For the meal, Lydia served great platters of stewed beef with plenty of gravy, mashed potatoes, sweet potatoes, fried mush, beet pickles, large slices of bread from big oven-baked loaves. For dessert they ate large pieces of fresh grape pie.

Reuben had swept the barn floor and hung lanterns from the beams. He knew that as soon as supper was over, the young folks would want to go to the barn and play party games: bingo, six-handed reel, O-hi-o, twin sisters, skip to my Lou, and maybe a little old-fashioned ring. Some of the boys had not found red ears of corn, and here would be a chance to make up for the loss.

Rosanna had never heard these party songs. She was especially delighted with the rhythm of O-hi-o. Little Crist was her partner for the first play, but soon other boys came around. When they played six-handed reel, Ben Sharp was her partner. Ben was tall and husky, and when they "balanced off," she thought Ben would swing her off her feet.

What a wonderful evening, with songs she had never heard, action she had never seen, and new friends that showed her every consideration. When the clock pointed to 1:30 a.m., Sam came around and announced, "Get ready, girls. It's time to go home."

Rosanna and Leah got to their room a little after two o'clock. Tired? Yes, but happy! Rosanna had resolved to have nothing to do with the boys until after she was seventeen. But as she dozed off, she was pleased with the thought that the nicest boy at the party, the one everybody called "Cristli," had been her partner.

In the cornfield the next day, the girls were rather sleepy, but they tried hard to keep up their usual pace. If a party left them unfit for work, they knew Momli would not be inclined to let them go next time. One could afford to make almost any kind of sacrifice for pleasure like that. So they used every ounce of will-power to keep awake and to keep going.

Evening seemed a long time in coming. When the supper dishes were done, two sleepy girls asked whether they might not put off the knitting till tomorrow evening. Momli smiled wisely. *"Jah, well,"* she agreed.

❧ ❧ ❧

Rosanna and Leah had never been to a Sunday evening singing. As they heard others talk about the singings, they had a great desire to go to one. But would they dare to ask permission so soon after the cornhusking?

Leah had an idea. "Rosanna, I think I heard Pap say that preaching will be at our house in three weeks. Let's get the boys to ask him to have a singing here in the evening. They generally have a singing in the evening at the same place where preaching was held that day. Then we'll already be at the singing, and we'll not need to ask Momli to go."

Rosanna thought it was a fine idea. They told Sam about it, and he agreed to help.

Preparing for preaching was soon uppermost in the family's mind, and it was a strenuous job. The houseyard was raked and swept. Every porch was scrubbed with silver sand to make it white and clean.

On Wednesday a few women came to help scour the tinware. On Friday others came to help bake great loaves of bread in the big oven. On Saturday a dozen women came to help bake apple pies and half-moon pies.

All day Saturday the menfolks were busy cleaning the stables and the barnyard and getting the preaching benches down and dusting them thoroughly. Early on Sunday morning, the men removed all partitions, placed the benches throughout the house, and put the big German hymnbooks, the *Ausbund*, on the singers' table. It was a busy week.

Sam was responsible for parking the carriages and unhitching the horses. He had asked Ben Sharp and Siever Yoder to help him. This gave him a chance to scheme with them: "The girls would like to have a singing here this evening. Will you boys ask Pap?"

The boys were eager to cooperate. When preaching was "out" and dinner was being served, the boys watched for Bishop Shem. As he came out from the first table, the boys approached him. "Shem, we would like to have a singing here this evening. Is that okay with you?"

He did not dare seem too easily convinced, so he answered, "*Ach*, what do you want a singing for?"

"We want to learn some new tunes, and your son Yost knows so many of them. If the singin's here, maybe he'd be willing to stay and teach us some."

"*Jah, well*," Shem agreed. He liked his son Yost, who was one of the acknowledged leaders of singing. The boys knew this mention of Yost was good strategy. Yost was already married, and married folks did not usually attend singings. But when they appealed to Yost with the angle that he could teach some tunes the youth didn't know, he could not resist. Yost was willing to sit and sing by the hour on almost any occasion, especially when someone wanted to learn from him.

Ben and Siever passed the word around to the young folks. Soon after the early autumn sunset, buggies began coming in over the hill to Bishop Shem's place. Boys were bringing their sisters and maybe a sister's friend, but not their own girlfriends.

Among the Amish, boys were rarely if ever seen driving in daytime with their own girlfriends. Great secrecy surrounded their social relations, making this the one time when hedging on telling the truth was permissible. When a boy was charged with having a girlfriend or a girl with having a beau, both would deny the accusation to the last, even if true. Everyone expected them to play this game.

Hence, they never wanted to be together alone in daylight. Boys did not take their girls to singing, but they did take them home afterward, in the darkness. A boy never went alone to his girl's home in daytime. He did not enter the house in the evening when he called on her till after her parents retired.

At a singing, two or three tables were set end to end along one side of the living room for the singers. The girls sat back of the table along the wall, while the boys sat on the other side. Even though only German hymns were sung, a singing was not counted as a regular worship service. Yet during the singing of any hymn, all persons present were supposed to join in singing or abstain from conversation. Sometimes the boys forgot and annoyed the singers by talking too loudly, making it necessary for the man of the house to exhort, "Let us have order." (These Amish customs surrounding courting and singings continue into the present.)

As Rosanna and Leah were hostesses this evening, they did not sit at the singers' table but left space for visiting girls. Yost Yoder, the singer, took his place at the head of the table. Next to him was Little Crist and Ben Sharp and other young men who were anxious to learn to sing.

Back of the table were the girls. Hannah Yoder, the singer's daughter, had a wonderful voice, clear and resonant. Beside her were Sarah and Franey, Little Crist's sisters, and many others, filling the table entirely. When the tables were filled, others came and stood back of the young men, both boys and girls, until there were nearly a hundred voices singing.

Yost's first selection was *"Weil nun die Zeit vorhanden ist* (While now the time is at hand)." It was one of the easy slow tunes and appears on the next page.

These slow tunes are difficult to sing. They are a holdover from Alsatian or Pyrenean chorales, or the Gregorian chants which originated in Germany in the early part of the seventeenth century. When the Amish people left Alsace-Lorraine because of religious persecution early in the eighteenth century, they brought these chorales along to America and have used them unchanged ever since.

There is no part singing. Everyone sings in unison. Since the Amish do not have these chorales set to music, they must be passed on from generation to gen-

Amische Lieder.

Weil nun die Zeit vorhanden ist.

G'funge beim
Christian J. Yober und
Rheyben Kauffman, 1907.

Ausbund 789 (3)

1. Weil nun die Zeit vor - han - den ist,
2. Wenn un - ver - se - hens kom - men wird
3. Da - rum so laßt uns flei - ßig sein,

Daß wir hie müf - ften schei - den,
Chri - ftus am Jüng - ften Ta - ge,
Mit Bä - ten und mit Wa - chen,

So woll uns Gott zu die - fer Frift
Der Welt Rich - ter und grof - fe Hirt
Zur Him - mel Freud aus die - fer Pein,

Ge - nä - dig - lich ge - lei - ten,
Uns ftell zur Recht'n, und fa - ge:
Ent - gehn den Höl - len Ra - chen

Daß wir be - trach - ten fort und fort
Kommt her Ihr feid ge - be - ne - deyt,
Und na - hen uns zu Gott al - lein,

Sein jetzt ge - hör - tes hei - lig Wort,
Er - erbt das Reich in E - wig - keit,
Der fpeis uns wie die En - gel fein,

Und uns mö - gen be - rei - ten.
Euch rühr hin - fort kein Pla - ge.
Woll ih - nen uns gleich ma - chen.

eration by memory. Consequently, only young men and women with a keen sense of pitch and sound can ever learn to sing them, and many can never learn them well enough to lead in singing.

Little Crist and Ben Sharp wanted to learn to lead, so they followed with great care. After two stanzas had been sung, Yost turned to Little Crist. "Now, Cristli, you lead the next verse. If you stall, I'll help you out."

Cristli took the same pitch and led off. He got along fine for the first three lines, but when he swung into the fourth line, he ran into trouble. So Yost's strong voice picked up the tune instantly and put Cristli back on track. He finished all right but was rather flustered.

Next Ben Sharp, with still less experience, wanted to try the *Lob Sang,* always sung as the second hymn at preaching service. Since this hymn must be sung every church Sunday, it is more familiar than others. That's why beginners try leading it as their first attempt. Ben started out with colors flying, but before he was finished, Yost had to help him get through it, too. On the next page the *Lob Sang* appears with notes supplied, even though the Amish have only the words in their hymnals.

After they had sung several of the slow chorales, one of the girls announced, *"Wo ist Jesus, mein Verlangen* (Where is Jesus, whom I long for)?" to the tune of "What a Friend We Have in Jesus." The "fast" tunes are easily sung, but the chorales must be learned for preaching services; no fast tunes are ever sung there. Then Siever Yoder called out, *"Jesu, Jesu, Brunn des Lebens* (Jesus, Jesus, fount of life)!" to the tune of

"Come, Thou Fount of Every Blessing."

Everybody knew these familiar words and the tunes and joined in heartily. Even those in the kitchen and on the porches sang until the house seemed to vibrate with melody. Rosanna was thrilled almost to tears! She knew some German and joyously joined in the singing.

Between hymns or chorales, pleasant conversation is always permissible, since the singing is an informal meeting. When ten o'clock came, Yost arose to leave the table. That was a signal for the others, and in a few minutes, everybody was visiting merrily or getting ready to go home.

The young women gathered near the door, and presently one "boy" after another walked up to his "girl," extended his arm, and out they went together. Young men brought their own sisters to singing, but others took them home. Thus the singing afforded more than an opportunity for the youth to learn the hymns of the church. It was also a pleasant time socially where the young people got acquainted, made friends, and chose companions. This prepared them for marriage.

Bishop Shem and Momli sat near the bedroom door, enjoying the singing. The bishop spoke pleasantly to the young people as they approached him. They respected him both as their spiritual leader and their friend.

Momli had the double pleasure of hearing the singing and seeing Rosanna so filled with happiness that she could hardly contain herself. A little mist dimmed her eyes as she thought of Rosanna, the little

Das Lobsang.

K'funge beim
Christian Z. Yoder und
Rheuben Kauffman, 1907.

(Das zweite Lied jeden Sonntag).

Ausbund 770 (3)

1. O Gott Vater wir lo — ben dich
2. Off — ne den Mund Herr dei — ner Knecht,
3. Gieb un — ferm Her — zen auch Ver — ftand,

Und bei — ne Gü — te prei — fen;
Gieb ihn'n Weis — heit dar — ne — ben,
Er — leuch — tung hie auf Er — den,

Das du dich O Herr gnä — dig — lich,
Das fie dein Wort mög'n fpre — chen recht,
Das dein Wort in uns werd be — kannt,

An uns neu haft be — wie — fen,
Was dient zum from — men Le — ben,
Daß wir fromm mö — gen wer — den,

Und haft uns Herr zu — fam — men g'führt
Und nütz — lich ift zu dei — nem Preis,
Und le — ben in Ge — rech — tig — keit,

Uns zu er — mah — nen durch dein Wort,
Gieb uns Hun — ger nach fol — cher Speis,
Ach — ten auf dein Wort al — le — zeit,

Gieb uns Ge — nad zu die — fem.
Das ift un — fer Be — geh — gen.
So bleibt man un — be — tro — ren.

Irish Catholic baby; her father going off to find a place for the other children; his accidental death so that he never came for the baby; the other children in Philadelphia, now grown to be adults, faithful members of the Catholic Church; and Rosanna, so different!

Had she done right to bring her up Amish? But what else could she do? She had followed God's leading from day to day, and this is where it brought her. She believed it was pleasing in God's sight, and she was content.

When all the young folks had left, Rosanna slipped over and sat on the arm of Momli's rocking chair. Putting her arm around Momli's shoulder, she asked, *"Hab ich mich recht aagschickt* (did I behave all right)?"

"Jah, ich bin zufridde (yes, I'm satisfied)."

Rosanna kissed Momli on the cheek and ran upstairs to join Leah. As they prepared for bed, Rosanna shared her happiness with Leah: "My! Isn't it nice just to be alive? Isn't it wonderful to sing like we sang tonight!

"Why, sometimes I felt as if my body was getting so light I couldn't keep my feet on the floor. I thought sometimes the singing would just carry me away! Singing, friends, church, home! Isn't life beautiful!"

🙢 🙢 🙢

The next day, Bishop Shem had business at the blacksmith shop, operated by Jesse Horton, a deacon in the Lutheran Church. When Shem entered the shop, the rugged blacksmith remarked, "Bishop, I want to thank you for the beautiful singing you furnished us last night."

"Could you hear it down here?" asked the bishop, astounded.

"Yes, sir! The sound of the singing came rolling down along the creek like a great, heavenly anthem. It lifted my soul to the very gates of heaven, and I could not help but say, 'Hallelujah!' My, it was wonderful! We Christians have joys that the world knows nothing about.

"I couldn't understand all the German words, but I caught the spirit of the singing. I don't believe, Bishop, that any secular singing can ever have such spiritual fervor and such moral uplift as did the singing of those young people last night."

The bishop smiled with satisfaction.

"And how well behaved your young folks are!" the blacksmith continued. "After the singing was over, dozens of buggies drove out the road past my house, and I never heard a loud word out of any one of those young people. Bishop, I rejoice that you Amish people are able to train your young folks so well."

CHAPTER 9

Young Womanhood

A S R O S A N N A pondered these new joys and friends, and her relation to the church now that she had been baptized, she began to have the feeling of being grown-up. Already her reputation as a good worker was widely known. When people found themselves in need of extra household help, they would ask her to come.

Such service was a way for her to earn extra money. Yet Momli did not feel that she wanted Rosanna to be considered as a maid for anybody and everybody to hire. She made it a rule to let Rosanna go only when there was an emergency, and then only for a week or two at the most. Thus Momli felt that she could culti-vate in Rosanna a finer feeling of self-respect and make her a happier woman.

Momli knew that the Amish did not in any way look down on girls serving as housemaids but kept them on the same level socially as the rest of the fami-ly. It was even considered a mark of fine accomplish-ment for a young woman to be able to step into a home and do any kind of work rapidly and well.

Momli reasoned, We have always been together. Now that I am getting older and need her more at home, why should I let her work for other people all the time? Besides, the way things look, I suppose she will get married someday, and then I will have to give her up.

Rosanna, for her part, had a keen sense of obliga-tion to Momli. All that Rosanna was and all that she ever hoped to be was due entirely to Momli's noble ex-ample and loving guidance.

As the autumn leaves were turning from green to gold and scarlet and somber brown, preaching ser-vices were to be held at Nicholas Yoder's, along the front (Jack's) mountain. It was the time for fall commu-nion. Rosanna and Leah had been looking forward to partaking of their first communion. After they partici-pated in communion, they would be considered full members of the church.

At the supper table on Saturday evening, Bishop Shem announced, "Tomorrow is communion Sunday. We'll have to start to preaching a little early. Let's get everything ready this evening so we can start by half past seven in the morning."

When it was half past seven on Sunday morning, the womenfolks were all dressed and ready. Sam had the big bay horse hitched to the white-top carriage for his father and Momli. He and the girls followed in his buggy.

On the way across the low plateau running lengthwise through the valley, they could see across the long hollow to the home of Nicholas Yoder. White-top and yellow-top carriages and open buggies were gathering from all directions—the Kauffmans and the Zooks from down the valley, the Peacheys and the Hartzlers from up the valley, the Yoders and the Bylers from the back (Stone) mountain, the Detweilers and the Kanagys from the front mountain, to say nothing of the Riehls, the Swareys, the Rennos, and the Hostetlers from all parts of the valley.

By half past eight, Bishop Shem and the ministers began to move toward the house, followed by the old men. Other groups followed, and in a few minutes the services began. The familiar strains of the singing could be plainly heard at the barn. That served as a plain hint to all the young men and boys still there that it was time to go to the house.

🖙 🖙 🖙

The order of services on communion day was slightly different from regular preaching services in that it required three ministers instead of two. The first one opened the meeting. This was followed by the silent prayer. The second one quoted and commented on long passages from the Bible which related to the children of Israel searching for the Promised Land.

The third minister, usually the bishop, talked about the sufferings of Christ and explained communion, the bread and wine, and the practice of foot washing.

These last two sermons strained the preachers, mentally and physically, since so much of the Scripture had to be quoted verbatim. Some ministers worked so hard at their preaching that their clothing became saturated with perspiration while they preached.

The preaching was continuous, but when the noon hour arrived, a table was set in the summerhouse. One by one, men and women went out, got a bite to eat—from the bread, hot coffee, pies, beets, and pickles—and then returned to their places.

Since Christ was crucified about three o'clock in the afternoon, the bishop tried to terminate his sermon about that time and serve communion. As that time approached, the deacon went out and brought in the bread and the wine. After the bread was blessed by prayer, the bishop and some of the ministers passed the bread to each member. After the bread was served, the wine was blessed in the same way and then the common cup was passed to each member till all were served.

While the bread and wine were being passed, the bishop usually repeated some Scripture pertaining to the communion in a low voice as though encouraging the members in good works. When the bread and wine had been served, the services were closed in much the usual way: testimonies from all ministers and deacons present, a few closing words from the bishop, prayer, and the closing hymn.

The closing communion hymn always was *"Vo'm Hertzen will ich singen* (From the heart I will sing)." Just before this hymn was announced, the deacon went out and carried in towels and two pails containing warm water. While this hymn was being sung, the men paired off and washed each other's feet in the room where the ministers sat.

When each had washed the other's feet, they extended the right hand of fellowship and greeted each other with the holy kiss. The one said, "God be with us," and the other responded, "Amen. Peace be with us." When they had put on their shoes, they went to a receptacle provided for alms and left an offering for the support of any poor folks.

While the deacon brought in pails of water for the men, the hostess provided pails and towels in the kitchen for the women. There the women washed the feet of each other in pairs, just like the men in the other room. When the members had observed the foot washing ordinance and given their offering, they were at liberty to leave the services. After the last couple was finished, the hymn was ended and services were over, at about half past four or five o'clock in the afternoon. (These Amish customs for communion service persist into the present.)

❧ ❧ ❧

Rosanna was so impressed with her first communion that when it came time to go home, she came to Momli with a request. *"Ich will mit dir Heem geh* (I want to go home with you)."

When her emotions were stirred, nothing soothed

her so much as just being with Momli. She had listened attentively as Bishop Shem explained that the bread stood for the broken body of Christ, the wine for his shed blood, and the foot washing for a life of humble service. Rosanna was deeply moved.

As they drove back home, the big bay held his proud head high. He was all life and eager to go. But in the carriage, Momli and Shem and Rosanna were still held by the solemn spell of the communion service, and they were silent.

ஃ ஃ ஃ

As the Christmas season approached, Rosanna noticed strange young men and women at church and at singings. She was told that they were "Peckwayers," young Amish folks from that part of Lancaster County drained by the Pequea Creek. They were usually young folks who had come to the valley to visit. If they did not have any relatives, they came with someone who did and stayed with their friend's relatives.

Since Lancaster County has so many Amish, one group frequently did not know that other parties were visiting. Sometimes three or four groups were in the valley at once, and that made a good many visitors. But at this time of year, the valley folks were well provided with fresh meats from the fall butcherings, canned fruits and dried corn and tomatoes, and large bins of potatoes and apples. The food supply was good, but it did take extra work to prepare for visitors.

These young folks dressed much like the valley young folks. However, the Lancaster "girls" pinned the long ends of their *Halsduch* (cape) straight down over the bosom instead of crossing them in front. The "boys" wore their hair a little shorter and trimmed their beards a little closer. Sometimes the ministers and the bishop in the valley looked somewhat askance at these young folks, fearing that they might have a little pride in their neatness and might sow some of that seed in the minds of the valley young people. Most of them were fine singers. The visiting boys played corner ball well, but the valley boys could surpass them in wrestling.

Rosanna and Leah heard that on Thursday afternoon, there was going to be a corner-ball game at Christian Sharp's, the home of tall, husky Ben Sharp. The Pequea boys were going to play the valley boys, and after the game, there might be some friendly wrestling. Since Sam was going anyway, Momli agreed that the girls might as well go too. Rosanna and Leah were delighted.

It was a sunny afternoon in January. Ben had just covered the broad manure pile with fresh clean straw, and everything was ideal for a good game. The valley boys drew corners first. They passed the ball around swiftly and then threw it at one of the two Pequea boys in the middle. However, they were surprised to see how these Pequea boys could dodge the ball.

Ben Stoltzfus was probably the best at dodging the ball. When the ball was thrown low at him, he would jump into the air and almost turn a somersault, clearing the ball by two or three feet. When the ball was thrown high, he would drop so quickly that the ball would shoot over him and miss again.

After the valley boys had exhausted their corner

force, they had to take their turns in the middle. Again they were surprised to see how those Pequea boys could throw a ball. They would look one way and throw the ball the other with great accuracy, hitting an opposing player without apparently looking at him. At first the game was rather one-sided, but the valley boys were quick to learn. By the time the game was ended, the score was only twenty-five to thirty in favor of the Pequea boys.

When the wrestling began, the tables were turned. They threw their hats into a ring, and the hats that touched meant that the owners should wrestle. The first bout came between Siever Yoder and the agile Ben Stoltzfus. Siever was not regarded as a good wrestler, and Ben was able to put him away rather easily.

The next match came between big Ben Sharp and visiting John Lantz, also a big man. This looked interesting from the beginning, but Ben knew the technique of "side-holt" wrestling, and it was not long till John Lantz went over Ben Sharp's hip with a bang, and he was down.

The next match looked funny. John Fisher, a six-footer, was to wrestle Little Crist Yoder. Fisher looked at Little Crist with a bit of scorn in his eyes. The Pequea boys grinned, but the valley boys winked at each other in perfect confidence. When they were ready, Fisher swung Little Crist as if to throw him away, but Crist leaped across his outstretched foot with ease. He landed on his feet in perfect position to counter with a backward trip, which laid Fisher neatly on his back.

A shout went up from the watching valley young

folks, including the girls, grouped under the barn's overshot: "Cristli! Good throw!"

"*Der gleh Deihenger* (the little scoundrel)!" exclaimed a Pequea boy. "Throw me that way if you dare."

"Come on," Little Crist welcomed him. "I'm willing to try."

John Mast came forward with a confident swing. They took holds, and Little Crist asked, "Are you ready?"

"Go ahead," said Mast. With one quick twist, Little Crist seemed to brace himself under Mast, lift him off his feet, and swing him over his hip. Then Mast was down. Both groups cheered, for Mast was the confident challenger.

Rosanna had been standing among the girls. When she saw Little Crist wrestle with boys so much larger than he was, she almost held her breath. But when he downed the big fellows, she could hardly conceal her delight.

One of the girls commented to her, "I guess those Pequea boys don't know that Cristli is one of the best wrestlers in the valley."

Rosanna tried to answer indifferently, but the little Irish lilt in her laugh gave her away. It was a great afternoon. The Pequea boys won in corner ball, and the valley boys won in wrestling. But whether they won or whether they lost mattered little, for they were playing for fun and laughter more than for victory.

One reason why Little Crist wanted to do his best in wrestling was because he had seen Rosanna at the games and talked to her for just a moment. He thought he never saw her look so beautiful. He noticed too that some of the Pequea boys were engaging her in conversation, especially that John Mast, who had challenged him to wrestle. He felt especially glad now that he had downed Mast, for he thought it might have impressed Rosanna.

When the wrestling was over, Rosanna confirmed his hopes. "I'm glad you threw Mast," she told him. "I don't like him anyway."

That declaration was a source of real pleasure to Little Crist. Putting all these things together, he decided that he might not be unwelcome if he called on Rosanna that Saturday evening. The more he thought of it, the more he decided that "there was everything to gain and nothing to lose."

As Crist went home that evening, he could not forget Rosanna's red cheeks, her bright eyes, and her winning smile. When Saturday evening came, he put on his best clothes and acted as indifferently and unconcerned as possible. He did not want to attract any attention. However, his sister Sarah was alert: "Cristli, I believe you're going down to see Rosanna tonight!"

He tried to convince her otherwise. "No, I'm not. I'm just going to town for a little while." But he could not quite hide the combined joy and guilt that played about his mouth.

Sarah just looked wise and exaggerated the emphasis in her response, "Uh-huh!"

When Crist got to Belleville, he saw some boys who teased him a bit, too. With a great effort at self-control, he avoided suspicion. To throw them still further off the track, a little later he declared, "Well, I be-

CRIST SNEAKING OUT
TO VISIT ROSANNA

lieve I'll go home." Off he started for home.

When he came in so early, Sarah and Franey looked surprised, but he simply said, "I told you so." He yawned and headed upstairs, apparently to go to bed. However, before coming into the house, he had placed a ladder against his bedroom window. Instead of going to bed, he went down the ladder and through the fields to Shem Yoder's.

Crist had put a few grains of corn in his pocket, and when he reached the house, he made sure that the parents were in bed. Then he went to Rosanna's bedroom window, tossed a few grains of corn against the panes, and waited. In a moment he heard Rosanna raise the window quietly. "Who's there?" she whispered.

He whispered back, "Crist Yoder."

"I'll be down in a minute," she replied, trembling with excitement. In a few minutes, Rosanna opened the front door ever so softly, and Little Crist tiptoed into the kitchen.

Rosanna had felt all day that Little Crist might call that evening. She had made up her mind that if he did, she would be ready to invite him in. They sat in the kitchen by a dim tallow candlelight, because the kitchen was farthest away from the bedroom where the old folks slept. They must not know. Secrecy was of utmost importance.

After they had sat a while and the kitchen grew a little chilly, Rosanna stirred the fire and put more wood into the stove. Little Crist said, "Rosanna, what's the use of burning more wood? Aren't we going upstairs?"

"No, Cristli," Rosanna gently responded, "we'll do our visiting here."

Then Rosanna went on to explain what Momli had told her about bundling. This was the old custom of a courting couple going to bed together, fully clad, and piling on the covers to keep warm while visiting. "Now houses are better built and heated. There's no need to keep up something that's open to so much criticism.

"Momli says that Bishop Shem is opposed to bundling. I wouldn't disobey him for the world. Because bundling tempts youth to sin, the preachers are preaching against it, and parents are talking against it. Momli says that only a few of our people court that way anymore. She thinks that in a few years the Amish will no longer practice bundling at all."

Little Crist could see the reasonableness of Momli's teaching and responded thoughtfully, "I think you and Momli are right." The subject was never mentioned again.

They had a happy evening together, talking about the cornhusking, the singings, the corner-ball game, and especially the wrestling. Rosanna expressed surprise that Cristli could throw a fellow as big as John Fisher, but he merely laughed and quipped, "The bigger they are, the harder they fall." He added that being short had some advantages, too. The big fellows could hardly get a good hold on him, while he could get under them and throw them.

Rosanna asked what progress he was making with his singing. "I was up at Reuben Kauffman's a couple times lately," he replied. "I think I know three of the slow tunes now, well enough to lead them in preach-ing before long."

While Crist enjoyed singing, his real interest was horses. He told Rosanna how he was studying horses, and that his father had a fascinating horse-doctor book. From it he learned to tell the age of a horse by its teeth, the type that made the best buggy horse, the best hors-es for road and farm, where to look for the principal weaknesses and blemishes, and everything about a horse worth knowing.

"When I get that book mastered, they can't fool me on horses," Little Crist declared. The conversation about the horse-doctor book reminded Rosanna of how she had once studied, too, to become a teacher. When she told Crist about it, he complimented her by saying, "Well, I believe you would have been a fine teacher."

One o'clock came all too soon, and it was plenty late for the first call. As he said good-night, he added, "May I come again sometime?"

Rosanna replied, "Maybe, if you want to."

As Little Crist walked home across the fields, he experienced a feeling he had never known before. Wonderful joy and gladness and inspiration were surging through his whole soul and body. Every mus-cle was charged with super strength. He ran as lightly as a deer for pure joy. Rosanna's last words, "Maybe, if you want to," lingered like music in his heart and al-most seemed to lift him from the ground as he ran.

When he reached home, everybody was sound asleep. He took off his shoes on the porch, opened the great hall door slowly, tiptoed upstairs, and went to bed. He fell asleep while congratulating himself that he had fooled his sisters, made a good impression on Rosanna, and come in without anybody knowing it.

Next morning at the breakfast table, Little Crist put on his most innocent look. However, Eli and the girls seemed to share a secret that annoyed Crist just a bit. When Eli finally made some slight reference to a ladder, he was suddenly aware that he had forgotten to remove the ladder from his window when he made his silent departure in the evening.

Little Crist blushed with embarrassment when his mother commented, smiling, "People who play tricks must have good memories."

CHAPTER 10

The Visit

AUTUMN SOON cooled into winter. The leaves of gold and brown could hold on no longer, and the trees in the valley and on the mountainsides were stripped bare. However, another beauty had already arrived. As the wind whistled around the corner of the barn, it carried with it flakes of snow. Before long, Big Valley was wrapped in a mantle of white.

Just before Christmas, the trees were so covered with clinging snow that their branches looked as though carved out of white marble. Fence posts like white fairies stood hand in hand around the fields. The morning sun shone on this vast expanse of white with all its variations. Thus the great Kishacoquillas Valley, surrounded by high snow-covered mountains, looked like a real wonderland.

Sam had already prepared the big sled, and on Sunday they would all go to preaching in it. He had filled the sled with clean straw. What fun it was to sit down in the sled, cover up with warm blankets, bed quilts, and well-tanned sheepskins. They would glide noiselessly along the road or through the fields behind two spirited horses.

Nobody wanted to miss preaching when the snowy roads were well packed, and the horses delighted in showing their strength and speed. This was also the time for more singings and parties and for weddings. While Rosanna had enjoyed summer, she found winter still more enticing.

Little Crist's calls became more frequent. In fact, they became regular. Every two weeks on Saturday evening, he went to see Rosanna. He still announced his arrival with a few grains of corn thrown against her bedroom window. No matter how long a young Amishman would call on a young woman, the tension of secrecy was never relaxed.

How Crist wished he could bring his beautiful black buggy horse hitched to his new sleigh and take Rosanna for a drive on Sunday afternoon. But that was just not done, and custom had be to kept. At least, after singings and parties, he would take her home in the dark. How she loved to sit in his comfortable sleigh, behind that glossy black horse, which pulled them so quickly and quietly—because the church had decided that sleigh bells were worldly.

Rosanna hated to see the snow slowly disappear in the spring. Yet the green fields and the flowers and the warm sunshine seemed so beautiful to her, too, that the winter joys soon faded from her mind.

One day Rosanna walked to Belleville to do some shopping. She stopped at the post office and was thrilled to have a letter from Philadelphia. It was from her brother William. As she read it, she was filled with excitement. William said he would come up to see her and Momli for a few days in the summer, at a time when it suited best to have him.

Rosanna hurried home to tell Momli the good news. Momli, too, was glad that he was coming because she did not want Rosanna to be entirely separated from her family.

As they made plans, they were not much concerned about when it would suit them best to have William come. They were more interested in choosing a time in the summer when he would get the most enjoyment out of his visit. The family finally decided that the harvesttime would be most interesting.

Then the cherries would be ripe, the early harvest apples would be ready to eat, the clover fields would be red with bloom, and the wheat fields would be aglow with ripening grain. Besides, there would be ten or twelve harvest hands to cook for, and one more at the table would hardly be noticed. William might enjoy talking to these hardworking men, too.

Rosanna wrote him at once and suggested that he come about the tenth of June and stay at least ten days. She wanted him to see Amish country life when it was most interesting.

Before heading for Kishacoquillas Valley, William went to tell his brother and his sister about his journey. Margaret and John were tremendously interested. John suggested, "Find out all you can about that hexing business and the signs they paint on their barns to keep the hexes away." Margaret wanted to know whether the Amish really paint the front farm gate blue when there is a marriageable daughter in the family, and whether they actually powwow to stop the flow of blood or to take away pain.

Rosanna's brother traveled by train from Philadelphia and recognized many things he had seen ten or twelve years before. That was his first trip to Thompsontown and Jericho to see Rosanna when she was just nine years old. Soon after passing Mifflintown, he found the train plunging into the Juniata Narrows. The track ran alongside the long waterway cut between Blue and Shade mountains by the Juniata River.

William was impressed by the Susquehanna and the blue Juniata, the towering mountains hemming in the winding Juniata Narrows, the Reedsville Narrows, and now the expanse of the fertile, colorful Kishacoquillas Valley, framed between two mountain ranges.

While riding the stagecoach from Reedsville to Belleville, the city man was awed by the scene: deep green cornfields, silver-green fields of oats just out in head, rose-red clover fields like great gardens, and golden wheat fields waving majestically. He had never seen such splendor of color in nature, nor had he ever known the scent of new-mown hay.

As William walked across the hill from Belleville to Bishop Shem Yoder's house, he paused many times to enjoy the beauty of the landscape, so quiet, so clean, so peaceful! "Rosanna is better here than in the noisy city. I'm glad Elizabeth did not let me take her back to Philadelphia with me when I visited her before," he mused.

Rosanna was watching for him. When she saw a stranger coming in across the hill, she ran to meet him, so glad to see her real brother again. William took off his hat, put his arm around her, kissed her. "Rosanna, is it really you? How you've grown!" he exclaimed.

"Yes, William, I'm your sister."

As he looked at her more closely, he said, "I'm sure you are. Nobody but the Irish could have hair and eyes and cheeks and a lilt like that. I've always prayed that the Virgin Mary would take care of you, and now I know she has."

"Maybe she has," responded Rosanna, not well versed in the work of the Virgin Mary, "but I think Momli helped her a great deal."

"That's true. God bless her," William agreed, making the sign of the cross in front of his face. Rosanna did not know what that meant, and she didn't ask, but she was confident that it was all right.

When they reached the house, Momli greeted William more cordially than was her custom. She was a woman of few words, but she wanted William to know that he was most welcome. While she never could give Rosanna up, she did want Rosanna to keep in touch with her brothers and sister.

When the men came in to supper, Bishop Shem

received William warmly. "William, I'm glad you came to see Rosanna and us; you are very welcome in our home."

Sam came in and shook William's hand. In Sam's strong grip, William's white slender hand seemed lost.

William remembered that the titles *Mr.* and *Mrs.* are not used much among the Amish. So he called everybody by their first names, to the delight and satisfaction of Bishop Shem. When they sat down to the table, all bowed their heads in silent grace. William crossed his hands and seemed to feel the presence of God. When grace was finished, Bishop Shem instructed, "Now, William, reach and help yourself."

The supper was a marvel to William—large platters of fried ham (such ham!) and fried eggs, huge pieces of homemade bread fresh from the oven, dishes of mashed potatoes, pitchers of gravy, stewed tomatoes and corn, and to top it all off, big pieces of fresh cherry pie and gingerbread. When different family members were through eating, William noticed that they did not leave the table. When the last one had finished, they all bowed their heads again, and he knew it was for the grace of thanksgiving.

William stayed for a week. As he watched Rosanna at work, he marveled at how much she did and how little it seemed to tire her. She milked the cows, worked in the garden, carried large buckets of milk to the pigs, fed the chickens, gathered eggs, washed, ironed, baked, and even helped in the harvest field sometimes.

When he asked Rosanna whether she ever got tired, she laughed. "Oh, a little, sometimes. But I do this kind of work all the time. I'm used to it and don't mind it."

William watched everything with great interest— six men mowing grass in a large field, turning hay and heaping it, pitching hay, and the harpoon hayfork taking up great loads of hay and dumping them into the mow.

Then wheat cutting came, with four or five cradlers, six or eight men binding the sheaves, and two boys gathering sheaves while two men shocked the wheat. Twelve or fourteen men sat down to the table at once, but busy as they were, William noticed that the silent grace was never omitted. He marveled at how fast and how much these men ate. When grace was finished, Bishop Shem would always say, "Now men, reach and help yourselves," and many of the men followed his invitation literally.

During the noon hour after the meal, sometimes two of these young huskies would tussle. The roughness with which they threw each other about made William respect their strength. These young Amish fellows were just as eager to have William tell them about Philadelphia as he was eager to know about the country. He talked about the city at various times, and one or another of them would exclaim, "My! I wish I could live in Philadelphy."

William also observed that the harvest hands were not all Amish. The Amishmen wore homemade clothes—white muslin shirts, broadfall pants, no suspenders, hooks and eyes on their coats and vests, high-crowned and broadbrimmed homemade straw hats, long hair, and beards. If a man had short hair, William knew he was not Amish. Both groups worked well together. It was generally conceded that, because of their heavy work, the Amish were a little stronger and had a little more endurance than the others.

They told William about the time Isaac Axe, a tall slender carpenter of the Lutheran faith, was helping make hay at Lame Yost Yoder's. He was asked to pitch hay on one side of the wagon from Little Crist, who drove the team and loaded hay from his side. Isaac commented, "Well, today the work will be easy." Lame Yost happened to hear him, so in private, Lame Yost told his son, "Spunk up, Cristli. Show Isaac that you can give him all he wants to do."

By four o'clock that hot afternoon in June, Isaac cried uncle. "Cristli, I've had enough. I'll have to lie in the shade a while. I hope your mother has onions sliced in vinegar for supper. If she doesn't, I can't go it any longer."

William enjoyed all these tales of strength and endurance told by the young fellows. However, he reminded himself to ask about the things his brother and sister wanted to know about. One evening when the work was done, Rosanna and Momli were sitting on the high front porch plaiting straw to make hats for the men. William approached them with his questions.

"My brother, John, wants to know whether the Amish people believe in hexing. He read in the *Public Ledger* that they do."

"We know that it exists some places among those speaking Pennsylvania German," Momli admitted, "but we do not practice it nor pay any attention to it. I know of only one old Amish woman who was ever suspected of hexing, but nothing was ever done about it, and now it has all been forgotten."

"Don't your people paint signs and symbols on your barns and outbuildings to keep bad luck away?"

"No, we do not generally paint our barns at all. Some people whitewash them, but they must be plain white. Signs and symbols would not be allowed by the church. I have often heard that in Snyder County and in Berks County, some people believe in hexing, but none of our people live there."

"My sister Margaret read that when a family has a marriageable daughter, they paint the front farm gate blue. Is that true?"

"No," replied Momli, "we never announce anything about our boys and girls so far as marriage is concerned. They are completely free to choose whom they will. Our only wish is that they marry someone in our own church. To marry someone outside our church generally causes a good bit of trouble, and if they marry outside the Amish faith entirely, they are excommunicated."

"And what does that mean?" asked William.

"When persons are excommunicated, their membership is taken away, and we do not eat or drink with them. They dare not sit at the table with other members but must eat separately till taken into the church again. The Bible says, 'With such do not eat.' We do not do business or work with those excommunicated or accept anything from them [1 Cor. 5:11]."

"That's pretty severe, isn't it?"

"Yes, but it's the best way to bring them to repentance," affirmed Momli, somewhat sadly.

"Do the Amish believe in powwowing to stop pain and bleeding?"

"Yes, indeed," assured Momli. "Many of our people can powwow, not only to stop pain and bleeding, but also to cure *rot Lafe* (bilious chills), the 'take-off' (wasting-away ailment) in children, wildfire (erysipelas), and *püscht Bloder* (pinkeye)."

"How is it done?"

"There are several different ways, but they are all based on the Bible. Everything is done in the name of the Father."

"I am learning to powwow," Rosanna remarked. "Already I can stop bleeding and take away pain. Crist King is teaching me to cure wildfire. His way is good.

"When Dr. Bigelow had the wildfire so bad and didn't get better, he sent for Crist King. Crist powwowed for him. The first day he was better, and the second day he was almost well. Dr. Bigelow didn't believe in powwowing and said it was just an old woman's notion. But Crist King cured him when he was so bad the doctors gave up. I guess now he'll be more careful what he says."

William and Momli talked on and on. She told him all about his father, Patrick McGonegal, and his mother, Bridget O'Connor, when they began housekeeping in Half Moon Valley. As she recounted these things, William could faintly remember the little home where he was born. He recalled Reuben Kauffman taking them to the railroad station, and what his father said when Reuben refused to take money for bringing them to the station: "I'm sorry to leave these Amish people. They are so kind when one needs help."

When Rosanna told him that Reuben Kauffman lived nearby, William declared, "I'll have to go and see him before I leave."

"Now, William, tell me about my sister, Margaret," Rosanna begged.

"Rosanna, you'll be proud of your sister when you see her. She's a beautiful young woman, tall and graceful, with lovely manners. She attended St. Mary's Academy for three years and is quite well educated. At present she is assistant librarian in the academy, and that's a fine position."

"Momli and I planned for me to be a teacher, but later we thought best to change," shared Rosanna. There was a touch of pathos in her voice which William noticed but thought best not to question.

The most unusual experience for William came on Sunday, when he went to preaching with the family. He sat on the front seat of the carriage with the bishop so he could see the homes and the fields and the people more plainly as they drove. Reuben Kauffman took William with him into the house for the church service.

William could not understand anything that was said. Yet the somber attire of the people, their deep spirit of devotion, the great volume of the chorale singing, and the rhythmic flow of the German preaching reminded him somewhat of his own church and challenged his deepest reverence and devotion.

When preaching was over, William was invited to share in the regular preaching dinner. He enjoyed the homemade oven-baked bread, the apple pies, the moon pies, the coffee, and the hot bean soup. After dinner, he joined the group of men standing in the yard, talking quietly. William had never seen so many men with beards, broad-brimmed hats, and somber clothes as he did that day.

Some of the men he recognized from the harvest field at Bishop Shem's, and he was pleased that many of them came and talked pleasantly with him. Others soon learned that he was Rosanna's brother from Philadelphia. Men gathered around curiously to hear the fluent English speech of this young man from the big city. They were pleased to hear him speak well of their beautiful mountains, the fertile fields, and the abundant harvest. This they took as a compliment to their hard work and thrift.

During the last few days of William's stay, he and Rosanna talked a great deal about their personal aspirations. William told her of his plan to own and manage a large department store in Philadelphia someday. He confided to her that he hoped to marry Mary McCarthy. "She's a beautiful young woman. After we're married, I want you to come and stay with us a while, just as long as you like."

Then William asked Rosanna whether she had any definite plans for her life. Rosanna, feeling that it was right to trust one's brother, told William about Little Crist Yoder, what a fine young man he was, and that they had never considered marrying anybody but each other.

"Crist's father would like to divide his farm and let Crist take part of it. If everything works out as planned, we may be married in January. I wish you could come to our wedding. An Amish wedding is a big affair."

Rosanna had never even told Momli about their plans, but she felt she should confide in William, her brother.

The day of William's departure arrived all too soon. Bishop Shem claimed that he had some business in Lewistown and thought it would be nice if Rosanna and Momli would go along. They would take William to meet his train. Nothing could have suited Rosanna better, for she had some important business in Lewistown, too.

While Momli and Rosanna took William to the train, Bishop Shem attended to his business affairs. Momli had no fear this time that William would try to kidnap Rosanna as he had earlier intended, when she was nine. William had been so polite and thoughtful in her home that she wanted to show him her deep appreciation by going to the train with him.

William thanked Momli for her hospitality and told them both good-bye. Then he boarded his train, and in a few minutes he was lost to sight where the Blue Juniata winds through the foothills of the Alleghenies.

On the way to pick up Bishop Shem, Rosanna told Momli about her plan to marry Little Crist in January. If Momli would give her consent, she would buy the makings for her wedding dress today, since Lewistown was the place to buy dress material. Momli wasn't really surprised at this announcement. She had been hearing about Lame Yost dividing his farm. That meant that somebody would likely get married, and everything pointed toward Little Crist and Rosanna.

"Well," responded Momli, "Cristli is one of the best young men in the valley. If you wish to get married, I have nothing against it." So it was settled.

On the way home, the Bishop was unusually jolly. When Momli asked him what made him feel so good, he shared, "I have just had a great honor shown me and the Amish people today. I needed three hundred dollars to pay for some fattening steers this fall. When I asked lawyer Culbertson whether he would lend me the money, he stated, 'Yes, sir, with pleasure.'

"When I said, 'Fill out a note for six months, and I'll sign it,' what do you think he told me? 'Bishop Yoder,' he declared, 'I do not want your note. Your word is just as good as your bond to me. Pay me back whenever you are ready. I have learned that you Amishmen, wearing hooks and eyes on your clothes, never borrow more than you can pay back. And when you say you'll pay it, you never fail to keep your word.' Now, what do you think of that?"

"*Der Herr sei gedankt* (thank the Lord)!" exclaimed Elizabeth. "We will not fail him."

"Now, Rosanna, since Pap has told us what makes him feel so good, don't you think you ought to tell him what makes you feel so good?"

"Yes, I'll tell him. Pap, today I bought material for a wedding dress."

"Well, that *is* news, now isn't it?" He laughed more heartily than usual. "If Cristli Yoder is the lucky man, I give my consent gladly."

"But you mustn't tell anybody," insisted Rosanna.

"I'll not tell anybody but Momli," agreed Shem.

Then Momli laughed, which was rather unusual.

On the way home, the white-top carriage could hardly carry its load of happiness.

CHAPTER 11

The Wedding

FOR THE REMAINDER of the summer, time sped rapidly for Rosanna. As usual, she was helping Momli with all the fall work: cleaning the house and yard and garden, making soap, boiling apple butter, and doing the daily chores. If she changed the program in the slightest degree, some keen-minded Amish woman would sense "something in the wind," and Rosanna's secret would soon be known to everybody.

The only visible sign of her intentions was the fact that Momli's flock of turkeys was a little larger than usual. Even Leah was not told of the plans. When

Rosanna was making her wedding dress and Leah hinted at a wedding, Rosanna replied casually, "I've been needing a new dress this long time. I'm just getting one ready for winter." She could get away with that reply because her wedding dress was to be the same pattern and style as her other dresses.

During November and December, at least eight couples in Bishop Shem's congregation were married. People teased Rosanna and Little Crist, "Look out now. You'll be next."

Crist just shook his head sadly. "Not for a while yet. Times are too hard to get married now." So well did he play his part, putting a little touch of regret into his voice, that even his closest friends were persuaded. "Doesn't look as though Crist and Rosanna are going to get married this winter."

But Rosanna and Momli were busy, making plans secretly. They decided that Thursday, January the twenty-first, was to be the wedding day. Amish custom required them to be published two Sundays in advance. At the close of the preaching service on Sunday, January tenth, their marriage would be announced at the close of preaching service.

When Little Crist came to see Rosanna these evenings, he no longer announced his arrival with a few grains of corn. He could see when other lights were out and all were in bed except Rosanna, who awaited him in the kitchen by the glow of a tallow candle. Then he stepped quietly to the door and slipped in.

Now they had a lot of things to talk about—the date of the wedding; who would be Crist's *Schtecklimann*, a minister acting as a go-between in presenting a formal proposal for marriage; who the waiters would be at the wedding dinner; who would be the *Schnitzler* (meat carver); where the marriage service would be held; and how many would be invited to the wedding dinner.

When Rosanna told Little Crist that she and Momli had chosen Thursday, January the twenty-first, as the wedding day, Crist thought a few minutes and then agreed. "That will suit me fine. By that time, we will have all our wheat hauled to market, the wood cut and brought home for summer use, and the logs hauled to the sawmill to make posts and lumber. I want to get all this work done so Pap and Eli will not have so much to do when I'm gone."

When the holiday season was over, it was high time for Little Crist to arrange for his *Schtecklimann* to go secretly to see Bishop Shem and Momli and get their consent to his marriage with Rosanna. A young man usually chooses the minister whom he likes best in his own congregation. The one Little Crist liked best was Crist L. Yoder.

Little Crist went over to see Crist L. in the evening just before Crist L. went to bed. No one must know about this, so he went as late as he dared. This mission is always an awkward affair for a young man. He called Preacher Crist outside and told him why he was there. Little Crist was not surprised that Crist L. laughed a bit—good-naturedly, of course.

The next evening Preacher Crist went over to Bishop Shem's house just a little before their bedtime. When he entered, Sam and the girls had already gone to bed. After a few minutes of conversation, he delivered his message. "I have been asked by Yost Yoder's son Christian to come here and ask you folks whether you would be willing to give him your foster daughter, Rosanna McGonegal, in marriage."

The bishop spoke first. "He is an obedient member of the church, a good worker, and liked by everybody. I believe he would make any girl a good husband. I have nothing against it."

After a moment's silence, Momli expressed her agreement. "I feel the same way."

So the matter was settled.

The next evening, Preacher Crist went over to Lame Yost's house, called Little Crist out, and reported, "Cristli, I've been to see Bishop Shem and Elizabeth, and they're both willing to let you marry Rosanna."

Little Crist thanked him and added, "We have chosen Thursday, January the twenty-first, for our wedding day. Will you see to it that we are published on Sunday, the tenth? That will be two Sundays before the wedding." Preacher Crist said he would do that.

When Little Crist came into the room again, Sarah asked, "Cristli, what did Preacher Crist want?"

Little Crist never batted an eye. "He wants me to help them saw wood next week."

"I guess!" returned Sarah, with a suspicious little laugh.

Little Crist's next job was to buy some gray material for his wedding suit and take it to Franey Yoder, who was expert in making clothes for Amish folks. She was especially good at making a man's *Mutze*. This was a frock coat with hooks and eyes, a split tail, and no rolling collar. It was the required wedding garment for a young man.

Since Little Crist had not yet been published, Franey rolled her wise old eyes but kept discreetly quiet. She was not going to lose her business through too much talking.

Sunday, the tenth, came. Little Crist put on a brave front and went to preaching as usual. The boys noticed that he tied his horse where he could make an easy getaway. When he joined a group of young men, big Ben Sharp teased, *"Well, heit denk ich gebts mohl ebbes* (well, today I guess for once there'll be something doing)."

Crist put on his most innocent look and casually inquired what was going to happen.

Ben laughed. *"Der Gaul is hendich* (your horse is handy)."

Little Crist thought preaching services were never so long as that Sunday. He felt, too, that all eyes were on him, and yet nobody knew anything about it except those pledged not to reveal the secret. Finally the main sermon was ended, the prayer read, the benediction pronounced, and all were seated. Everybody listened almost breathlessly. This was the time when couples soon to be married are published by the deacon.

When the place for the next preaching service was announced, Deacon John Hostetler intoned slowly, as though teasing the congregation a bit by keeping the news from them as long as possible, "It has come to pass that a brother and a sister have agreed to enter the bonds of matrimony, namely, Yost Yoder's Christian and Rosanna McGonegal."

The moment this announcement was finished, Little Crist arose, went out, got his horse, and drove off to Bishop Shem's house as fast as he could go. Rosanna was awaiting him, for a girl never went to preaching on the Sunday she was to be published. This was the first time Little Crist ever went to see her in the daytime. No more secrecy now! He and Rosanna were published. Everybody knew.

On this special day he ate dinner with Rosanna and a few chosen friends. Later, when the bishop and Momli came home from preaching, he visited with them for a while. Now all shyness was gone.

When preaching was out and the girls were talking, Sarah declared, "Well, when I saw that Rosanna was not at preaching today, I was just sure that she and Cristli would be published. But he was pretty sly about it. Now I know that he is not going over to Crist L.'s next week to saw wood, the little fibber. I thought he was fibbin' when he told me. Crist L. was his *Schteck-limann,* I'll bet you a dollar."

❧ ❧ ❧

The next big job for Crist and Rosanna and Momli was to decide whom they would invite to the wedding. First of all, Little Crist's uncles, aunts, and cousins had to be invited. Since Rosanna had no kinfolks in the valley, Momli and Bishop Shem's near relatives were invited instead. Then there were a host of Crist and Rosanna's young friends who were not related. When they finally had the list completed, they found it contained more than two hundred names.

"Well," commented Momli, "the house is big. We

have plenty of turkeys and chickens and ham and beef, and we can easily bake enough bread and pies and cakes. We have lots of canned fruit and apples in the cellar. Rosanna is a good girl, and she must have a nice wedding."

"*Jah, well, ich bin zufridde* (all right, I'm satisfied)," agreed Bishop Shem.

Written invitations were not to be used. It was Little Crist's job as bridegroom to drive around for the next week and personally invite the two hundred people to his wedding. Many were eager to know just who was invited to the wedding. When women would meet each other, one would say to the other, "*Hoscht du en Stuhle an die Hochzich* (do you have an invitation to the wedding, a place to sit at the feast)?"

For the next ten days, considerable effort was put forth to get ready for the wedding. This was a large affair, as usual for the Amish. The house was cleaned thoroughly and the tinware polished. The floors were scrubbed with silver sand to make them immaculately white. Temporary tables were built, and everything was tidied up in general.

A day or two before the wedding, a number of women and men came to help in dressing the turkeys and chickens and baking the pies and bread and cakes. They were directed by a family friend who agreed to serve as hostess for the festive meals.

Early on the wedding day, these same persons came again to roast the turkeys and chickens and fry the ham. The men handled the huge pots and kettles and removed partitions, as for church services. The helpers placed the temporary tables around three sides of the living room, the downstairs bedroom, and the dining room. One table was in the kitchen. The food was ready at the right time, and they set the tables. There were ten tables, each from fifteen to twenty feet long—enough to accommodate two hundred guests. As customary, the best food was placed on the corner table, where the bridal party would be seated.

While the hostess and twenty-five helpers were preparing the noon wedding feast, the bride and groom and all the invited guests were at an Amish neighbor's house. There the marriage service was being held.

That morning the order of service was practically the same as for a regular preaching service on Sunday. The house was filled with benches as usual. The bridal party sat on two rows of chairs facing each other, the boys in one row, the girls in the other, close to where the bishop and the minister stood while preaching.

When the first hymn was announced, the ministers headed toward an upstairs room prepared for them. The whole bridal party followed to the stair door. Here the two young men and the two young women attendants took seats provided for them. The bride and groom followed the bishop and the ministers to an upstairs room for counsel. Here the bishop and the ministers instructed the couple to be married in the ethics of Christian marriage—the husband's duty to his wife, and the wife's duty to her husband.

After this guidance, the bride and groom returned downstairs. When they reached the stair door, the best man and his partner led the way to their regular seats while the groom and bride and the other couple followed. The singing by the congregation continued until the ministers returned from the upstairs room. Then the singing ceased and the minister speaking first stood up. He preached for some twenty minutes, and then all knelt in silent prayer except the bridal party, who stood, facing their chairs. After the prayer, everyone stood while the regular Scripture was read, and then they sat down.

The bishop's sermon consisted of long passages of Scripture quoted verbatim from the Bible. These passages were chosen to portray home life and social relationships, to instruct in proper living. This was a standard sermon, given at every wedding. At a certain point in the sermon, about twelve o'clock, the bishop reached Tobit and the account of Tobias and Sarah becoming betrothed and married.

This story provided an opportunity for the bishop to say, "We have before us a brother and a sister who have agreed to enter the bonds of holy matrimony, namely, Christian Yoder and Rosanna McGonegal. If there is any brother or sister present who can give good cause why these two should not be married, let that one speak now, for after this no complaint will be heard." The bishop paused a moment in silence, then continued. "There being no objection, you may present yourselves for marriage."

Little Crist and Rosanna then stood, joined right hands, stepped forward, and were married in a simple ceremony similar to that of other denominations—but with no wedding ring or bridal veil. Before God and the congregation, they made a covenant of lifelong faithfulness to each other. The bishop called for God's blessing upon them and pronounced them husband and wife.

After they sat down, the services were closed with testimony from ministers and deacons present, a few more words from the bishop, a prayer from the prayerbook, the benediction, and the closing hymn.

When the hymn ended, the bridal party stood up first. The girls put on their wraps and the boys their overcoats. They met at the front door and proceeded to the front gate, where hostlers had brought the three buggies driven by the groom and his two attendants. The bridal party and all invited guests headed to the bride's home for the wedding dinner.

About one o'clock, when everyone had arrived, Bishop Shem stepped to the door and announced, "Dinner is now ready." He directed the guests where to sit. First, the bridal party was seated at the *Eck*, the corner table, from which they could see everybody and everybody could see them. The bridal party sat behind the table along the wall, Rosanna to the right side of the corner, and Little Crist to the left. The best man and his partner sat next to the groom and the other couple beside the bride.

The unmarried girls filled in back of the tables along the wall around three sides of the room. The unmarried young men sat facing the girls on the opposite side of the tables, their backs to the empty square, the middle of the room. The young and middle-aged married women then took their places, next to the wall, around three sides of the table in the dining room. The young husbands, especially the singers, sat with their backs to midroom, facing the women. In similar manner, the older men and women sat at a table set up in the bedroom, or at one in the kitchen.

Rosanna and Crist waited patiently while Bishop Shem directed the guests where to sit, not individually but by groups. When all were seated, the bishop took his seat at the singers' table in the dining room, paused a moment, and then said, "If we are all seated, let us pray." All bowed their heads in silent prayer.

For the noon meal, they had roasted turkey, stewed chicken, fried ham, mashed potatoes with gravy, sweet potatoes, corn, green beans, peas, carrots, bread, butter, apple butter, jellies, pies, and cakes. Although an Amish wedding dinner is not exactly a religious meal, it is always orderly. A little fun for the bridal party is traditionally provided by the *Schnitzler*, a young man who is a close friend of the bride and groom. He carves the turkey on the corner table and sees to it that the bridal party is well served.

The *Schnitzler* for Rosanna and Little Crist was Dixie Dave Yoder, called that because he had done some traveling in the South. He was a jolly fellow and a good conversationalist. When he had served Little Crist a large piece of exquisite turkey, he kidded, "Remember, Cristli, how well I'm serving you today. When once you keep a house, I'll be in for dinner, and then you serve me as I'm serving you and Rosanna today."

"Bring your turkey with you," joked Crist, "and I'll do it."

When the people were about finished eating, Reuben Kauffman announced the first hymn, *"Wacht auf, ruft uns die Stimme* (Awake, the voice is calling us)."

This hymn is always sung first after a wedding dinner and is quite difficult, but Reuben was equal to the occasion. Wedding guests generally bring their own singing books with them, a small book of German hymns. Everybody had a hymnbook, and all loved to sing the wedding hymns.

They sang in unison, following the custom in Germany over two hundred years ago. The great volume of vocal music filled the house with melody and all hearts with joy and gladness. When the sound of this great chorale died away, pleasant conversation was resumed.

Then Yost Yoder, Bishop Shem's son, the singer, announced *"Fröhlich pfleg ich zu singen* (Joyously do I sing),"* and the visiting ceased. He began with a strong voice and a fine tremolo, and everyone joined in heartily. Those who had served as cooks in the kitchen came crowding to the doors of the room where the singers sat. Others stood in midroom, behind the seated men, and raised their voices with the others in an impressive blending of faith and goodwill.

Everybody sang except Little Crist and Rosanna— brides and grooms never sang on their wedding day. They were both good singers, having sung these great wedding hymns many times. It was almost more than Rosanna could bear, and some said that they thought they saw her eyes moisten during some of the hymns.

The first three hymns were distinctly wedding hymns and must be sung in their regular order. The third was *Schücket euch ihr lieben Gästen* (make yourselves comfortable, beloved guests)."

Hymns and conversation alternated pleasantly till

about four o'clock, when all the young folks arose from the table and headed for the barn. Sam knew what they expected. He had swept the barn floor the day before and had everything in readiness. It was a beautiful sunny winter day, so the doors and windows were left open much of the time. As they went to the barn, Rosanna observed, "Why, this is a summer day instead of winter. They say a nice day means much happiness. I hope it comes true this time."

"We'll just make it come true," declared Little Crist.

At the barn they played the regular party games: bingo, skip to my Lou, there goes Topsy through the window, O-hi-o, and six-handed reel. Crist and Rosanna joined in heartily, for they knew that according to custom, this was their last chance. Married people rarely if ever took part in party games, although it was not forbidden by the church. When married, they have joined the older folks and seemed to feel they should leave the playing to younger ones.

As soon as the young folks went to the barn, the cooks came to clear off the table, wash the dishes, and reset the tables for supper. Not nearly everything was eaten. Much that remained from dinner was warmed up for supper. For fear there might be a shortage, Momli reinforced the meat supply with roast beef and dried beef, replenished the bread and cake plates, and added stewed and canned fruit.

When darkness began to fall, Reuben Kauffman was sent to the barn to tell the young folks to come to supper. At dinner the girls sat back of the table and the boys on the opposite side. Now at the supper table, all the boys had to sit with partners. Each boy had to take a girl to the table whether he wanted to or not.

Young married men enjoyed standing at the door till every fellow had found a partner. If any young man pretended to be too timid to ask a girl, the married men brought him to the door forcibly. At the same time, they grabbed a girl by the hand and sent these two in together. After they were inside, all resistance ceased, and together they went to the table. It was obvious that these young fellows wanted to take girls to the table, but it was not considered proper to seem eager to do it. So they acted timid and bashful.

With the exception of the young folks, the seating at the supper table was about the same as at noon. During the meal, there was lots of lively conversation. When they had finished their supper, Ben Sharp announced a hymn of the slow-chorale type, and once again the singing rose to inspiring volume. This time, however, no special hymns were required by custom. After two or three of the slow chorales had been sung, Siever Yoder announced, *"Wo ist Jesus, mein Verlangen* (Where is Jesus, whom I long for)?"* They sang it to the tune of "What a Friend We Have in Jesus." From there on, more and more of the selections were sung to "fast tunes."

At suppertime, wine was provided. Bottles of wine were placed here and there on the table, for was not wine served at wedding feasts in Bible times? While many took a sip of wine, nobody ever drank heavily. (Later, when temperance began to be advocated, the custom of serving wine at Amish weddings was discontinued.)

The wine was a excuse for much kidding. If between hymns a guest wished to crack a joke to someone's mild embarrassment, he put a little wine in his glass, held it high, and announced something. One such toast was sprung by Lewis Riehl: *"Es gilt dem Hochzeiter, wo er die Leeder vergesse hat* (a toast to the bridegroom, when he forgot to take the ladder away from the window)."

All who knew the joke laughed heartily. Eli had told Lewis that Crist had put a ladder to his window to slip out the first night he went courting and forgot to remove it. When someone proposed a toast in this fashion, nobody drank wine except the person proposing the toast, and in this way toasting did not lead to excess or rowdiness.

Later in the evening, Little Crist held his glass high with a bit of wine in it and announced, *"Es gilt dem Lewis Riehl, wo er eigschlofe is in der Gmeh* (a toast to the time Lewis Riehl fell asleep during church)." Everybody laughed uproariously, for all remembered when Lewis had been out rather late one Saturday night, went to sleep in preaching the next day, and fell off his bench.

Yost Yoder, the singer, toasted Ben Sharp for the time he called the wrong girl in the dark as he was leaving a Sunday evening's singing. So there was lots of fun at Rosanna and Little Crist's wedding. About two hundred good friends had gathered to do them honor, and they lingered around the heavily laden tables.

When things were at their height, four men who had helped in cooking and serving, came in with long-handled pewter or brass dippers to take up a collection for all the cooks. As coins were dropped into the dippers, the men shook them vigorously, making all the clatter possible. Thus they let everyone know how hard they had worked to prepare and serve the fine meal, how poor they were, and how much they needed the money. If someone pretended not to hear or to be unwilling to give, they shook their dippers at his ears with such terrific din that he was glad to throw in a coin.

Siever Yoder passed the dipper at the corner table, and when he came to the bridegroom, Little Crist ignored him. Then Siever shook the dipper as noisily as possible and proclaimed, "Oh, Cristli, look what a fine dinner and supper we've prepared for you. Think, oh, bridegroom, how we slaved that you might eat this day like a king. Have mercy on us poor men and women, and give freely of your unbounded wealth. Set a good example to these other banqueters that they may give freely, for all my brother and sister cooks will bear witness that we sorely need the money."

The higher the flow of Siever's oratory, the louder the guests laughed, until finally Little Crist dropped a silver dollar into the bowl. This coin changed the tone of the rattling. Siever in make-believe gratitude bowed and thanked the bridegroom for his wonderful generosity.

In a new outburst of oratory, Siever announced, "Today we serve a noble man, a man of wealth, a man of generous disposition, a man who sympathizes with the cruel position of the poor. With our humble hearts aglow with gratitude, we thank you, good sir."

The collection was divided among the twenty-five cooks and helpers, who used the money to buy some little souvenir by which to remember the pleasure they had at Rosanna's wedding. These cooks were all friends, in comfortable circumstances, but it was great sport to play the part of needy servants and extract money from their banqueting friends.

When the singing and pleasantry had continued until near nine o'clock, the young folks arose from the table and went to the barn again. There they played the same kind of party games as in the afternoon. About eleven o'clock they returned to the house, again in couples, nibbled a bit at the food, and sang and joked as before. About one o'clock, the bride and groom retired, and that was the signal that the wedding was over.

As they were leaving the table, Reuben Kauffman remembered that he had helped Rosanna and Little Crist get together at her first cornhusking. He had known Rosanna from her babyhood in Half Moon Valley and had always taken a keen interest in her welfare. Now Reuben looked admiringly at the bride and groom. "My, what a beautiful match! She is a black-eyed, Irish brunette, and he is a fair-haired, blue-eyed German blond, a perfect matching of opposites! What a pair!"

Rosanna's blue wedding dress and her white kerchief and apron seemed to enhance her red cheeks and bright eyes. Little Crist's gray suit, his slightly trimmed beard, his hair just as short as allowable—all made him look every inch a man, even though he was small. Many a young fellow in that group knew the iron of his muscles in wrestling and had great respect for his strength.

Before going to their room, Rosanna suggested, "Let's look at the wedding presents." One of the bedrooms upstairs had been set apart for gifts. Waiting for them on the bed, on the bureau, on the chest, and even on the floor were the tokens of love and friendship— dishes, lamps, tablecloths, towels, clocks, handkerchiefs, saws, hatchets, hammers, wrenches, and even an ax for Little Crist.

Probably the most beautiful present came from Philadelphia, a linen tablecloth from John and William and Margaret. Rosanna, her eyes dimmed with gratitude, said to her bridegroom, "My, Cristli, isn't it nice to have good friends! In the years to come, we'll prove to them that we were worthy of these beautiful gifts, won't we?"

The cooks began to clear away the food and take down the temporary tables. By now, the guests, somewhat weary of feasting and jesting, began putting on their shawls and bonnets and hats and coats. Goodnights echoed throughout Momli's spacious house, and Rosanna's wedding was over. Amish weddings are all like Rosanna's, although some are not quite so large.

CHAPTER 12

The Dower

T HE SECOND DAY after the wedding, Rosanna went home with Crist to the big stone house where Lame Yost and his wife, Catherine, lived. For several years, Rosanna had known Crist's sisters, Sarah and Franey, but she had never been in their home except on such special occasions as preaching or a singing.

Rosanna had always wanted to visit with Catherine, his mother, for she seemed such a kindly person, but custom simply did not allow it. She wondered, too, what kind of man Lame Yost was. He looked rather stern, but his voice was low, and it had a musical note in it that attracted strangers and inspired confidence.

Lame Yost was not a fluent talker, but Rosanna thought as she spoke to him on her first visit that she detected a note of appreciation, which made her feel much at home. Crist's mother was more talkative, and it was not long till she and Rosanna visited quite comfortably. Eli, the younger son, was a bit timid at first. Right from the start, however, the girls with their many mutual interests made Rosanna feel welcome and at home.

Rosanna looked around at the large well-furnished house, the well-spread table, and the other signs of plenty everywhere. She could not help but have a deep feeling of satisfaction that she had been privileged to cast her lot with folks like this. The family members were highly respected by everybody, in good standing in the church, comfortable in material things, and above all, happy and content in each other's presence.

A few days after the wedding festivities, Rosanna reminded Little Crist, "For the next few weeks, we will have to visit all our uncles and aunts and cousins. You know they will expect us."

When the first weekend approached, they went over to spend the night at Uncle Christian's. He was known as "Charley Crist" because one night before he was married, he went on horseback to see Solmy, his girlfriend. As he crossed a wooden bridge near her home, he called to the horse, "*Schleich, Charley, schleich* (sneak, Charley, sneak)." Some boys happened to hear him, and ever after that, he was called "Charley Crist."

Solmy was a gracious mother, and she heartily

welcomed the newlyweds. If at any time they felt timidity, it was soon dispelled. What a supper awaited
them—stewed chicken with waffles and gravy, candied
sweet potatoes, creamed sweet corn, snow-white
mashed potatoes, and all sorts of jellies, jams, cakes,
and cookies. It was almost a second wedding dinner.
Rosanna had never lacked anything, but this seemed
like sheer luxury.

On Sunday evening they went to Uncle Nicholas's, over by the front (Jack's) mountain. Here another
feast was prepared. During the night Rosanna was
awakened, she thought, by the cry of a wildcat or a
panther reverberating along the mountainside. When
daylight came, they looked out the window and saw in
the orchard two full-grown deer. They had come
down from the mountain. By pawing the snow away,
they were able to eat the grass in the orchard.

The next night they went to Uncle Eli Zook's, and
so on, until all the uncles and aunts and cousins had
been visited. Little Crist told Rosanna, "I wish we
didn't have to spend so much time visiting, but since
this is the custom, we'll have to do it. It won't be long
now till spring, and I must be attending sales and buying some farm machinery and horses. I don't want to
be behind with my work when spring comes."

A month before the first of April, Lame Yost noti-
fied the man in his tenant house that he would have to
move. This was merely a formality. Peter Anthony, the
big strong German, well knew that Little Crist would
want the tenant house until his father had finished the
new house and barn for him on the west division of
the farm.

Rosanna knew that she would not have to live in the tenant house for long. Thus, she did not move all her things in, but waited to move them in the fall when the new house and barn would be completed. The first summer, Little Crist shifted along with as little machinery and as few horses as possible. When fall came, the real moving took place.

On the day they moved into the new house, there was considerable activity, both at Lame Yost's big stone house and at Bishop Shem's house. There was a hint of rivalry as to which household would contribute most to this young couple as they began farming in earnest.

Shem's son, Sam, brought Rosanna's things up on the two-horse wagon, things which Momli and the bishop had given to help her set up housekeeping. On the wagon were a table, a bureau, a cupboard, a stove, a bed, bedclothing, a half dozen chairs with a rocker to match. Behind the wagon trailed a horse and harness and the best cow in Bishop Shem's stable.

Rosanna had been a good girl and a hard worker. She had helped in the harvest field and at cornhusking. Always she had been ready for every household duty. Now was the chance for Bishop Shem to show his appreciation. So he presented her with the best cow, besides chickens, hams, potatoes, and flour.

From the big stone house, for Little Crist, came a bed and bedding, a Windsor desk, a set of dishes, some handworked linen, a tablecloth, a horse and harness, a harrow and a cow, again the best in the herd. Lame Yost Yoder had a large farm, a big house and barn, and a high financial rating in the community. He was not going to give his oldest son a shabby horse or a worthless cow!

When his horse had run away five years before, throwing him from the carriage and breaking his leg, it had lamed him for life. Little Crist, then only sixteen, assumed the responsibility of the farm in such a manly way that nothing was lost of crops or cattle. Such a son deserved the best. So the horse was to be his own choice. Little Crist picked Harry, the big dapple gray Percheron gelding, weighing 1,700 pounds, and as beautiful as an Arabian stallion.

Setting up these young folks in housekeeping that fall was a real occasion. It was the delightful union of two families of high standing. Eli twitted Leah, and Sam teased Sarah and Franey. Lame Yost and Bishop Shem sat by, smiling at the jokes and clever remarks bandied back and forth among the movers.

Momli and Catherine busied themselves making the beds and arranging the dishes and the linens with hands whose every touch conveyed a blessing. Sometimes they did not utter a word for a long time as tears moistened their eyes.

Momli was thinking of the little Irish baby she had raised to womanhood, from whom she had never been separated. Now she must give her up. Catherine was thinking of her firstborn, the son so dear to her mother heart, who must now leave her fireside. Of course, Rosanna and Little Crist were not going far, but still they were going. Today for the first time, these two strong, pious women felt that they had a sacred common interest.

Sarah, Franey, and Leah made themselves responsible for preparing and cooking the dinner. When the large platters of stewed chicken, fried ham, and mashed potatoes had been put on the table, together with a variety of vegetables and bread and all the jams and jellies and gravies, Sarah went to the door and told her brother, "Cristli, call the men to dinner." When they were ready to be seated, Little Crist said to Bishop Shem, "Shem, you take the head of the table."

The bishop replied, "Oh, no, Cristli. Today you are the man of the house, and the man of the house always takes the head of the table."

Little Crist, taking his place at the head of the table, smiled and invited, "Will you all be seated?" After the silent grace was finished, Crist attempted to fill his new role properly by saying, "Now, you must all reach and help yourselves." That's what every Amishman is expected to say immediately after the blessing when there are guests at the table.

It was a jolly meal in the large square kitchen in the new house. Rosanna presided in a general way, but Franey chased the flies, Sarah attended to the water and coffee, and Leah replenished the chicken and ham platters when they got low.

As they ate, Bishop Shem volunteered a little pleasantry. *"Well, Yoscht, denks du die Kinner kenne haushalde* (well, Yost, do you think these children can keep house)?"

Lame Yost pondered a moment and then countered, *"Well, wann du die Rosanna so gut ufgezoge hoscht as ich der Crist hab, glaab ich geht's* (well, if you raised Rosanna as well as I raised Crist, I believe it will go)."

Catherine smiled with satisfaction, for she felt her husband had given the bishop a pretty good answer.

When all had finished eating, Little Crist paused a moment. They all bowed their heads in a silent grace of thanksgiving for the meal. As they left the table, the men lingered in the kitchen while the girls who had waited on the table ate their dinner. To show their gallantry, Eli and Sam waited on them. As the boys served, they made many blunders, some intentional, some from lack of practice. But they justified themselves by saying that strong men are not supposed to do housework.

🙠 🙠 🙠

The evening shadows deepened and the cricket's chirp echoed in the crisp October air. Little Crist and Rosanna sat alone by the kitchen stove, reviewing all the activities of the day.

Rosanna commented, "Well, we have a lot of things to be thankful for. We have a new house and barn, two horses, two cows, a plow, a harrow, a table, a stove, a cupboard, two beds and bedding, plenty of quilts and blankets, a desk, a bureau, dishes and chairs, and about everything we need."

"You missed a very important item which I have," objected Crist.

"What is it?" asked Rosanna thoughtfully. "I thought I named everything."

Crist took her in his arms and declared, "I have Rosanna McGonegal, the nicest girl in the world!"

CHAPTER 13

Keeping House

 I T W A S N O T L O N G till spring now, and Little Crist was busy going to sales and buying a few more horses and cows and some farming implements. His specialty was horses, and one day he told his father, "If I see a horse that is offered cheap, I'll buy him, feed him up, sell him, and try to make some money."

"It's pretty risky business. You can't see inside of 'em, and sometimes they're rather weak," cautioned his father. "But if you're careful, you may make a little."

Crist studied his horse-doctor book diligently until he thought he knew a good deal about the age of a horse by its teeth and the location of the most common blemishes—ringbone, spavin, and eye weakness. He believed he could also tell a lot about a horse's constitution by the shape and position of its feet.

After a while, he heard that Nancy Jake Yoder had a horse to sell, but he also knew that this Jake, one of widow Nancy Yoder's sons, was about the shrewdest horse trader in the whole valley. There could be no harm in looking at the horse, he decided. Nancy Jake lived along the back (Stone) mountain. When Crist went over to see him, this Jake said, "Yes, sir, Cristli, I have a horse to sell."

"Is he sound and all right?"

"I'll show you the horse. The buyer must be the judge."

Jake trotted the horse out, and Little Crist noticed that he limped slightly on his left hind leg. When the horse came to rest, Crist examined his leg and diagnosed, "Ringbone."

"Are you sure?" asked Jake.

"Well, he has a slight limp when he trots, and he has a bit of enlargement above the pastern joint. He might do me for light work if I keep him off the road, but he's not worth much money. He may go bad at any time."

Jake blinked his wise old eyes. "You blasted little jockey. I didn't think you'd notice that, but you're right. I keep only first-class horses, so you may have this one for half price."

The deal was made. Crist took the horse home, laughing up his sleeve because he had learned from his book how to cure ringbone, a secret few men knew. If he cured this horse, he could sell him for a fine prof-

it, and Daddy Yost would smile. The cure was simple—
the application of a salt-and-vinegar solution daily,
and thorough rubbing three times per day.

Crist applied the remedy vigorously. To his delight, after a month's treatment, he saw that the ringbone was considerably smaller. By midsummer, the
ringbone as well as the limp had entirely disappeared.
Horses at that time of year were in heavy demand, and
buyers were numerous.

Dave Mutersbaugh, a horse buyer from Lewistown, stopped by one day. "Cristli, do you have any
horses to sell?"

"Oh, I have one or two I might sell if anybody
wants them badly," admitted Crist nonchalantly.

"Trot 'im out, then."

Crist brought out the bay he had treated for ring-
bone. He was a beauty and had fine knee action. As
Crist trotted him up and down, Dave commented,
"Pretty nice horse. Is he sound?"

"So far as I know."

"What do you want for him?"

"Two hundred dollars."

"Oh, you're too high!" Dave exclaimed.

"All right, if you don't know a good horse when
you see one, nobody loses but you." Crist led the
horse back into his stall. Little Crist's indifference and
what he had just said irked Dave considerably. After a
bit more pressure from Dave, during which Crist
maintained his show of indifference, Mutersbaugh declared, "I'll take him." He counted out ten twenty-
dollar bills and led the horse away.

Little Crist could hardly wait to get to the house to

tell Rosanna how fortunate they were. He had bought a horse for one hundred dollars and sold him for two hundred, after keeping him only three months—one hundred dollars clear gain!

Rosanna smiled and slipped into a little Irish brogue, imitating her Irish neighbors and her brother, William. "Cristli Yoder, a schmart man it is that you air. Some day you'll be the horse king of the Kishacoquillas."

Crist was pleased with her praise, especially with her last phrase, "horse king of the Kishacoquillas!"

Soon the fieldwork began in earnest. One day as they were eating dinner, Little Crist suggested, "Rosanna, when we are working in the fields, ring the dinner bell at quarter after eleven, and we'll unhitch at once and come home. If we are working about the barn, then ring the bell when dinner is ready, and we'll come at once. If you always ring the bell when you have the meal ready, we will come promptly and not lose time. With this understanding, both you and I can get our work done to the best advantage.

"Before we were married, I helped Jake Hartzler build fence one day. The church they belong to does not allow dinner bells, and when Motley blew the dinner horn, we went right on working for almost a half hour. When we finally got to the house, dinner had stood on the table and was cold. Motley was disgusted because the good dinner she had prepared with so much care wasn't at its best. I saw then how wrong it is for men to treat their wives that way. I made up my mind to treat my wife better if I ever had one. What do you think of my idea, Rosanna?"

"That suits me fine. Down at Bishop Shem's, Momli always blew the dinner horn ten minutes before dinner was ready. That gave the men time to get in and wash for dinner. But sometimes when Sam wanted to finish a job, he would go on working till he was through and come to dinner late. Momli never said much, but the bishop saw that it made things unhandy for the women folks. He finally told Sam that from now on, when the dinner horn blew, he should drop his work, come to dinner, and finish afterward."

So their dinner-bell agreement was made and carefully adhered to. When Crist and Rosanna sat down to a meal, the food was always hot and inviting.

Rosanna was just as determined to get ahead as Little Crist was. The chickens were laying well, and the cows gave good milk. Rosanna was making two or three nice rolls of butter per week above their need. These she took to the store, and the butter and extra eggs more than paid for the groceries they bought. She felt happy that she was keeping up her end of the housekeeping.

One day when Ann Roper came over from the village to buy some cream, she exclaimed, "My gracious, Rosanna! Don't you find this awful hard work—feeding chickens and pigs, cooking, and milking cows? Do you ever have time to play cards?"

Rosanna stopped polishing her tinware for a moment, turned, and looked at Ann. There was a touch of pity in her voice: "No, Ann, I don't have time to play cards, and I wouldn't play cards even if I had time. I think it's a waste of time. Besides, our church doesn't allow card playing.

"Anyhow, this is not hard work. With a new house and barn, a sober and industrious husband, new furnishings in the house, beautiful horses to work and drive, and a chance to buy our farm when we wish—well, feeding chickens and pigs and making butter and cooking are not hard work. They're pleasure and enjoyment! We're having fun!"

"Rosanna, I envy you. You're a happy woman. I wish I had your philosophy of life." Ann had a note of disappointment in her voice.

Rosanna was happy in her new home, but from the first she went to see Momli each week. When she knew that Momli had company, she frequently went down to help her. Even though Momli had always been a strong, healthy woman, she was beginning to age a bit. While she would never complain, work did not go quite so easily for her as in earlier years.

Momli frequently came up to spend the day with Rosanna, too. She was devoted to her husband, Bishop Shem. Leah, his daughter, was kind to her. But Momli somehow felt that Rosanna was her own daughter. She had taken her in as a little baby five days old and raised her to womanhood. Now to be separated from Rosanna was more of a burden to Elizabeth than she had expected. She never came to see Rosanna without bringing something for her in her basket.

One day in the early spring, Rosanna looked out the window toward the barn and saw Momli coming under the barn's overshot with her basket. Rosanna was so glad to see her again that she hurried out to meet her. When they came into the house, Momli took the covering off the basket. "I brought you a can of to-

- 181 -

ROSANNA KNITTING WHILE
MOMLI VISITS

matoes and a can of sauerkraut."

Then she repeated, "A can of tomatoes and a can of sauerkraut."

When Rosanna seemed a bit worried about this soliloquy, Momli reminisced, "I was just thinking. One day long ago, over in Half Moon Valley, I took your mother a can of tomatoes and a can of sauerkraut. Come to think of it, I carried them in this very basket. That was thirty years ago, before you were born. How pleased your mother was! I'll never forget her, so strong and beautiful!

"If the doctor had only treated her right when you were born, we might have her with us yet. But then I never would have had you. In his sermon, the bishop sometimes quotes the hymn, '*Was Gott tut, das ist wohlgetan* (what God does is done aright),' and I guess it's true."

As they sat and talked, Rosanna began to knit a little stocking. A look of deep satisfaction brightened Momli's face, but she did not comment on what she saw until she was leaving for home. "*Wann du mich mohl brauchst, kumm ich* (whenever you need me, I'll come)."

Rosanna and Little Crist were nearing the second summer of housekeeping when their firstborn came. The baby was a little boy and according to custom was to be named after his paternal grandfather. Yet Little Crist did not want to be selfish, so he asked, "Since your father is not living, would you be willing to name our baby after my father?"

"I'm perfectly willing," agreed Rosanna. "And would you let his middle name be McGonegal?"

That, too, was an old custom, and so the baby was named Yost McGonegal Yoder.

Baby Yost was the first grandchild in both families, so he was popular. Lame Yost frequently came to see his little namesake. One day he promised Rosanna, *"Wann er mohl gross genung is, kaaf ich ihm en paar Hosse* (when he is big enough, I'll buy him a pair of pants)." At preaching services, Catherine and Momli vied with each other as to which grandma would get to hold the little newcomer.

Baby Yost grew well. When he was about a year and a half old, a little sister joined the family. Little Yost took great interest in her, but Rosanna was the one most pleased of all. Now she had an opportunity to honor Momli in the finest possible way. She named her little girl Elizabeth. How she had hoped the second baby would be a little girl, so that she might show Momli how grateful she was to her for all she meant to Rosanna!

When Rosanna told her that she would name the little girl Elizabeth for her, Momli reacted with joy and happiness. Little Yost now had to share the attention of Momli, but to Grandpa Yost, he was still *the* boy.

With two little ones to care for, Rosanna found that she needed help. In the community was a middle-aged woman who had no home of her own. Rosanna asked her to come and help care for the children and assist with the work. This woman was Mary Ann Carson, a Scotch-Irish Presbyterian. For many years she had kept house for John Armstrong, but when Armstrong died, she was without a home.

Mary Ann gladly came to help Rosanna. As she

worked in the home, she became much more than merely a housemaid. She became a friend.

And as the years passed, this friendship between Rosanna and Mary Ann ripened into a mutual dependence. When Mary Ann was out of work, she always knew she was welcome at Rosanna Yoder's. There she would go for a week or a month and stay as a helping guest. Mary Ann was an intelligent woman. She spoke good English and understood Pennsylvania German but refused to speak it. As a result, Rosanna's children grew up learning to speak good English along with the Pennsylvania German. They were bilingual right from the beginning.

Mary Ann liked little children. She became fond of Little Yost as he followed her about, trying to say one English word after another. Baby Elizabeth smiled and cooed and prattled as though she too were trying to learn to talk English. All this was a great satisfaction to Little Crist and Rosanna. When they had occasion to go away for an evening or to attend preaching in stormy weather, they could with perfect confidence leave the children with Mary Ann.

By this time Little Crist was getting his farm well organized. He had to be away from home rather frequently now because he was buying and selling more horses. It was clear that if he wished to have the fieldwork done in time and in season, he needed a hired hand. The first one to work for him was Siever Yoder, whom he had known for many years. Since he knew Siever was reliable, he felt justified in buying and selling horses even more widely.

Often in the fall of the year, Little Crist would go

over to Stone Valley to Hetty Porter's or Sam Powell's, or to Hiram Ross's across Broad Mountain, and occasionally as far west as Ennisville or Neff's Mills. Sometimes he'd buy three or four horses on one trip. Crist knew that feed might become scarce during the winter in Stone Valley. As cold weather approached, he could buy horses more cheaply there.

One fall he went over to Hetty Porter's and asked, "Hetty, have you any horses to sell?"

"Yes, I'll sell any horse in the stable. I have too many to keep over winter. Besides, I need a little money to pay my taxes."

Crist walked into the stable and looked them over. He noticed a dapple-brown steed, his favorite color, that had the makings of a fine horse. It had good large feet, straight, well-boned legs, was broad across the chest and between the ears, and had large intelligent eyes and an honest-looking face.

"What'll you take for that horse, Hetty?"

"He's a good one," said Hetty. "I'll take one hundred and fifty dollars for him. He's worth more, but my grain is too scarce to keep him over winter."

Crist had schooled himself to bargain a bit, no matter what price was asked. But when Hetty mentioned one hundred and fifty dollars for that fine horse, he did not have the nerve to offer less. He would have felt guilty of taking advantage of a woman when she had to sell. So he said enthusiastically, "Here's your money, and I hope it will help you out."

Hetty's husband had been killed by the kick of a horse, and she was trying to raise her four boys and two girls on the farm. Crist had too much of the golden-rule principle in his heart to press for the lowest price with a woman like that. As he bridled the horse and led him away, Hetty almost wept in gratitude, but she managed to say, "I hope you have good luck with him, Cristli."

Never had Little Crist bought a horse with such possibilities—five years old, as pretty as a picture, and as sound as a dollar. He called the horse Harry, after Hetty's oldest son, and he never went to the stable without the sight of Harry filling him with satisfaction. He instructed Siever, "I want you to curry Harry thoroughly every day, and if we work him, then twice a day." Crist regularly fed the horses. Since proper feeding was an art, he assumed that responsibility himself.

By spring, Harry had gained considerable weight, and that, together with Siever's currying, made him a handsome horse indeed. When Siever led him out to water daily, Harry had the spirit of a mountain deer and the gentleness of a mother sheep. Crist reasoned that a horse with such a disposition would make a wonderful leader. He could hardly wait till spring farming came to hitch him in the lead, put a single line on him, and teach him the meaning of *gee* (turn right) and *haw* (turn left). But Little Crist discovered someone had already taught him well, for he was as much at home in the furrow as an old fire horse on the way to a burning building.

The more Crist worked Harry as a leader, the better he liked him. He mused, "I must keep that horse to stabilize my rapidly changing team. Harry will make any horse work alongside him."

However, one day Dave Mutersbaugh came

around to buy horses. As he entered the stable door, he was ready for a deal. "I need a good horse. Do you have any to sell, Cristli?"

"Yes, sir, I'll sell any horse in the stable except Harry, the front one."

Dave looked them all over and then asked, "What's your price on that front horse?"

"He's not for sale," declared Crist emphatically.

"Well, if you would sell him, what price would you ask?"

Finally Little Crist responded, "Well, if any man would be fool enough to give me three hundred and fifty dollars for him, I guess I'd let him go."

"Sold!" stated Mutersbaugh as he reached for his wallet.

"But," protested Crist, "he's not for sale."

"Come on," scolded Dave. "You can't back out now. You said you'd take three hundred and fifty dollars for him, and here's your money."

"I'm a man of my word," Crist replied, "and I said I'd take three hundred and fifty dollars for him, if any man was fool enough to give it. But Dave, I didn't class you in that crowd."

"Cristli, do you know why I'm giving it to you? I know a man who has five horses that look exactly like him. If I set this horse among them, you couldn't tell me which was your horse. He wants the sixth horse, and he'll give me five hundred dollars for this horse. One hundred and fifty dollars sure profit makes most any man a little foolish, eh, Cristli? That six-horse team will be worth five thousand dollars."

As Harry was led out the lane, he looked back and

whinnied as if he were trying to say, "Good-bye, master. I'm sorry to leave you." Cristli Yoder almost wept.

Afterward, when talking about Harry, Crist would say regretfully, "That horse could almost talk English. I know he understood English and German, for no matter how far away he was, if I told him to come to me, he would come. If I told him to go forward three steps, he went. If I told him gee or haw, he would turn right or left, he did so willingly. Yes, sir, that horse could almost talk.

"If I ever buy another like him, I'll not sell him for any money. Horses like that just seem to bless our stable with peace and prosperity."

CHAPTER 14

Margaret's Visit

ROSANNA'S BUTTER and egg production was increasing. The cows gave a fine grade of milk. Her springhouse, through which a fresh limestone spring flowed in a constant stream, was so cold that butter and milk were kept sweet for the longest possible time. This enabled Rosanna to make a fine quality of solid butter, eagerly sought by the nearby townsfolk.

Butter was selling for ten to twenty-five cents per pound. When dealers came to buy butter and took fifteen to twenty-five pounds at a time, it was bothersome to get a pencil and paper and figure the amount due. She knew that some of them were not above making slight "errors," always in their own favor.

Rosanna had an idea. She noticed on the back of an almanac a pyramid-shaped multiplication table which went as far as twenty-four times twenty-four. Rosanna decided to memorize the entire table. Then if someone bought seventeen pounds of butter at nineteen cents a pound, she wouldn't reach for a pencil to figure it out. Instead, she could offhandedly say seventeen times nineteen is three hundred twenty-three, or three dollars and twenty-three cents. Rosanna enjoyed the mental exercise of learning the table.

She had gotten as far as the twenty-first line when Little Crist came home from town one day with a letter postmarked in Philadelphia. Rosanna opened the envelope eagerly and unfolded a letter from her sister. Margaret was coming to see her in July! For years they had been corresponding now and then, but Rosanna had a deep desire to see and know Margaret, her only sister.

Rosanna replied at once, expressing her great delight. She assured Margaret that she awaited her visit with great anticipation and pleasure. Rosanna asked Margaret to let her know which day she would arrive so someone might meet her at Reedsville and spare her the lumbering stagecoach ride to Belleville. About the middle of July, another letter said Margaret would arrive Thursday evening, July twenty-fourth.

When the day arrived, there was real excitement around the Yoder house. Cristli hitched his fastest horse to his yellow-top carriage and drove to Reedsville to meet the four o'clock train. He wanted to be there early to give the horse a bite to eat, a drink of water, and a short rest. That would ensure that the trip back home could be made as fast as possible.

When the train arrived at Reedsville, Little Crist was on the platform looking for someone whom he had never seen. Only three ladies got off the train. He knew one of them, Mrs. Rice, the grain merchant's wife. The other two looked more like shoppers than travelers, but he stepped up to these ladies and inquired, "Are either of you ladies Margaret McGonegal?"

When they both replied, "No, sir," Crist hardly knew what to do. That was the last train of the day from the east, so all he could do was drive home and tell Rosanna that Margaret did not come. Rosanna was greatly disappointed, but she consoled herself with the thought that Margaret was a woman of affairs. If she missed connections at Harrisburg, as doubtless she had, Margaret could take care of herself for the night.

Next day there was no message, but Rosanna had a feeling that Margaret would arrive on the stagecoach that evening. She set her house in order, washed and dressed little Yost and Elizabeth, put on her own good dress, and awaited the arrival of the stagecoach at about six-thirty. When the time drew near, she could scarcely wait.

Rosanna watched and listened, and just a minute after six-thirty, she heard a heavy vehicle rumble over the wooden bridge a quarter mile down the bend of the road and around the low hill. "Oh, that must be the stage," she murmured to herself. In another minute, she heard the familiar clatter of the horses' feet, and then the stage appeared with the horses in a fast trot. That must be Margaret! But Rosanna waited till the horses swung in toward their outer gate at the road and stopped.

Then she saw a woman dressed in black alight from the stage and heard her ask, "In this road?" Rosanna could wait no longer. She hurried out the lane to meet the visitor, still wondering whether this really was her sister. When they met face-to-face, there was no doubt.

Margaret threw her arms around Rosanna and exclaimed, "My sister!" For a moment both were so overcome that neither could speak.

When the first wave of emotion subsided, they looked at each other for unmistakable signs of family resemblance. Margaret was taller, but both had black wavy hair, dark-brown eyes, red cheeks, and rather dark complexions.

Margaret spoke first. "I kept thinking as I came, maybe this is not my sister after all, but there is no mistake. We're both as Irish as St. Patrick himself. God bless the Irish!"

As they walked in the lane together, Rosanna told Margaret how Cristli had been to Reedsville to meet her the day before. When she did not come, they were worried for fear something might have happened to her.

Then Margaret told her that the train from Philadelphia arrived at Harrisburg after the westbound train had left, so she had to stay there overnight. "The agent told me," reported Margaret, "that this connection is often missed because the schedule is tight. He assured me that I would have no trouble today. Indeed, I had no difficulty finding my way out here."

When they reached the house, Margaret was charmed with the chubby-cheeked children. While she faintly remembered the Amish in Half Moon Valley, she had forgotten that little boys were dressed like miniature Amishmen—with long pants and the same cut of coat, hair, and hat as Daddy's. Now she saw three-year-old Yost with his long pants, broad-brimmed hat, little white muslin shirt, and no suspenders. Her amusement almost overcame her delight.

As Margaret looked at Yost, she commented, "Even though he has a big hat and long hair, you can't hide the Irish in him."

Little Elizabeth, the toddler, was wearing a little white cap, a pink dress, and long apron, like a pinafore. Margaret found her quaint and adorable.

When Margaret met Little Crist, she recalled Reuben Kauffman back in Half Moon Valley. She was only seven years old when they left that valley, but she remembered Momli and how kind she was to the children in their great sorrow from losing their mother. She asked to see Elizabeth again. Margaret remembered her as Elizabeth since Rosanna had later called her Momli.

Even though Margaret had known Amish folks when she was a little girl, the sight of all these men and women in their quaint garb made her feel as though she were in a foreign country. The men were all rugged looking, but as she looked at them more closely, she noticed that they had fine complexions, clear skin, and red cheeks. While the men all wore beards, they shaved the upper lip and the upper part of the cheek so that their complexions often showed off to good advantage.

The women all wore white caps and dresses made of perfectly plain material without ruffles or lace. Their cap-encircled faces, because of so much outdoor work, carried a deep tan which city ladies often coveted. What impressed Margaret was the fact that everyone bore the stamp of health and strength. She observed no intoxication, no poverty, nobody destitute among them.

Such equality and uniformity, Margaret had never seen before. None of the Amish were rich and none were poor. In cut of garment, there was absolute uniformity, yet with some variety in the subdued solid colors. Margaret noticed that these plain people were not only modest in their dress but in their speech as well. Most of them spoke in short sentences and in low tones. They seemed to be somewhat reluctant to initiate talk with outsiders but were quite friendly once such a conversation started.

Margaret had lived in the city ever since she was a little girl. The pure clean air, the unobstructed sunshine, the abundant foliage of the trees, the delightful freshness of the fruits and vegetables on the table, and the aroma of the country-cured ham—these all filled her with wonder and delight. Little Crist had a fine field of second-crop clover in full bloom. Margaret walked through it every day and filled her lungs and her soul, as she said, with the rich perfume of that beautiful field.

This was blackberry season, too. One day they all went to the mountain to pick blackberries. Margaret thought blackberries grew on trees. She was thrilled when she found that she could walk up to a bush, pick berries, and eat all she wanted, with perfect freedom. At first she was afraid and asked, "Cristli, are you sure there are no bears or alligators in these bushes?"

Crist was tempted to tell her that there were no alligators, but she had better keep a sharp lookout for whale and buffalo. But since he did not wish to make fun of her, he answered truthfully that they were safe and that any animals would already be scared off.

In a surprisingly short time, Rosanna and Crist had gathered three large buckets of blackberries. When Margaret saw them carry these buckets filled with perfect berries, she thought she had never seen such abundance before. In the city one had to pay for every berry, and here you carried them away in bucketfuls, and nobody seemed to care. What luxury!

As they drove home behind Crist's spirited driving horse, Margaret could not help comparing its speed and spirit with the lumbering horsecar in the city. There the horses had to be urged with a whip to make them go, but this horse had to be held in tightly and calmed by soothing words to keep him from running too fast. It seemed that every minute of the day had either a surprise or a thrill for her.

That evening as they sat and talked, Margaret observed, "I notice that you do not have window curtains, nor pictures on the walls, nor carpets on the floor. Is there a reason?"

"Yes," replied Rosanna. "Our church believes in

nonconformity. 'Be not conformed to this world' (Rom. 12:2). The church does not allow curtains or carpets or pictures. We are taught to practice plainness in clothing, in manners, in speech. Even our carriages are different from other people's. Our preachers continually warn us against 'worldliness.'

"But then, we make up for some of the beautiful things you have by keeping our floors scrubbed, our tinware polished, and our table linen white and beautiful. We're allowed to have beautiful flowers in the house and in the yard and garden. And we dare have good-looking horses, too. How Cristli admires and enjoys handsome horses! You noticed that the horse we drove for blackberries today had plenty of spirit, and he was beautiful, too."

"Beautiful!" exclaimed Margaret. "His sides were so glossy you could almost use them for a mirror. As for spirit, I thought every minute he would run away, but I got an awful thrill out of it. So different from those poky, old, overworked trolley horses!

"I noticed something else," Margaret went on. "When eating, almost everybody uses a knife more than a fork. At first I was slightly shocked, but now I believe I know why. Your knives are broad at the end, and your forks have only two tines. For a working man to use a two-tined fork would be too tedious and slow. They can eat faster with a knife."

"Well, I never thought about it, but that does seem like a good reason," responded Rosanna.

"I notice, too, how well-behaved your children are. Why, it seems to me that all they do is eat and sleep and play and grow. I don't believe I've heard one of them cry since I arrived. How do you do it?"

"First of all," explained Rosanna modestly, "we believe good health comes from good food, and second, we insist on obedience. You see, obedience is the underlying principle of the Amish religion. We are taught to obey God, as his commandments are set forth in the Bible. And then we willingly obey the bishop and the ministers, whom we feel are chosen by God to teach and direct us since they are selected by lot."

"By lot? What do you mean?" Margaret wondered.

"That's our method of choosing a minister. Since our ministers are men who have to make their own living, receiving no pay from the church, we have in each congregation a bishop, a deacon, and three or four assisting ministers. They are generally farmers or carpenters and cannot devote much time to study and the preparation of sermons. We have three or four ministers so that not too much responsibility or duty falls on any one of them.

"When a minister dies or gets too old to preach, the bishop takes a vote of the church as to whether another minister should be chosen. If the congregation votes unanimously for it, the bishop sets a Sunday, generally communion Sunday, for the election. When the proper time comes, the bishop and one assisting minister withdraw to an upstairs room prepared for them. The deacon stands at the stair door and another minister at the top of the stairs.

"One by one, the male members then go to the deacon at the stair door and whisper the name of the man they believe best qualified for the ministry. When the men have finished voting, the women pass to the stair door, and each quietly mentions the man they feel best qualified for the ministry.

"When all have made their nominations and the votes are counted, the deacon takes as many hymn-books from the singers' table as there were men voted for and gives these hymnals to the bishop, who has counted the votes. The bishop places a small piece of paper in one of these hymnbooks. The ministers and the bishop then go downstairs and place these books in a row on the singers' table. The bishop calls the names of all the men voted for. Each one in the lot steps up to the table and chooses one of these hymnals until each candidate has a book.

"The bishop then takes the book from the man nearest to him and opens it. If the slip of paper is not in that book, the man is free. The bishop takes the book of the next man and opens it. He continues down the line until he finds the book containing the slip of paper with the Bible verse, such as 'The lot is cast into the lap; but the whole disposing thereof is of the Lord' [Prov. 16:33]. The bishop announces the name of the man holding that book, and he is elected by lot as the minister chosen by God."

"Chosen by God!" Margaret exclaimed. "He must feel like Moses."

"Well, yes," agreed Rosanna, "but he does serve in a team with the other preachers. Every church Sunday, they withdraw to a room upstairs and share counsel. Yet the responsibility of the ministry is such a serious matter that men shrink from it. Occasionally someone selected has felt not able to fill the office so overwhelmingly that he refused to serve and begged to be excused. But that is rare.

"Ministers feel themselves chosen by God. They consecrate themselves to God's service and do the best they can. By this method of choosing a minister, we feel that we give God the greatest possible chance to choose the right man for us, and thus our obedience and respect is easy."

"Rosanna," Margaret responded, "your ideas and teachings about obedience and nonconformity remind me of some of the practices of the Catholic Church. You know our orders of sisters wear a plain black garb, which carries out your teaching of nonconformity, and the priest certainly does insist on obedience to the rules of the church."

Then Rosanna had some questions. "Margaret, tell me something about John and William. Are they doing well?"

"William is always concerned about my welfare and happiness, and he frequently speaks of you, Rosanna. The priest is fond of him. In fact, he thought William should study for the priesthood, but William is set on business. He's clerking in a large store alongside another clerk whose name, I think, is Wanamaker, John Wanamaker. They're good friends, and someday they want to go into business together and have a large department store.

"Brother John is a typesetter at the *Public Ledger*, and I think he's getting along well. I'm afraid he likes his wee drappie (drinking) too well. However, William and the priest are watching him closely. I hope they can keep him on the right road."

After they had talked freely about their different churches, Rosanna asked Margaret whether she would care to go along to preaching on Sunday. Margaret thought a moment. "Since it's all in German, which I don't understand, I am sure Father Calahan would not object."

When Sunday came, preaching happened again to be at Reuben Kauffman's. They were all in the carriage ready to go soon after eight o'clock, farmers' time—always at least a half hour fast. But going to church early was not out of the ordinary for Margaret since she usually attended early mass.

They drove up the road and soon found themselves in a long procession of white and yellow carriages. While they approached the barn, carriages in groups of twos and threes were coming from all directions. Rosanna and Margaret walked to the house. The houseyard was already dotted with groups of men moving slowly toward the porch to go inside.

The two sisters found the kitchen and the summerhouse and the porches filled with women and girls. They went to the summerhouse to remove their wraps. Everyone was curious to know the identity of this well-dressed, stately woman with Rosanna. Crist's sister Sarah glanced at Margaret and whispered "sister" to a clump of girls. Everybody knew that Rosanna had brothers and a sister in Philadelphia. So that satisfied their curiosity. Anyway, it was time to go into the house and find seats.

Lydia, Reuben's wife, recognized Margaret as Rosanna's guest, shook hands with her, and welcomed her. Then she told Rosanna, "I've placed two chairs in the bedroom for you and your sister, where you can see and hear well." Lydia knew that it would be a considerable strain for the visitor to sit on a backless bench for three hours if she were not accustomed to that.

When they were seated, Margaret noticed that all the men in the house sat with their hats on. To her, this was a peculiar sight. But soon she heard a man say something in a firm voice, and with a swish every hat was off.

In a moment, he began to sing, and others joined till all were singing. What Margaret thought was a command was just Yost Yoder announcing the first hymn. Afterward Rosanna explained that at preaching the men never take off their hats until the first hymn is announced, and then all hats are removed at once. Margaret had never heard singing like that. It had some similarities to the chanting of the priests but was not exactly the same. The unison of the men's and women's voices in the Alsatian chorales moved her deeply. When a chorale swung into a minor key, it almost made her weep.

Margaret observed everything carefully—the singing, the beginning sermon, the silent prayer, standing during the reading of the Scriptures, the main sermon and testimonies, the prayer read from the prayerbook, the benediction—when everybody, even the children, bowed the knee—and the final hymn.

Although she could not understand German, she noticed the solemn countenances of those men and women, their respectful silence, and their spirit of devotion. This all filled her with a sense of divine presence. She was impressed that the Amish folks, slightly stoical, came to preaching services not for entertainment but for worship. Strange as it may seem, she felt much at home with them.

Margaret liked the dinner, the moon pies, the hot bean soup, and especially the efficient promptness with which it was served. The bean soup, made in a fifty-quart kettle, had a delicious flavor she had never tasted before. Rosanna explained that bean soup made in large quantities is always better.

❧ ❧ ❧

When the Lame Yost Yoder family returned from preaching that afternoon, they discussed Rosanna's sister. Franey commented that Margaret was tall and good-looking, wore a silk dress that must have cost a lot, walked straight, and talked with a clear voice. Eli had seen Margaret at a distance, too, and eagerly listened to what Franey was saying about her. He was rather glad next day at the dinner table when his father said, "Go over to Cristli's this evening, Eli, and ask him whether he needs any seed wheat."

Eli really wanted to go over and talk to Rosanna's sister, but to go without a reason might look as though he had some particular interest. He could not have anyone thinking that. Eli had never talked to a city lady before, and he was concerned about how he would look to her.

He was astonished to find how friendly and common she was. Almost before he knew it, they were talking like old friends. She told him about the city, the high buildings, the big stores, the horsecars, and the theaters.

Eventually Margaret wondered, "Eli, I have heard that there are ghosts in this valley. Did you ever see one?"

"Do you mean spooks?"

"Yes, that's what I mean."

"Oh, yes, I've seen some myself," Eli claimed. "About a mile below Belleville, there's a little ravine called Kootcher's Hollow. The road runs in the middle of it, and often when people ride through there at night, a dog without a head runs along inside the fence. Sometimes he comes through the fence and jumps right up on the horse just back of the rider.

"Last fall Siever Yoder and I were coming home from a cornhusking about two o'clock at night. When we approached Kootcher's Hollow, Siever said, 'I wonder if we'll see old Shep tonight. I'm going to call him.' 'Don't you dare,' I replied, but when we were riding into the hollow, Siever called, 'Here, Shep, here, Shep.' Before we could count to three, that headless dog jumped through the fence and right up on the horse behind Siever.

"When I saw that, I rode off at full gallop. Poor Siever urged his horse with all his might, but his mount could scarcely get off the spot. When Siever finally got out of the hollow, his horse was covered with sweat and foam. Siever was frightened almost to death."

"Really?" exclaimed Margaret, her eyes wide with wonder.

"Also, up on the mountains, I know a big rock," continued Eli. "Under that rock, right where you can see it plainly, are thousands of dollars of money in gold. But you can't get it. The minute you go near it, a thousand snakes shoot their heads out all around it, and nobody has the nerve to touch it.

"Then, over in the Seven Mountains, there's an old hotel where wheat haulers often stop overnight. A man once lived there who stole some money. After he died, lots of men saw his ghost walking around that area at night and heard him say over and over again, 'Where shall I put it?' One night a half-drunk teamster saw him and heard him say over and over, 'Where shall I put it?' The teamster replied, 'You fool, put it where you got it!' Nobody ever saw or heard that ghost again. That just put him to rest."

"Eli, you frighten me." Margaret shivered. "Are there any ghosts around here?"

"Well, I never saw any right here, but I have heard some pretty funny noises in the barn."

Although several persons in the valley admitted that they had seen things they could not explain, most thought Eli had a rather vivid imagination. But for Margaret, it was a great evening. Never before had she met anybody who claimed to have really seen a ghost. It was a wonderful evening for Eli, too. He had found someone interested in his spook stories.

🐦 🐦 🐦

The days passed all too fast for Margaret and Rosanna. Every day brought new experiences for Margaret—a trip to the top of the back (Stone) mountain, where the whole valley was in plain view; a trip to the big mill with the overshoot wheel; watching four spirited horses hauling a big load of oats; the cool orchard shade, where it was so pleasant to read; the delicious milk and ham and eggs, and the fresh fruits and vegetables. The greatest joy of all was learning to know her beautifully quaint little niece and nephew and her adorable sister, Rosanna.

Margaret would never forget her visit with Reuben Kauffman and with Elizabeth. They both had known Margaret's parents well. Reuben spoke almost eloquently about his friendship with her father, Patrick McGonegal, while Elizabeth shared touchingly about her great love for Bridget, Margaret's mother.

The last evening Margaret was with them, Crist went to Belleville and told Tommy Horton, the stage driver, "Come over in the morning. Rosanna's sister is returning to Philadelphia and wants to catch the train at Reedsville."

The next morning, Rosanna listened for the rumble of the stage across the bridge. When Margaret came, that rumble had filled Rosanna with joy. When she heard it this morning, her heart was pained with emotion. It signaled a farewell that she dreaded.

With Margaret gone, the house seemed empty. If it had not been for the cheerful prattle of little Yost and Elizabeth, she could hardly have endured it. Rosanna seemed to sense something more than just the sadness of parting. Some faint foreboding was gnawing at her heartstrings. She felt that Margaret would come to visit her again, and for a moment her heart was light. Then a sinister premonition returned like a dismal shadow of doom and disaster, slowly approaching. She could not see the sorrow, but she felt the withering blight of the oncoming shadow.

Could it be that some unseen hand was trying to point out dangers that were lurking around her children, ready to destroy them? This was the type of vague intuition which sometimes brings warnings to the minds of women, even when they are not yet able fully to interpret them.

CHAPTER 15

The First Sorrow

A S BISHOP SHEM grew older, he became stricter and more conservative. He insisted that everything had to be kept just as it was years ago. But various members in the church felt that some rules could be cautiously changed for the better without yielding to worldliness.

Since the beginning of the church in this area, men had worn white muslin shirts for both work and dress. At work they soiled easily, and it took a tremendous amount of rubbing to get them clean. Some of the women began making colored shirts, blue or brown, for their men to wear while working. The bishop preached strongly against this laxity and worldliness. He even threatened excommunication if the offending ones did not put away the worldly, colored shirts.

Several women did not have time to make straw-hats for their men. Their husbands went to the store and bought strawhats, which were both lighter and more comfortable. This too met with disapproval.

Bishop Shem called for his church to keep the older style of having white-topped or the newer yellow-topped carriages. But some young men in his congregation were not satisfied with the yellow oil-cloth and chose to run with black-top carriages, which also protected against rain but were more durable. This was breaking the old rules (*alte Ordnung,* old order), which was *verbodde* (forbidden).

The bishop also thought some of the girls showed pride in wearing their caps (prayer head coverings; 1 Cor. 11) too far back on the head and showing off their beautiful, wavy hair. They also used broader cap strings with larger bows beneath their chins. A few even became so worldly that they tied their cap strings loosely, allowing the bow to rest on the chest instead of being drawn tightly under the chin, as tradition pre-scribed.

All these encroachments of worldliness and mani-festations of pride were objectionable to the bishop and his supporters.

In the congregation was a bright young minister, Christian K. Peachey, who rather sympathized with the offenders against custom. He felt that simplicity of attire was the duty of all Christians. But at the same time, he felt that the principle could be preserved even if some hardships were avoided. Word slowly leaked out that Crist Peachey was in favor of colored shirts, carriages topped with black, and store-bought straw-hats. People gradually learned that he was not entirely averse to the girls setting their caps back a bit to show their hair and using broader cap strings to make larger bows.

At the singings, the boys and girls talked about it. Some felt that they should obey the bishop. Others felt he was too strict and that Crist Peachey was more nearly right. At preaching, little groups of men engaged in low-voiced conversation, and it was soon observed that these little groups were composed of men who were either for the bishop or for Crist Peachey. There never was any open disputing. Men and women and young people just quietly took sides according to their convictions or their inclinations.

This went on until the bishop felt a little uneasy about Crist Peachey and his views. One Sunday the bishop preached a rather strenuous sermon condemning those who were not faithful to the rules and the old order of the church. Crist Peachey felt the rebuke keenly, but he did not feel guilty. Many of the members sensed that the sermon was aimed directly at Crist and his sympathizers. This sermon stirred things up even more than before.

When communion came, the ones siding with Crist Peachey refused to commune because there was a lack of harmony in the church. Among those who did not feel like taking communion were Reuben Kauffman, Ben Sharp, Little Crist, and many others and their wives. Even the bishop's own son, Yost, the singer, was on the Peachey side. Finally Ben Sharp suggested that the group see Crist Peachey and propose to him that they all withdraw and start a new church.

Preacher Crist agreed that if they were dissatisfied with the strict enforcement of the old rules and order, maybe they could advance their spiritual lives better by withdrawing. He agreed to be their minister. As the new idea of separation became known, more people expressed sympathy with Crist Peachey. The new group decided to hold their services at Ben Sharp's on the same Sunday the bishop's group held the regular meeting at Nicholas Yoder's. Thus church fellowship was somewhat disrupted between the two groups, and many families were divided.

Little Crist, Rosannà, Sarah, Franey, and Eli went with the Peacheys, while Lame Yost and Catherine stayed with Bishop Shem. Shem's son Yost left his father, but his daughter Leah stayed with him. Many families that were undecided at first eventually came over to the Peachey Church (later called the Renno Church), which allowed black-topped carriages.

Less than ten years after the division, the Peachey congregation far outnumbered Bishop Shem's group, the *Alt Gmeh* (Old Church, later called the Byler Church), with mostly yellow-topped carriages. Bishop Shem was not strict enough for some ultraconservatives in the Old Church, who split to form the Old School, the Nebraska Amish Church, with the older-style white-topped carriages.

There was no change in creed or dogma between the factions, merely a difference in the application of the Scripture, "Be not conformed to the world." Yet even with the separation, members of the Renno and the Byler groups would still share communion with each other on occasion.

❧ ❧ ❧

Not long after Margaret's visit, the hot August days came with burning severity. Flies were more persistent pests than ever and harder to control. (Screen doors had not yet come into use.) For catching flies, Rosanna had a common device made of an ordinary crock with the bottom broken out, inserted into the top of a two-bushel burlap bag. To hold the bag in place, a string was tied tightly around it just below the rim of the crock. Apple butter or molasses was smeared around the inside of the crock.

This flytrap was then placed where flies were thick. The flies were attracted by the molasses and went into the crock to eat. When the inside of the crock became lined with flies, someone would quickly spread a cloth over the top of the crock, shake the flies down into the bag, give the bag a twist to keep them there, and then set the crock for another catch.

Despite all precautions, children were frequently stricken with cholera infantum. Already there had been several deaths, so Rosanna watched her children with the greatest of care. One day she noticed that Elizabeth cried a little and was listless and sleepy. Little Crist called the doctor immediately, but the doctor treated the case lightly and assured Rosanna that the child would soon be all right.

By the next afternoon, fever began to develop, accompanied by vomiting and much internal distress.

Crist went for the doctor again, but he still showed little concern, gave a few drops to allay the fever, and assured Crist that there was nothing to worry about. He said he would drop in the next day, perhaps, to see the child.

Momli came up in the evening, and when she saw her little namesake, she told Rosanna, *"Des Kind is schlimm* (this child is very sick)." Again Crist hurried to bring the doctor, but he was out of town. His wife promised to send the doctor over just as soon as he returned. He did not come. Toward morning the baby developed cramps and finally convulsions. As they sat by the cradle watching, applying hot compresses while waiting for the doctor, little Elizabeth breathed heavily a few times and was gone.

Rosanna's grief could hardly be described. For the rest of her own life, she held the opinion that if the best doctor had been available to give proper treatment, little Elizabeth would still be with her. Rosanna felt that their great sorrow came through carelessness of the doctor, who treated the case lightly. She gave up her little girl, so beautiful and promising, named in honor of Momli. It was a grief almost too heavy for her to bear.

∽ ∽ ∽

It was not long till the corn shocks dotted the fields once more. The frosty mornings opened the chestnut burrs and turned the bright green of summer into the brown and the crimson and gold of autumn.

Since the death of Elizabeth, Momli came up more frequently. She hoped she could help to lighten the sorrow that weighed so heavily on Rosanna's heart. Today she had brought her knitting, and as they sat knitting or patching, they talked. Momli thought she noticed the weight of Rosanna's sorrow slowly lifting since she talked with greater freedom than she had for a long time.

When evening began to fall, Momli arose to go. As she said good-bye, she added, *"Wann du mich mohl brauchst, dann kumm ich* (whenever you need me, then I'll come)." What a comfort for Rosanna was contained in those few thoughtful words! Elizabeth might not have been able to spell *appreciation* or define *gratitude*, but she lived out and inspired these ennobling qualities every day of her life.

 🖋 🖋 🖋

When the fall work was done and snow flurries again began to streak the mountainside, Rosanna noticed that butter prices were improving. She decided to churn all she could. During Margaret's visit and baby Elizabeth's sickness, she had interrupted her project of learning the twenty-four lines of multiplication. But now that her work confined her more to the house, she began again to study these advanced tables.

Rosanna was impressed with the advantage of knowing these math answers. Just a week ago, the butcher wanted to charge her $2.07 for sixteen pounds of beef at twelve cents per pound. But since she had already mastered the sixteenth line, she corrected him, "Sixteen pounds at twelve cents a pound would come to $1.92."

The butcher figured again and was somewhat embarrassed. "You're right," he admitted.

When she told Cristli about it in the evening, he commented, "I'm glad you caught that old rascal. I always thought he'd cheat if he could. Now he'll think twice before he tries to cheat you again. I think I'll take you along when I go out to buy horses. Your multiplication tables might help me."

Rosanna replied with a twinkle, "These are egg, butter, and meat tables, not horse tables!"

"You're right, Rosanna, they're not 'horse stables,' " Crist said with a laugh. "But seriously, we must be on our guard. Honesty is part of our religion. Some people have no religion, and some who seem to have religion, don't let it interfere with their business. If they can cheat a bit, they'll do it. Since we try to be honest, we expect everybody else to be honest, too, but then we become an easy mark for rascals. Now that you know those tables, the butter buyers and the butcher can't cheat you. If I get stuck with feed bills and horses, I'll get you to figure out my problem."

One day Little Crist came home from having some new horses shod at the blacksmith shop. He hurried to the house and told Rosanna, "I have some good news for you. I've just seen the new doctor. He was at the shop getting his horse shod, and I talked with him."

"What does he look like?"

"Oh, he's a fine-looking man. His name is Hudson. He is big and handsome, and has a nice voice so that when you talk to him, you just can't help but like him."

"Well," noted Rosanna, "you know we'll need a

doctor before long, and I just could not think of using that doctor who neglected Elizabeth so badly. If you think Doctor Hudson is all right, let's get him for when I need him."

"I hoped you'd say that. I asked Jesse Horton about him. The blacksmith says this doc went to medical school for four years, so he's well educated. People say that other fellow went away to school only a year or two. Jesse thinks that Dr. Hudson will put the other fellow out of business, and I believe it, too. I'll see Dr. Hudson soon and tell him that we want him when you need him."

"My, I don't know when I was so glad. I dreaded seeing that other doctor come into my house again," confided Rosanna.

Crist noticed that the news of the new doctor was a tonic for Rosanna. The burden of doubt and fear that had haunted her ever since the death of Elizabeth seemed to vanish, and she talked of the coming event with confidence and pleasure. When Crist saw Dr. Hudson one day in town, he told him that they would need him before long.

Dr. Hudson promised, "I'll be over to see your wife soon, just to get acquainted. I'll give her some suggestions that may make things easier for her."

When Dr. Hudson called a day or so later, he showed such interest and concern that Rosanna's confidence in him was established at once.

When the baby was born, Dr. Hudson's skill and training soon had the child and the mother comfortable, resting, and doing well. The baby was a little boy, whom they named Levi. Crist reasoned that from the sturdiness of his little body, he would someday make a good harvest hand. During all these days, Momli was by Rosanna's side constantly, and she never lacked any comfort that Momli could supply.

When Rosanna was able again to look after her household duties, she found that Mary Ann Carson, her maid and friend, had done her usual splendid job of keeping the household running smoothly. Everything was in order.

Little Crist went to Belleville one evening to buy the groceries but did not return as promptly as usual. When he came back, Rosanna asked, "Cristli, is anything wrong that you stayed so long?"

"Yes, Rosanna, I'm afraid there is. I stopped to listen to the men talking about the war, and I'm afraid some of us Amish people will either have to pay our exemption or go to war or to jail. Today Sike Brindle, Dave Fultz, Ed Stumpf, and Jesse Horton left for Washington, and people are afraid that more will be called.

"Lincoln called for seventy-five thousand volunteers, thinking the war would soon be over, but last week there was a bad battle at Bull Run. They say the South is enlisting men by the thousands. Of course, I won't go to war and kill. That's plainly against the Bible. I want to be loyal to the government, but between God and country, God must come first."

"But there's another way," Rosanna reminded him. "Lincoln said that those who don't want to go to war because of conscientious scruples may be excused by paying a three-hundred-dollar exemption. And your pap pledged that if you are drafted and can't pay your exemption, he'll pay it for you."

"That's right. I'd forgotten about that."

Later, several Amishmen were drafted. Some paid their exemption promptly. For those who did not have the ready cash, the church paid it.

In preaching one Sunday, the bishop asked all members to remain after the singing of the last hymn. He counseled them, "These are dangerous times. The war is raging, and we do not know who will be called next. Let us pray for deliverance from sinful requirements, and let us remain steadfast in the faith.

"If any one of you is drafted and you cannot pay your exemption, make it known without delay to Deacon Jonas. We'll make up the money at once and free you. At present, there's something over a thousand dollars in the alms treasury. If necessary, we can borrow from that fund until we have time to replace it.

"Also, if any man outside our church is drafted, a Lutheran or Presbyterian or Methodist whose conscience is against war, you may wish to help him pay his exemption if he is not able. I believe that would be right in the sight of God.

"Now, if there is nothing else, I will not detain you any longer." Then after pausing a moment and hearing nothing, he dismissed them, "Go in peace."

🙖 🙖 🙖

The December winds began carrying more and more snow so that by Christmastime the mountains and the valley were covered with white powder. Sleighing was good everywhere. One of Crist's great delights was to hitch two fine horses to the big bobsled, bed it well with clean straw, cover the straw with sheepskins and blankets, bundle up Rosanna and little Yost and the baby, and go to preaching on Sunday.

In most things, the Amish religion discouraged the principle of the beautiful rather than cultivating it. However, when horses are well cared for, they grow handsome. Since there never was a church ruling against beautiful horses, Little Crist bestowed most of his aesthetic inclinations on horses. You could have a prancing team dash into the barnyard where preaching was to be held. The team might attract ever so much attention, but since nobody could lay his finger exactly on the spot where pride could be located, it could be neither condemned nor punished.

There was some subtle rivalry among Nancy Jake, Reuben Kauffman, Ben Sharp, and Little Crist in seeing who could drive the finest team to church. Yet none of these horse fanciers would ever admit that he was trying to outdo the others. Nancy Jake liked the ponderous Percherons, Ben Sharp preferred the swift-footed Hamiltonians, and Little Crist leaned toward the general-purpose Corn Planters. Reuben Kauffman appreciated fine horses of any kind.

It was a pleasure now to go to preaching. The Peachey (Renno) Church was growing rapidly, and there was perfect harmony between members and ministry. The congregation was made up largely of forward-looking youths and middle-aged men and women who believed in plainness and simplicity but not in too much unnecessary sacrifice and severity.

Crist Peachey had been made bishop since the division, and his leadership inspired the utmost confidence in the members. He demonstrated an unusual

GOING TO PREACHING
IN THE BOBSLED

degree of common sense, a fine conception of justice, a thorough understanding of the Scriptures, and fine tact in leadership. The bishop was a successful farmer. He kept his 140-acre farm in top shape. It was well equipped with buildings, machinery, and livestock. The layout was all paid for, and he was known to have considerable money in the bank.

His prosperity and management in material things were vital factors in establishing confidence in his religious and spiritual leadership. The Amish believe in self-sufficiency, and they strive to maintain it through hard work and good management. If he had been shiftless and careless in material things, he could never have built up such a healthy congregation. But with his strong personality and his evident wisdom, his leadership was never disputed. His opinions on church affairs were eagerly accepted as authoritative, and the members gladly obeyed.

Bishop Crist never resorted to anything that even bordered on coercion. Since he was called to the ministry and later to the bishopric by lot, he felt called of God. He consecrated his life to the upbuilding of God's kingdom, and no one ever doubted his dedication for a minute.

Everyone saw that the glory of God motivated the bishop to lead out, with no thought of personal aggrandizement. God prospered him in every way. Neither favoritism nor revenge ever entered into the discipline of a member. Those disciplined felt that justice tempered with mercy was meted out to them, and they were edified and satisfied. On this account, his church moved forward without dissension or discord.

Life moved on pleasantly for Little Crist and Rosanna as they prospered in material things, deepened their friendships, and felt a growing sense of responsibility in the church and the community. Experience in horse buying and selling had given Crist self-confidence, and with the added knowledge came both pleasure and profit.

Crist was being recognized as an authority on horses. Younger men would ask him to go with them to appraise a horse they were thinking of buying. They trusted that if there was anything wrong with a horse inside or outside, Little Crist Yoder could detect it.

Both Crist and Rosanna loved to sing, and in the long winter evenings, they would often sit and sing some new chorale they had heard. Many times neighbors and friends would come just for the joy of spending an evening singing together, or to learn a new chorale that to them was especially difficult.

In the preaching services, Little Crist led many of the hymns. According to custom, Rosanna never led any hymns in preaching services. But at weddings where women were allowed to lead hymns, she enjoyed a little friendly competition with her husband. Even at weddings, women were not supposed to lead any of the first three hymns, which must be sung in regular order. After that, however, anyone wishing to lead was free to do so.

As the years passed, more children came to the family. Three years after Levi was born, John arrived.

Seven years after that, Joseph, the youngest of the family, was born. Rosanna did not expect Joseph to live. He was so small at birth that he had to be carried on a pillow. Even the courageous Dr. Hudson had little hope for him.

One day Rosanna asked, "Doctor, may I feed him diluted cow's milk sweetened with brown sugar?"

"Feed him anything you like," said the doctor. "He's not likely to make it anyway."

However, in Rosanna's heart, there was no giving up. She fed her scrawny little baby weakened cow's milk sweetened with brown sugar and, surprisingly, he began to grow. One day when Doctor Hudson came to see the baby, he observed, "Why, Rosanna, this little scamp is growing. I believe you're a better doctor than I am. What did you do for him?"

"Cow's milk and brown sugar, and—you won't laugh if I tell you what else I did, will you? Since he was wasting away, I asked Mattie Hartzler to come over and measure him for the 'take-off.' She found that he had it, so she powwowed for the 'take-off,' and he's been improving ever since."

"Well, I'll be hanged! I don't know what the 'take-off' is, and I don't know what powwowing is, but I know that this little buster is getting better. So I'll not condemn powwowing. You Amish people seem to have a patent on that.

"I heard about the time Dr. Bigelow had erysipelas so bad that he was half afraid he'd die. When he finally sent for Crist King to powwow for him, he got better at once. Perhaps it's a form of faith healing or mental healing. I confess I don't understand it. But if

Mattie Hartzler can powwow for your sick little baby and help him to health, I'm for it. The time may come when we'll all understand it better and maybe use it instead of so many pills and powders."

Rosanna was surprised and gratified at the sensible attitude Dr. Hudson took toward powwowing. However, no matter what his opinion might have been or what he might have said, nothing could shake her faith in powwowing. She herself had stopped the dangerous flow of blood for many a man and beast when they had met with serious accident.

Neighbors far and wide knew Rosanna's power over pain. When someone suffered unbearably, they would come to her or send for her, and she would powwow to stop their agony. In a few minutes, the pain would be gone so the patient could rest comfortably.

Bill Kosier, a hard-working carpenter, lived at the back (Stone) mountain. About every two years, he would get a severely sore eye, as painful as a boil on the eyeball. The Amish name for it is *püscht Bloder* (pinkeye). When the pain in his eye became unbearable, he would come to Rosanna.

After she would powwow for him on two consecutive days, the inflammation would clear up. The pain would disappear, and Bill would say, "Rosanna, I don't know what in the world I'd do if it wasn't for your powwowing. When my eye hurts so bad that I can hardly stand it, the pain begins to ease up the minute you are through powwowing the first time. You're better than any doctor. Let me pay you for it."

"Oh, no. If I took money for it, the powwowing

wouldn't do any good. If I can help you, I'm satisfied."

Perhaps the faith Rosanna had in powwowing is related to the faith that can "remove mountains" (Mark 11:23). How little we really know about the possibilities of that faith described and practiced so long ago.

CHAPTER 16

The Boys

THE TRAINING OF Amish children begins early in life. The first general lesson is obedience. Parents such as Crist and Rosanna were careful not to issue many orders or commands. But when they gave a command, it had to be obeyed at once and without any back talk.

One of the first lessons in obedience and endurance came as Rosanna took her children along to preaching. The little ones were required to sit with their mother and keep reasonably quiet for almost three hours. Children might sleep if they wished, but they must not disturb the services. Any child who cried too much would be taken out and quieted and brought into the services again. One who repeated the crying stunt too often would be taken out of the house beyond hearing distance and punished.

The children quickly gained the impression that to be taken out of preaching services was no lark. They learned to endure the long services without much complaint. To make the burden a little lighter, however, the hostess provided a snack in the middle of the services. She brought a well-filled platter into the room where the mothers and the children were seated and gave each child a piece of half-moon pie. This helped to break the monotony.

A key virtue in Amish training is learning to work. There is always much work to do, and Amish parents are sure that idleness leads to wrongdoing.

At the age of six, Rosanna's boys were required to fill the woodbox each evening without being told to do so. It was their regular duty. They also were given the responsibility of putting bedding in the cow stable and tying the cows for milking. These tasks were assigned to Yost and Levi as they came along, and when they realized that these jobs could not be neglected without reproof or punishment, they did them without complaint.

To complain would be to show weakness and a lack of manly strength, and no red-blooded Amish boy wants to be a weakling. The general scorn for weaklings is a tremendous stimulus for young Amish boys and girls.

For the next few years, when the March sun had dried off the fields, Little Crist took the two older boys out to the field with him to help in the first spring job —picking stones off the field that would later be mowed for hay. That job is a backbreaker, and many boys hate it. But since there were two, Yost and Levi, almost the same size, a little rivalry could be established that helped greatly in carrying on.

When the boys were tired, Little Crist would say, "Come on, boys. We'll soon have this job done, and then we'll begin to plow." Plowing is always a challenge for boys, and they delight in doing it. A boy who can handle a plow and shows himself a good horseman is practically considered a young man.

Crist saw the time approaching when the boys could work with the horses. He took care to have on hand good and reliable lead horses which the boys could work and drive with less danger. One of these was a roan called Charlie, and the other was a big bay named John. Yost, being the oldest, was given his choice of leaders for plowing. He chose Charlie, and that left John for Levi.

The first day's plowing was a great occasion for these boys. They did their best to see which one could plow the straightest furrow. During the first day, Little Crist went first with one son and then with the other to show him how to hold the plow, how to swing it around at the end of the field, how to say "gee" and "haw" to direct the horses right and left, and how to manage the plow when it struck a rock. The boys knew all these things fairly well from following along when their father or the hired man plowed. But they needed practice to learn how to do it themselves.

When unhitching time came in the evening, Little

Crist purposely remained in the background to see whether they could unhitch and take the teams home without help. He was gratified to see these little chaps unhitch the horses properly, lead them to the fence so they could climb up and jump onto the leader's back, and ride home. At the supper table, only one subject was discussed.

"Well, I plowed more furrows than you did," Yost bragged to Levi.

"Maybe you did," Levi retorted, "but I plowed mine straighter than you did."

When the boys had gone to bed, Little Crist told Rosanna, "Mother, I'm pleased with the way those two little shavers plowed today. Why, they already plow as well as many grown men. When they get a little more practice, they'll be hard to beat."

Rosanna answered with a little tease in her voice. "It's the Irish in 'em that makes 'em good workers."

As the parents talked of the interest and effort these two lads put into their work, they rejoiced that their early training was already well begun.

One day as Little Crist was out in the field along the road, where the boys were plowing, Robert Maclay drove by. He was a Scotch-Irish Presbyterian gentleman who did not use nicknames and called people by their right first names. Robert looked in and saw these two boys plowing, so he stopped and greeted Little Crist.

"Well, Christian, I see you're getting considerable help with those boys plowing, and they're doing it well. Soon you'll need more land. How would you like to come up and farm one of my places? My homestead contains 150 acres. I'm having a little trouble handling it well, but I believe your management would suit me fine. Would you consider farming my homestead? Take your time to think it over."

With that, he drove away.

At the supper table that evening, Cristli told the family what Robert Maclay had said. As they talked about it, the boys showed strong interest in the idea.

"Then we'd have six horses, wouldn't we?" suggested Yost.

Levi, twelve years old, observed, "There isn't enough work on our seventy acres to keep all of us men busy, and I'd rather farm another place than hire out to work."

"I think Levi is right," agreed Rosanna.

From that time on they seriously considered farming the Maclay place. It was a little over a mile away, but Robert Maclay was one of the finest Christian gentlemen in Kishacoquillas Valley. He was Lincolnesque—tall and slender, with a well-trimmed beard and a shaved upper lip. Robert spoke slowly, in low, well-modulated tones. He was well read, lived by the golden rule, and possessed a great deal of common sense.

On his homestead he had a fine white colonial house and a large barn. Apart from one large hill, the fields were level and easily worked.

"We'll consider well before we decide," declared Little Crist. "But one thing is sure. With four boys coming on, we must have more land to farm or let the boys work out for other people. I believe we'll all be better off if we keep the boys at home."

This met with Rosanna's wholehearted approval, and the decision slowly formed to accept Robert Maclay's offer.

Throughout the summer, Little Crist was amazed to see how rapidly the work was completed with the help of Yost and Levi. John was large enough now to do some of the chores at the barn. Finally the corn was all husked and put away, and the boys were off to school. By that time, the family had fully agreed to take over the Maclay farm next year if a satisfactory agreement could be reached. Accordingly, Little Crist went to see Mr. Maclay one day to make final arrangements, if he could.

As he approached the house, Little Crist was impressed with the fine dignity of the homestead. He liked the large white colonial house, the towering maple trees in the yard, the flourishing garden, the well-chosen shrubbery, and the general air of culture and serenity.

As he entered the house, he noticed at once the great height of the ceiling, the stately hall, the heavy rugs on the floor, the long draperies, the pictures on the wall, and the piano standing in one corner of the parlor. At first he was somewhat overwhelmed. Everything was so different from the plain Amish homes to which he was accustomed.

However, charming Martha Maclay, the lady of the house, soon made him forget all his timidity. It almost seemed to him that she had been expecting him and was glad he came. Indeed, Robert had told her about Little Crist Yoder and how he hoped that Crist would decide to farm their homestead. She called Robert from the library. He came into the parlor, shook hands with Little Crist, and made him feel like a long-looked-for guest.

Little Crist finally said, "Well, Robert, we've been thinking about your invitation to farm the homestead, and we've about decided that if you still wish us to farm it, we'll try to do that."

"Christian, this makes us happy indeed," Robert stated. "I told Mrs. Maclay that I hoped you would decide to farm for us."

"On what terms would you expect us to farm?"

"I'll furnish the land and half the commercial fertilizer and seed and pay all the taxes. You furnish the machinery and half the commercial fertilizer and seed and do the work. Then we'll divide the crops evenly. Would that seem fair to you?"

"I think that would be a just bargain, and I'm willing to farm for you on those terms."

"Shall I have an article of agreement drawn up for both of us to sign?" asked Robert.

"Robert, I'll take your word if you take mine, and we'll not need a written agreement."

"Your word to me is as good as your bond, and we'll not bother about the article," agreed Robert. "Begin work in the spring when you see fit."

For many years Little Crist farmed Robert Maclay's big spread with never a word of disagreement. Mutual respect and confidence grew deeper as the years came and went.

Farming the Maclay place not only made more work for the men but also for Rosanna. When they worked at Maclay's, she had to pack dinner, which they took with them. But at harvesttime and threshing time, she prepared the meals at home, put the food in large kettles and crocks, loaded them into the carriage, and took them to the Maclay farm. There in a large, cool basement, she served the many workers.

This was hard work for Rosanna and the hired girl, but there was always a jolly social atmosphere surrounding a group of harvest or threshing hands. The fun and pleasure of it all just about made up for the hard work.

For Rosanna, there was the added pleasure of meeting Mrs. Maclay, one of the most refined and cultured Christian women in all the valley. Martha Maclay graciously extended every possible favor and courtesy to Rosanna. These two women, so different in manners and customs, were almost identical in ideals and aspirations. Rosanna was not quite so soft-spoken, but she cherished the same things in her heart. And Martha took such an interest in the boys that they came to look upon her as a near relative.

✒ ✒ ✒

Rosanna's brother, John, who worked at the Philadelphia *Public Ledger*, had never been to see Rosanna. But when Margaret returned after one of her visits, she gave such a glowing account of the beautiful Kishacoquillas Valley and its quaint inhabitants. As a result, he wanted desperately to visit his Amish sister and her family. John had heard about threshing grain, and he wondered just how it was done. So he wrote to Rosanna and told her that he would like to visit her during the threshing season.

Rosanna sent him a letter and invited him to come in September. Besides seeing them thresh, he could watch them making cider, and better still, see the beautiful green of the mountains turn to still more beautiful crimson and gold.

John had never traveled much outside the city. However, he recalled that some years before, Margaret had told him about the close connection at Harrisburg, the change of cars at Lewistown, and the stagecoach ride to Belleville. To make the trip in one day, he left Philadelphia early in the morning. He had never seen a real mountain, and when he approached Harrisburg and saw the foothills of the Alleghenies, he was charmed with their towering grandeur.

As the train roared through the Juniata Narrows and the Reedsville Narrows, he concluded that his sister must live in a mountain hut. But when he boarded the stagecoach and entered Kishacoquillas Valley with its broad, well-kept fields, he felt he had reached the land of real "milk and honey." He saw many things he had never observed before and wanted to ask the stage driver about them. But he decided to conceal his ignorance of the country and have Rosanna and the boys give him his information.

Crist and little Joseph met John in Belleville at the end of the stagecoach line. If Margaret had not warned him about the quaint dress of the Amish, he doubtless would have been startled when he saw Little Crist's broad-brimmed hat, his long hair and beard, and a little boy dressed just like him. But when John alighted from the stage, Little Crist approached him with a smile. "Are you John McGonegal?"

"Yes, sir, and no doubt you are Rosanna's husband, and this is your little boy."

"Yes. Come with us," invited Crist. As he led John to the yellow-top carriage, John wanted to stop and look at everything. He seemed to be in a foreign land, but the gentle voice of Little Crist assured him that he was in good hands. Rosanna met John at the house-yard gate. He looked into her dark eyes, observed her wavy hair, and thought he heard an Irish ring in her voice. Not till then could he believe that this was really his sister.

They had held supper until Uncle John arrived. When they were seated, he noticed that not a word was spoken, but before eating, every head was bowed during a period of silence. Margaret had told him about the silent grace which the Amish observe before beginning a meal.

John did not quite understand when Little Crist said, "Now, reach and help yourself." There was plenty within reach, but the idea of reaching for it instead of waiting for it to be passed was new to him. However, Rosanna came to his rescue and helped him to the most delicious ham he had ever eaten, fried eggs—dozens of them, he thought—and mashed potatoes and gravy. He had never seen oven-baked bread such as Rosanna put on the table, and the butter was golden yellow.

Yost and Levi were a little shy of their city uncle. As the meal progressed, they mustered up courage to ask some questions about the city. Uncle John, for his part, was interested in their sunburned hands and faces, their long hair, and their homemade clothes.

Most amazing of all to Uncle John was the air of responsibility these young Amish lads assumed toward the work of the farm. When the meal was finished and the grace again observed, the boys were off to do the evening chores. There was no conference about how to share the work. Everyone knew their job, and they went right at it, determined to do it quickly and well.

Rosanna left Mary Ann, her trusted friend and helper, to clear away the dishes. She and her brother sat on the high front porch just outside the living room and visited. Rosanna wanted to know all about Margaret and brother William.

"Well, you know Margaret married Will Reese. I'm not so sure about him. He's a rover. Last time I heard from her, they were in Arizona with wild Indians for neighbors. But Margaret seems to be happy. She says the Indians often come with their ponies, and she rides one to the nearby village. Margaret says the Indians are nice to her. They call her White Swan.

"William is still in the big department store, but I am a little alarmed about his health. He's developing a cough that sounds dangerous to me. William doesn't get the outdoor exercise he should. And, now, Rosanna, tell me about the Amish. Are you happy?"

"Well," began Rosanna, laughing, "I was only five days old when I decided to turn Amish, and I really didn't have much to say about it. One of the finest women in the world took me just to help our father out, and when he never came for me, she just naturally raised me Amish. I have never known anything else.

"Don't you think I have reason to be happy? My

husband is sober, faithful, devout, industrious, thrifty, and everybody thinks well of him. I have four boys I believe will become good men. There's not much more in the world for anybody, is there?

"Of course, our clothes are not like city folks' clothes, but then, if you think about it, clothes add but little and detract but little from the joys of life, as long as they're clean and decent. One thing we Amish people never worry about is changing styles. We never change the cut of our dresses.

"When sister was here to visit, she was fussing because her dress was a year old and out of style, and it made her a little unhappy. My clothes never make me unhappy. Naturally, I like to have dresses of good material, but I'm rather glad that I do not need to worry about changing styles. It must be wasteful, too, to have to throw a good dress away just because it was last year's model. We wear our dresses out, every one of them. We throw nothing away."

"But tell me, Rosanna, why don't Crist and the boys wear suspenders? I should think they'd lose their trousers."

"The church says suspenders are worldly, so we don't allow them. Besides, we make all our men's clothes, and we fit the trousers so that the waist band comes just above the hip bone. By making it a little snug, the trousers never slip down. Going without suspenders in hot weather is a little cooler and it also gives greater freedom to the shoulders in working."

"That makes sense. But don't the men suffer with their long hair?" John wondered.

"They never knew any other way, so they don't

mind it at all. I'll admit there is no advantage in long hair except in winter, when it keeps the ears warm. But one of the great principles of the Amish church is to stand against worldliness."

"I see," responded John. "It's the same principle that our Catholic sisters practice in their orders by clothing themselves in their special habit. Maybe from the religious standpoint, the Amish people aren't so far wrong, after all."

Little Crist planned his threshing to come during John's visit. One evening he announced that the next afternoon they would bring the threshing machine and the rotary horsepower machine and set it up to be ready to begin threshing the following morning. John was tremendously interested in seeing the big red thresher drawn by four horses coming in the lane, followed by the more modest-looking horsepower device.

The thresher was drawn to the barn bridge, turned around, and two horses hitched to the back of it to pull it into the barn. Then the horsepower rotary was placed some twenty feet from the entrance to the barn floor. A line of connected rotating shafts conveyed power from the center of the rotary to a jack placed at the edge of the barn floor. The jack was a transfer unit with gears that used the power from the shafts to run a flywheel. The crew connected an eight-inch-wide belt between the flywheel of the jack and the pulley of the threshing machine.

The horsepower apparatus was a low, cog-wheeled machine with five long, equally spaced arms extending out from its center in all directions. Two horses were hitched to the end of each arm. When the ten horses walked around in a circle pulling the arms, they furnished rotary power to run the threshing machine. One man stood on the center of the horsepower unit with a long whip and saw to it that each horse pulled its share. The horses stepped over the rotating power shaft when they came to it.

This threshing outfit was owned jointly by Little Crist and three brothers, Nancy Jake, Nancy John, and Preacher Sam Yoder. They helped each other thresh, and this cooperation was called "back help." The mother of these three brothers was named Nancy. So to distinguish two of her sons from other Jake and John Yoders, they were given nicknames.

Nancy John owned two farms adjoining Little Crist's farm, and he certainly did love to feed a threshing machine by forking sheaves into its mouth. There was quite an art in doing it properly, with sheaves evenly spaced and heads first. That way, most of the wheat and grain would be separated from the straw.

When Nancy John and his boys arrived the next morning, Little Crist introduced him to John McGonegal. After a few words of greeting, Nancy John asked, "Did you bring your woman with you?"

"Do you mean my wife?" asked Rosanna's brother.

"Yes, your wife."

Calling a man's wife his "woman" was unusual for John McGonegal. Afterward he told Crist, "At first I didn't know what he meant. If anybody in the city would ask you whether you brought your woman along, you'd feel like giving him a crack on the jaw."

When the men had gathered for the threshing, twelve in all, the driver cracked his whip, and the ten horses began to move around in the circle, at first straining but steadily pulling to build up momentum. John watched the shafts vibrate and rotate as they picked up speed. The cogwheels in the jack started to sing.

Nancy John mounted the footboard of the thresher. Now the cylinders were whirring like a swarm of angry bees. When the threshing machine got up to speed, Nancy John began feeding sheaves into the roaring and shaking contraption. Other men passed sheaves of grain to him from the mow. Straw began flying out of the barn front above the overshot and onto the strawstack. The precious grain flowed into a storage bin.

Just before dinner, John McGonegal went into the house and found a long table set for fourteen men. He wondered whether these men, so busy with work, would observe the silent grace before beginning the meal. John was eager to know whether their religion extended that far.

In a few minutes, Rosanna rang the dinner bell. John heard the driver's repeated "whoa, whoa" and the slowing down of the singing, shrieking wheels, till everything was quiet. The horses were unhitched, watered, put in the stables, and fed. Then, to wash for dinner, the men gathered at the yard pump, where Rosanna had placed basins, soap, and towels.

When the last man was ready, Little Crist called, "Come in, men, and be seated." The men found places and waited. When all were seated, Little Crist took his

ROSANNA'S BROTHER JOHN
AT A THRESHING MEAL

place at the head of the table, bowed his head, and every man whether Amish or not did the same. John McGonegal couldn't help but respect and admire men who took their faith seriously in every phase of life. When grace was over, Little Crist invited them, as Amish hosts always do, "Now, men, reach and help yourselves."

John McGonegal was given a place at the end of the table where he could see everything and where he would not be jostled too much by the men. As he looked, he marveled at that meal—platters filled with fried ham, stewed beef, mashed potatoes, and a rich brown gravy that would stimulate any appetite. Beside these rib-stickers, there were string beans, beets, pickles, apple butter, jelly, honey, and plates of golden butter.

When John thought all were filled, Rosanna brought grape pie, cherry pie, gingerbread, and layer cake. The city man noticed that these hungry threshers were equal to every course. He was entertained, too, by the wit and humor that passed back and forth during the meal. At threshing time, one grace at the table was considered sufficient. When the men had all finished their meal, Little Crist moved his chair back. This was a signal for all the men to leave the table.

After dinner, the harvest hands found a shady spot on the porch or lawn to visit, rest, or take a nap. The dinner bell had rung at eleven-thirty, and at one o'clock, Little Crist announced, "Time to hitch up, boys."

John was surprised to see how quickly the ten horses were bridled, hitched to the horsepower, and ready to go. He noticed how the driver started the horses slowly. There was a low murmur of the revolving wheels at first, and as the speed increased, the siren song of the machine became higher and higher till it was running at full speed. The threshing at Crist's place lasted well into the second day. John wrote a short sketch on "Country Threshing" for the *Public Ledger*.

The days passed all too quickly for Uncle John, but Yost and Levi did manage to share some special treats with him. They took him fishing one night with the scoop net and squirrel hunting one afternoon. Another day they went on a mountain trip to see where the chestnut trees would soon drop their bright brown fruitage. Once they took him to the blackberry patches to see whether some late berries might still be hanging or whether they might chase a few cottontails out of the bushes.

John enjoyed all these experiences immensely. Finally, however, his vacation ended and he had to return to the city. On the way home, he managed to think up a few good fish-and-bear stories. These he shared generously with his city pals, who had never been to the country and stood around in open-mouthed wonder.

꧁ ꧁ ꧁

Rosanna always had a hired girl to help her. Nevertheless, the work necessary to run two farms was more than she could endure. One summer when she was taking harvest and threshing meals regularly to the Maclay farm, Little Crist noticed that Rosanna was more tired than usual. Mary Ann Carson's efficient work did not relieve her sufficiently.

So Crist assigned young John to the house to help there for two or three days each week. This gave considerable relief, for John had already learned to cook a fine meal. With a few suggestions from his mother, he could bake fairly good bread.

Yet even with this extra help, Rosanna caught a bad cold, which speedily turned to pneumonia. Dr. Hudson, her favorite doctor, was called at once. While he was not an alarmist, he declared frankly, "Rosanna, this is a serious case of pneumonia, and we'll have to work together carefully."

She assured him that she would carry out every suggestion. But day after day, her bronchial tubes closed more and more until finally even the optimistic Dr. Hudson feared for her life. He took a special interest in Rosanna.

Many times when the good doctor had cases where pain baffled him, he would send for Rosanna to powwow and relieve the pain. With her help, erysipelas patients improved at once. If little children had that wasting-away sickness for which there seemed to be no medicine, they began eating and resting immediately after Rosanna began the powwowing for the "take-off." The doctor could not afford to lose her from his community practice.

Doctor Hudson came to see her twice each day, laying on poultices, plasters, and hot and cold compresses. Finally one day, the tightness on her chest seemed to relax, her breath came easier, and she fell into a long restful sleep.

When she awoke she said, "Doctor, I'm better. That painful breathing is gone."

Dr. Hudson replied good-naturedly, "Better? I should say so. You've been getting better for the last two hours."

"What? Did I sleep two hours? And were you here all that time?"

"Was I? Well, I should say so! For a while, you were too ill for me to leave you. But now, young lady, the crisis is over, and you're better. You'll soon be well again."

Those reassuring words took a load off her heart. They came from a doctor in whom she had absolute faith, and they were reinforced by the confident look in Little Crist's face. Rosanna could feel her pulses quicken and could almost sense her circulation carrying off the infection. After that, Dr. Hudson came only once each day, and then less frequently.

As the doc arrived one afternoon, the convalescent was sitting out on the high front porch admiring the garden filled with luscious red tomatoes, and the orchard laden with red apples. When the doctor found Rosanna there, so much improved, he chuckled. "I suppose the next time I come, you'll be out on one of those trees, picking apples. Well, let me warn you! You've been a pretty sick young woman, and a few days' rest will be the best investment you can possibly make."

"Don't you worry, Dr. Hudson. I'm going to rest in the fresh air and sunshine till my cheeks get rosy. Then Cristli will make me go to work for fear I might run off and leave him."

"Yes, I can picture you running away from a husband like Cristli, and from boys that show the strength and responsibility your boys do. Lady Rosanna, you're a queen on a throne, and it would take a ten-mule team to pull you off. We all know that," the doctor teased.

During Rosanna's sickness, Momli was at her bedside most of the time. By now she was getting quite old, and walking did not go so well. Rosanna sensed that Momli was failing rapidly, and it gave her no small concern.

As soon as Rosanna had regained her own strength sufficiently, she went to see Momli and was convinced that her fears had been well founded. For some years Momli had known she had a heart condition. Now at times it was becoming acute, making her quite weak.

To conserve her own strength, Rosanna had the boys hitch faithful Old Charlie to the carriage. She took little Joseph along to open the gates as she drove down to Momli's every day. When Momli finally was confined to her bed, Rosanna asked Mary Ann Carson to come and supervise the work at home while she stayed with Momli day and night.

How Rosanna loved this woman who had done so much for her! Now that Momli needed her so much, she could not leave her. Momli must have every attention of love and service that could possibly add to her comfort and happiness.

One day as Rosanna was adjusting Momli's pillow to make her more comfortable, Momli confided, "My time is short now, but how glad I am that Patrick McGonegal brought me his little baby to take care of for a while. Rosanna, you have been such a good daughter to me."

Rosanna smoothed her hair and kissed her wrinkled cheek. "You have done more for me than I can ever pay back. As long as I have anything, you shall never want."

Rosanna stayed faithfully at Elizabeth's bedside. One evening, as the twilight gathered in the valley, Momli's breath came slower and slower until it was no more. She did not suffer but seemed to fall into a peaceful sleep that carried her tired spirit into eternity. Bishop Shem, now in his mid-seventies, had lost his second wife.

When Elizabeth's body was laid away, no real daughter ever mourned her mother more sincerely than Rosanna grieved for Momli. It was the closing of a beautiful, unselfish life, and Rosanna honored and cherished her memory as long as she lived.

CHAPTER 17

Casting the Lot

AT PREACHING ONE Sunday, Bishop Crist Peachey said, "Some of our ministers are getting well along in years. I would like the congregation to consider whether we should choose a new minister in the near future. We will take the voice of the members next church Sunday. If the vote is unanimous, we will choose one on communion day, which comes in four weeks." This was according to custom, since all decisions must receive a unanimous vote to be approved.

As Rosanna and Crist drove home from church that day, he said little, and Rosanna knew what was on his mind. He feared that the lot would fall on him and he would have to preach thereafter. Rosanna had the same strong apprehension. Wishing to ease his mind, she asked, "Cristli, how many do you suppose will be put into the lot if they make a preacher on communion Sunday?"

"Oh, I don't know, but I have an uneasy feeling that the lot will fall on me."

"I hardly think you need worry. You are already forty-four years old, and no doubt they will nominate younger men."

"Well, I hope they do, but somehow, I feel terribly uneasy."

No more was said then, but two weeks later, a vote of the church was taken on "making a preacher," and the vote was unanimously affirmative.

"Then," declared the bishop, "at the communion service in two weeks, we will cast lots for preacher, and may the Lord's will be done. Let us pray earnestly over this important matter, that nothing may in any way hinder the will of the Lord."

When the last sound of the closing hymn died away, a great many men that Sunday arose with solemn faces, fearing that the lot might fall on them. They wanted to yield to the Lord's will, but they also felt the great weight of a minister's responsibilities and their own sense of unworthiness.

On communion Sunday, preaching was at Dave Renno's. Knowing that communion services were always much longer than regular services, the people gathered early. By eight-thirty, the house was filled, and in a few minutes, Yost Yoder, the singer, announced the first hymn. Little Crist sat at the singers' table as usual, but his mind was so filled with a strange foreboding that he could hardly sing.

The preachers withdrew to the room upstairs for counsel, as usual. The hymn ended, and Reuben Kauffman began singing the *"Lob Sang,"* which did not need to be announced since it was always the second hymn. Ben Sharp led one verse of the third hymn, and then singing ended as the ministers returned from counseling.

Old David Peachey arose to "make the beginning," followed by silent prayer and the reading of the Scriptures while all stood. John Peachey then spoke on the prophets and patriarchs, which is the duty of the second speaker at the communion service. The bishop got up next and spoke of the Last Supper, the sufferings of Christ, and the communion.

When the bread and wine had been served and foot washing observed, the bishop stated, "According to the vote of the church two weeks ago, it is our duty now to cast lots that the Lord may choose a worthy brother to break unto us the bread of eternal life. After the singing of the hymn, the members of the church may remain seated so that we may attend to this serious matter."

After the closing hymn, all persons not members of the church withdrew. The ministers returned to the upstairs room where they had counseled earlier. When all was ready, Deacon Jonas Peachey took his position at the stair door and announced, "All the brothers who wish to place a name in the lot will come here and give me the name."

One after another, the men went to the stair door and placed a name in nomination. Jonas then passed each name to a minister at the head of the stairs, and that minister reported it to the bishop and an assistant, who kept account of all names submitted.

When the men had all given their nominations, the women took their turns in the same manner. The bishop and the ministers then counted all votes and dropped from the list any brother who had received fewer than three votes. On this particular day, seven men received enough votes to be placed in the lot.

Next, the deacon went downstairs, took seven hymnbooks from the singers' table, and carried them upstairs. The bishop wrote a Bible verse on a slip of paper and placed it in one of the hymnals. This time he used Acts 1:26, "And they gave forth their lots; and the lot fell upon Matthias; and he was numbered with the eleven apostles." The books were shuffled, taken downstairs, shuffled again, and placed in line on the singers' table.

The bishop announced those voted for, and Little Crist Yoder was one of the seven. Each man nominated was asked to come forward and choose a book. When each man had taken a hymnal from the lineup, the bishop took the book from the man nearest to him and opened it. Since the slip of paper was not in that book, he looked in the book of the next man, and so on, till he found the book containing the paper.

When the bishop asked Little Crist for his book, Little Crist handed it to him. The bishop opened it and announced, "The lot today falls on Brother Christian Z. Yoder. May God bless you, and may you consecrate

– 253 –

your whole life to God's divine service."

Despite Crist's courage and his surrender to the will of God, the gravity of the office filled him with concern. His eyes filled with tears that rolled down over his cheeks.

There was a deathlike silence, and with trembling voice he implored, *"Seind mir eingedenkt im Gebet* (remember me in your prayers)."

When they were dismissed that day, many a man took his hat and went out greatly relieved. But Little Crist took his hat, feeling a tremendous load on his shoulders and an ache in his heart.

When the men reached the yard, they gathered in groups of twos and threes, and there was only one topic of conversation—that the lot today fell on one of the best qualified men in the church, obedient to all the rules of the church, and strictly "in order," observing all regulations concerning dress.

A few of the men had the courage to come to Crist and wish him God's blessing, but Amishmen as a rule are rather reticent in such matters. All the ministers came to him, extended the right hand of fellowship, greeted him with the holy kiss, and invoked the blessing of almighty God upon him.

Bishop Peachey was especially helpful. He knew from experience what a staggering blow it was to a member to assume the duties of minister, to preach the Word of God without any particular training or preparation. But he assured Cristli that, heavy as the burden seemed now, the load would lighten in time.

This would come as Crist applied himself to the study of the Word of God, and as he understood the

BISHOP PEACHEY GUIDING
CRIST IN HIS STUDIES

Scriptures more and more. He would became experienced in preaching the Word. The consciousness of doing the will and the work of the Lord would someday transform these burdens into the joy of service.

Crist pondered the bishop's wise and sympathetic words during the days that followed, and they slowly lifted his spirit and gave him peace.

When Crist and Rosanna returned from communion that day, it was already almost dark. The new responsibility pressed heavily on both of them. Even the younger boys noticed their mother's tear-stained eyes. When they asked what was wrong, she simply said, "Pap was made preacher today. He's much broken up. Let us all be considerate of him."

Even the smaller boys, John and little Joseph, only five, seemed to sense the gravity of the situation. They kept quiet all evening, sharing the apparent burden and gloom of father and mother. The children knew that it was a serious duty to preach the gospel in the German language and to be God's direct representative.

Fortunately for Little Crist, his boys, Yost and Levi, were now quite grown up. They could easily take charge of the work both on the home farm and on the Maclay farm. John, too, was old enough to handle horses and work in the fields, so three teams could be kept going without their father working. Consequently, day after day and night after night, Crist applied himself to the study of the Scriptures.

After a day or two had passed, Bishop Peachey came down to offer further words of consolation and encouragement and direct him somewhat in his studies. An Amish minister was supposed to quote long passages of Scripture verbatim. For the next few years, Little Crist literally committed whole chapters of the Bible to memory.

A newly elected minister was not required to preach at once but was given two or three months to become adjusted to his new position and duties. After awhile the bishop would ask him whether he would be willing to present the opening sermon, about a half hour in length. If he began this short message and found that his preparation did not enable him to finish it, he was at liberty to sit down at any time. He could call upon some other minister to finish his part.

After a few attempts at "making the beginning," he was asked to preach the main sermon (*Gemeh halde*). This message generally continued for an hour and a half. Again, the beginner is permitted to take his seat at any time if he feels he has exhausted his preparation, and some other minister is asked to finish the sermon.

A new minister at his first attempt to preach has probably the most sympathetic audience in the world. Everybody is conscious of the tremendous difficulty of the task, and every listener is prayerfully supportive. How anxious the congregation is to find out whether he has a good voice, whether he quotes the Scriptures accurately, and whether he speaks with confidence.

The Christmas season was just beginning when the bishop proposed in the ministers' council at preaching, "Cristli, would you be willing to try preaching the beginning sermon next Sunday a week?"

"If you wish me to, by the grace of God, I'll do the

best I can," Little Crist solemnly agreed.

The two following weeks were weighty ones for Little Crist. He redoubled his efforts, studying more hours each day and much longer into the night. Rosanna shared the responsibility and explained to the boys, "Pap has hard studying to do for the next two weeks. Let's do the work so well that he will not need to bother about it at all."

"We can easily do it," responded Yost. "The field work is all done. So before school in the morning and after school in the evening, we can do everything. I'll take care of the horses. Levi will attend to the steers. John will take care of the cows. Little Joseph can see to it that the chip basket and the woodbox are always well filled."

"Yost, that's a good plan," Rosanna affirmed. "All that is left for Pap to do is to feed the horses at noon when you boys are at school. He'll enjoy feeding the horses. Besides, that'll take him away from his books, give him a little exercise, and do him good. I'm a little afraid sometimes that he's studying too hard."

The boys accepted their additional responsibility as a privilege just to show Pap that they meant to help him all they could. What a satisfaction it was to Little Crist when he went to the barn at noon to feed the horses and saw every horse well curried and slick as an eel. Levi had even curried the steers, and the cows were well bedded and clean. The entries and walkway under the overshot were "shoved" clear, scraped with the back of a rake. The manure pile was built up straight on every side, and the barnyard was raked and cleaned to perfection.

Crist knew how much extra work all this tidiness required. He felt a strange twitching at his heartstrings and mused, "Well, if the boys are standing by me like that, I'm going to do my best so that they'll never need to be ashamed of their father's preaching."

When Crist returned to the house for the noon meal, Rosanna noticed an unusual moistness about his eyes. "Cristli, isn't everything all right at the barn?"

"Yes, Rosanna, that's just it. Everything is done perfectly. My heart is so full of thanksgiving for such loyal boys that it makes my eyes get a little watery."

"Yes, we have much to be thankful for," Rosanna agreed thoughtfully.

✎ ✎ ✎

According to Amish tradition, as the boys grew up, they were required by their parents to conform to the church rules whether they were members or not. Around the age of fourteen or fifteen, depending a little on his maturity, a boy was required to wear a *Mutze* (frock coat) to the preaching service.

When Yost, the oldest son, came to this age, Rosanna told him, "Yost, you are about big enough now to wear a *Mutze*. I'll get you some nice black material, and you take it over to Franey Yoder. She can make a good-fitting *Mutze*, and you will look smarter if it fits well."

The first Sunday Yost wore his *Mutze*, he was self-conscious, as the boys usually are when wearing their new frock coat. He now looked like a full-grown man. To avoid being too conspicuous, he sought out his friend Joe Kanagy who had already begun wearing his

Mutze. By being with Joe, he thought he would not attract so much attention.

Yost was an obedient son. He was always willing to let his hair grow long enough to satisfy the preachers, go without suspenders, and wear his *Mutze* on all occasions when he dressed up. At the age of seventeen, he joined the church.

The second son, however, had a mind of his own. Levi had his hair cut a little too short, permitting the lower half of his ear to show. Then when he also wore suspenders and refused to wear a *Mutze,* his parents had much concern. They talked to Levi and urged him to become a member of the church and conform to its rules, but he could see no good reason for doing so.

Otherwise, the wonderful support that Rosanna and the boys gave Little Crist filled him with confidence and courage. It gave him much the same feeling that he used to have when he hitched four fine horses to a heavily loaded wagon. At the word to advance, every horse would square itself and crouch lower and lower so as to pull to the limit of its strength, if necessary. Teamwork, ah! that's what Rosanna and the boys were showing him. To some extent, it took away his fear of preaching and filled him with confidence and strength.

Little Crist had no feeling of exultation as they drove to church early on the Sunday of his first attempt at preaching. Neither was he greatly depressed. He felt a measure of calm composure instead of the nervousness he had feared. The gracious teamwork of Rosanna and the boys was now buoying up his hope, and his heart was filled with faith and peace.

While the first hymn was being sung, the ministers went to the counseling room prepared for them upstairs. At the right time, the bishop declared, "Today Brother Christian Yoder will make the beginning, and Brother David will preach the main sermon."

As the preachers returned, the congregation noticed that Little Crist led the procession. That meant that today he would make his first trial at preaching. Reuben Kauffman was leading that great hymn *"Weil nun die Zeit vorhanden ist* (While now the time is at hand)."

Little Crist himself had led that hymn many times and knew it word for word. He thought, How appropriate. Truly, my time is at hand.

The great chorale and the tremendous volume of the men's and women's voices mingling in unison lifted his apprehension. He felt strength flowing into himself to preach the Word.

When the last sound of singing died away, Little Crist arose slowly and deliberately looked over the whole audience. He cleared his throat a bit and began in a strong voice: "The grace of the Lord Jesus Christ be with you all. We have great reason this morning again to be filled with gratitude and praise for the wonderful mercy of God, and with the psalmist we can truthfully say, 'The Lord is my shepherd....' "

Crist spoke clearly and with confidence, and the people listened attentively. In that audience were scores of friends who were as anxious that he do well as he himself was. As he spoke, he seemed to read their prayerful concern for him in their pleasant, interested faces. He went on raising his voice a little higher and showing more and more confidence. Little Crist quoted the Scriptures well and made some appropriate comments.

Before he expected it, the clock struck ten. Crist knew he had spoken the usual half hour, so he closed his remarks in the customary way: "And, so, if you are of one mind with me, let us come before the Lord in silent prayer."

Among the Amish it is not customary to comment on a sermon to the man who preached it. But after church, David Byler, who was married to Franey and was Little Crist's closest brother-in-law, came to him. "*'Sis gute gange* (it went well), Cristli," he commented, and that was saying enough.

On the way home, Rosanna also remarked, "Cristli, it went well."

Crist replied, "And I guess it went poorly enough, too, Rosanna." But he was thankful that he did not need to take his seat and ask some other preacher to finish the *Anfang* (the opening sermon).

CHAPTER 18

The Family

LITTLE CRIST WAS encouraged by the fact that he did not need to take his seat before the half hour was up and ask some other minister to finish the opening sermon. So he applied himself vigorously every day to further Bible study as the boys went to the village school. He knew well that it would not be long now till the bishop would ask him to preach the main sermon, and he wanted to be ready as far as humanly possible.

While school was in session, the house was quiet during the day. He accomplished much in mastering the Scriptures. Only little Joseph was at home, and he spent most of his time outdoors playing with Old Porter. That faithful Newfoundland dog took great pride in protecting children in general and little Joseph in particular.

When a beggar came to the gate, Old Port was right there, telling him in the fiercest growl and bark not to enter. But if a neighbor stopped by, Old Port would meet him at the gate with a friendly wag of his tail. If the man entered and walked toward the house, Old Port would generally pick up a stick or a bone and walk along beside him as a friendly guide until he reached the middle of the yard. Then Old Port would drop the stick or bone he was carrying.

When the man stopped, all was well, but if he did not stop, Old Port would growl. Then if the man waited on the spot till someone appeared to invite him in, everything was fine. However, if the visitor did not stop for the growl, Old Port would bite him and fight him off.

Once when the threshers were at Little Crist's, he warned the men not to go into the yard to pump water for the horses on account of the dog. But Sike Brindle, a husky lad from the mountain section, boasted, "I'm not afraid of your old dog," and in he went. Old Port met him politely, but when Brindle got halfway to the pump, Old Port growled. Brindle paid no attention to him, so Old Port sprang for Brindle's throat with such a terrific bound that it almost knocked Brindle over.

Brindle saved his neck by throwing up his arm, which Old Port seized by the wrist and held till Little Crist came running into the yard, shouting, "Let go, Port! It's all right!"

The dog let go, but he stood right there as if to say, "I warned him, but he wouldn't stop. I thought it was my duty to stop him."

At first Brindle got angry: "I'll kill that old dog."

Little Crist replied quietly, "Would you kill a faithful watchdog for doing his duty?"

Brindle, seeing how wrong he was, walked away and said no more. He owned a few good hunting dogs himself, and when he thought a bit, he saw that the dog was entirely within his rights.

Late in the fall, when summer balm was yielding to winter chill, Rosanna heard Old Porter barking furiously at the yard gate. She went to see what the trouble was. As she had expected, there stood a beggar with a large bundle on his back. Thinking he might want some food, she went to the gate to speak to him.

He was a clean-looking German who spoke the German language well. When he saw that Rosanna was Amish, he asked, "*Werden Sie so gute sein mir ein wenig Mittagessen geben* (would you be so kind as to give me a bit of dinner)?"

Rosanna had been taught from girlhood never to turn away a hungry man who asked for food. "*Jah, des kann ich duh* (yes, I will)."

The beggar smiled at her Pennsylvania German, but he understood what she said. Opening the gate, she turned to Old Porter and told him to let the stranger through: "All right, Porter."

The beggar followed Rosanna and the dog to the house. The doors were closed because the day was chilly. Rosanna did not think to let Old Porter come into the house, as he often did. To guard her, he came onto the porch, stood on his hind legs, placed his front feet on the windowsill, and watched through the glass till the beggar was gone.

Rosanna set a good meal before this beggar: bread and butter and apple butter, ham, fried potatoes, some other leftovers from the cupboard, and plenty of hot coffee with rich cream. So grateful was the beggar that he talked freely of the kindness and hospitality of the Amish people. When he left, Rosanna asked his name.

"My name is Henry Fisher, and I come from the valley of the Rhine in Germany."

After that, Henry Fisher was a regular caller for years. At first he would come in the evening and ask to stay overnight. Since he was always treated courteously and never refused, he finally came and stayed overnight without asking. He was treated much like any other guest. Besides supper and breakfast, he was given a clean bed. In the evening he and the family would talk and visit like long-parted friends. No man ever went away from Rosanna's door hungry.

🙟 🙟 🙟

When Rosanna was a little girl, Momli had planned that she should be a schoolteacher. But when Momli married Bishop Shem Yoder, the schoolteacher idea had to be given up. Rosanna had never quite lived down that disappointment. As her boys went to school, she cherished a secret hope that maybe one of her boys would be apt in learning and might someday be a teacher.

She soon saw that Yost, her oldest son, would never be a teacher. He took after his father in wanting to be a horseman. But Levi, the second son, liked school and got along well. By the time he was in the third reader, it was clear that he was good in mathematics.

Levi's teacher was Old Dave MacNabb, Scotch-Irish and a devotee of arithmetic. How he delighted to watch Levi and his seatmate, John Axe, try to surpass each other in handling numbers. Many evenings John Axe would come to Rosanna's house, and these two boys would work arithmetic problems till the assigned lesson was mastered. Next day, when they gave perfect recitations, Old Dave would say, "Boys, I'm proud of you. Someday you're going to be men of affairs."

Rosanna rejoiced in Levi's application to his books. If he had an unusually difficult problem to solve, he would sit up till midnight or later rather than give up. Yet she always had the feeling that Levi's ability in arithmetic was largely due to prenatal influence. While waiting for his birth, she had been studying the twenty-four lines of multiplication to cope with the butcher and those who came to buy her butter.

When Levi finished the eighth grade, plus studying algebra and physics, he took the county examination for teachers, passed, and got a school. Rosanna's cherished ambition was realized—one of her boys was a teacher!

When the school year ended and the spring work was well under way, Rosanna remarked at the table one day, "I believe preaching will be here in four weeks."

"Let me see," responded Little Crist. "Reuben Kauffman's on Sunday, Ben Sharp's in two weeks, and then comes our turn. That makes four weeks. You're right."

To Yost and Levi, now well grown and feeling the responsibility for the looks of the place, preaching Sunday was a very important day. Many fine farmers would come to preaching, and they would notice everything about the place. These two boys intended to see to it that no one went away from Little Crist's place with cause for disparaging remarks.

During the whole week before preaching Sunday, they used every spare minute redding (tidying) up the place. Every board and stick had to be in its place, the barn floor cleaned out, and every piece of machinery properly parked. The wagon shed had to be swept, and every wagon and carriage lined up straight.

Then on Saturday, just preceding the service, several women came to help Rosanna bake apple pies and half-moon pies. Little Crist gave the boys all day to finish cleaning up the premises.

At the barn, they cleaned and swept from beginning to end every stable and entry and the walkway under the overshot. The manure pile was stacked up with sides as smooth as a brick wall and as straight as a line in all directions. The house yard and the whole barnyard were swept from end to end. Every stick, stake, stone, and piece of stubble was removed so that each man, as he drove into the barnyard on Sunday morning, could not help but be attracted by the tidiness of the place.

The preaching benches had to be taken down from their place of storage above the overshot, dusted and washed if need be, and placed in the house to be dry and warm by morning. The partitions between the living room, bedroom, and kitchen were removed.

On Sunday morning the people began to gather, and Yost and Levi hustled around, helping them unhitch their horses and take them to the stables. They were alert for any comments, and they did not have long to wait.

As they hurried the horses past men standing in small groups, they heard one say, "*Es guckt verderbt schee doh* (it looks mighty nice here)." Others observed, "*Doh ist es awer sauwer* (it's very clean around here)," or "*Die Buwe kenne awer schaffe* (these boys can really work)."

When Yost and Levi happened to pass in some unobserved place, they smiled or winked, delighted. They had their reward.

🌿 🌿 🌿

In Belleville one day that fall, Little Crist was approached by Charlie Rodgers, a witty old Irish Catholic. "Cristli, it isn't going so well wid me just now havin' considerable rheumatism and stomach misery and all," complained Charlie. "I'm wonderin' whether you couldn't bring me a load of firewood someday. And would you mind speakin' to some o' your Amish brethren and ask them if they would be so kind as to bring me a load, too? And if it's a frolic ye'll be havin' for me, I'll ask Molly and the girls to make ye's all a good dinner."

"I'll see some of my neighbors, and maybe we can have a wood frolic for you."

"Well, if ye'll be so kind, I'm sure the saints'll be

blessin' you for your kindness."

While in town that day, Little Crist happened to
. see Preacher Nancy John Yoder, his brother Nancy
Jake, Reuben Kauffman, and Ben Sharp. They each
agreed to bring Charlie a load of good cordwood or
poles on the following Thursday.

Later in the day, Little Crist saw Charlie and reported, "Charlie, I've seen four of my neighbors, and
they all agreed to bring you a load of wood next Thursday, a week from today. Will that suit you?"

"Suit me, me man? Nothing in the world could
suit me better, and I'll be askin' Molly to pray the blessin' of the saints on ivery one o' ye. And we'll be havin'
the dinner ready for you when you get there."

On the following Thursday, these five farmers
went to their woodlands on the mountain and gathered up a load of wood for Charlie Rodgers. They all
had about the same distance to go and arrived at Charlie's house around eleven o'clock in the forenoon.
Nancy Jake with his fine team of dapple gray Percherons came first. With horses prancing, he drove up to
Charlie's woodshed with a fine load of wood.

Charlie was standing, waiting, and smiling, "Ah,
begorry, Jacob, it's a fine team o' horses you're drivin'
today, and it's a fine load of wood you've brought me,
too."

"Yes, sir," said Nancy Jake. "They've about pulled
my arms out trying to hold them back."

The other four men arrived soon after with their
own particular variety of fancy team. Knowing that
Charlie had no suitable stable for the horses, they all
brought horse feed. When the wood was unloaded,

they fed their horses at their wagonbeds.

As these five crack teams were hitched all around Charlie's modest home, old Bill Cogley, another Irishman, walked by and shouted out to Charlie, "By the saints o' Killarney, Charlie, are ye havin' a horse show here today?"

"Not just exactly that, but it looks enough like it. You see, Molly has a birthday today, and some of our Amish friends are helpin' her to celebrate by each bringin' her a load of firewood."

"Well, it's a lucky man ye aire at that for havin' a wife with such prosperous influence and friends," declared old Bill.

By this time Molly and the girls had dinner all ready. She went to the door and called to her husband, "If the men be ready, Charlie, bid them come in."

Charlie took the head of the table. He knew that the Amish always observe grace before beginning to eat, so he asked, "Riverent John Yoder, would ye please be askin' the blessin'. I'm not so divlish good at it myself."

Demure as Amishmen usually are, that request just about broke them up. Rev. John did ask the blessing, but the men all noticed that there were little hitches in his voice which were caused by his determination to resist laughing.

When the blessing was over, Molly said, "Now neighbors, ye'll be noticin' that I can't set the table you Amishmen are used to. But you're as welcome to the wee bite we have as the flowers o' May. For the great kindness ye've shown us today, we should be givin' you a banquet instid o' this humble fare."

One of the men replied, "Molly, you have plenty. If you had any more, you would overfeed us and make us sick."

For years to come, when these men met, one or the other would say, "Riverent John, would you please ask the blessin'? I'm not so divlish good at it myself."

Charlie Rodgers sounded the praises of Little Crist and the Amish neighbors who filled his wood-shed to the limit. It was well known that Little Crist rarely refused anything a poor person asked him for. Many a man would come to him for a bag of wheat when poverty was knocking at his door. Little Crist knew and the man knew that he probably could never pay for it, but he got the wheat just the same. More than one young woman from the village came to Rosanna for a loan or advice, and she never went away empty-handed.

🙠 🙠 🙠

Little Crist had been carrying on large-scale farm-ing, managing the Robert Maclay homestead besides his own place. This was now about to receive two seri-ous jolts. For some years Yost had been paying atten-tion to Barbara Peachey, the only child of Bishop Peachey. Barbara so charmed Yost that he was never interested in anyone else. As he became of age, they were married.

Their wedding was an exact duplicate of Little Crist and Rosanna's wedding, twenty-five years be-fore. The marriage services were at Dave Renno's. The wedding festivities were held at Bishop Peachey's, the bride's home, with over two hundred guests. There was the same menu of turkey, chicken, pie, and cake. The same three wedding chorales were sung in order after the dinner meal. Party games for the young folks were played on the carefully swept barn floor. Two boys and two girls were waiters. There were best men, the *Schnitzler* (meat carver), the wedding presents, and finally the pseudo-collection for the cooks.

They began housekeeping on the 140-acre farm owned by the bishop, the homestead. Yost's gifts from home and his dowery were the same as his father had received when he and Rosanna moved into the new house Lame Yost had built for them—a horse and harness, a plow, a harrow, a cow, two pigs, a few chickens, dishes, a tablecloth, blankets, quilts, and comforters.

About this time, Levi received his certificate to teach school. That left only John and little Joseph to do the work. Since there was too much work on the two farms for them to keep up, Little Crist decided to give up farming the Maclay farm. He was sorry to do this, not because of a lessened income, but because it severed his close relations with Robert Maclay.

For more than ten years he had farmed this fine place, and never was there a word of dissension between them. Robert was always satisfied with the work in the fields and never questioned the division of the grain. He was pleased with the quiet, respectful conduct of the boys and men as they had occasion to work about the barn.

Little Crist went over to tell Robert that he would no longer be able to farm his place because of two of the boys leaving home.

Robert responded warmly. "I'm sorry indeed to

have you discontinue. Your work and your fair dealings were most satisfactory. I'll miss your boys greatly, for I look upon them as fine young gentlemen. But with Yost marrying and Levi beginning to teach, I can see how shorthanded you would be. I want to say again that to me, our dealings have been ideal and eminently satisfactory."

To this Little Crist replied, "Robert, I cannot say it so well as you do, but I want you to know that I deem you to be a most considerate and charitable landlord. I'm sorry that we have to stop farming for you. Our relations have been so pleasant. We all liked to come up here. Rosanna has enjoyed so much Mrs. Maclay's kindness to her and the boys."

When Yost went up to his wife's place to tend his father-in-law's farm, Rosanna was lonesome for her oldest child. Up to this time, the family circle had not been broken except once, when Little Crist went with the bishop to Lawrence County on a preaching tour for two weeks. At that time, the boys and Rosanna both missed him so much that it was difficult for them to carry on till he returned.

Yost had never been away from home, and now Rosanna could hardly bear it that he was not coming home each evening. He did make it a practice to visit his parents in the evening about every two weeks. Many times at the dinner table, Rosanna would say, "I believe Yost will come home this evening," and sure enough, when evening came, in would walk Yost. That happened so often that the family began to believe there was some connection between the minds of mother and son, almost telepathy.

When Mary Ann Carson grew too old to make a living doing housework, the Presbyterian Church arranged for her to live with someone near the church. But no matter where she was making her home, every now and then she would come to Rosanna's house and stay for a day or a week or a month.

Mary Ann would help a bit about the house, doing a little more than the trouble she caused. She was a light eater, and at Rosanna's house there was always plenty of food anyhow. Mary Ann's presence was no strain on the household. The whole family liked her company and conversation. The boys admitted that they owed their fluent English to her.

By now, Mary Ann was growing quite old, and the only place the church could get for her was at Lydia Esh's. That was about two miles from church and Rosanna's house. Nevertheless, about once a month Mary Ann would walk up for a few days and then wend her way back to Lydia's house.

One day in midwinter when the snow was deep and still drifting, she remarked to Lydia, "I hope when it comes my time to die, I can die at Rosanna's house. I have always felt so much at home there."

Only a few days later, Rosanna was at the window, looking out the lane, and marveling at the deep drifts of snow. Then through the snow-filled storm, she thought she saw something moving in the lane.

Rosanna looked intently until the gust of wind subsided. To her surprise, she recognized the form of old Mary Ann, laboriously working her way through the snowbanks toward the house.

"*Ach*, my!" exclaimed Rosanna. "There comes Mary Ann through the snowbanks in the lane. Somebody go and help her at once."

John seized his hat and coat, slipped on his boots, and was out in a few seconds. When he reached her, he asked, "Why, Mary Ann, aren't you nearly frozen?"

"Oh, no. I'm getting along pretty well."

John plowed through the snow, kicking it aside to make a path for her and in a little while had her safe in the house.

When she entered the kitchen, Rosanna greeted her. "Why, Mary Ann, weren't you afraid to start out in a storm like this?"

"No, I wasn't afraid. I somehow felt that I just had to come today. I've been on the road nearly four hours, but I'm so glad I'm here."

That evening Mary Ann visited with abandon and contentment. She seemed to be extra happy, as though she had finished a task laid out for her by an unseen hand. Rosanna sensed that there was something unusual about this visit.

The next day after the noon meal, Mary Ann dried the dishes for Rosanna, as was her custom. When the dishes were put away, she started to go into the living room. As she reached the door between the rooms, she fell. When Little Crist picked her up, the muscles of her face were strangely drawn, and she was unable to speak. She was paralyzed.

Crist and Rosanna quickly brought a bed down from upstairs, set it up in the living room for her, and gave her the best care and attention.

The doctor said, "It's a stroke. There's nothing to

– 276 –

do. Make her as comfortable as you can. Mary Ann can't live more than a few days."

She lived just one week. During that time, a number of her church friends came to see her. She tried to speak, but only Rosanna could understand what she said.

At the funeral, Lydia Esh told Rosanna what Mary Ann had confided to her only two weeks before, that she hoped she could die at Rosanna's house. Lydia had tears in her eyes. "The poor soul had her one great wish granted. It looks like divine leading."

After the funeral was over, Robert Maclay, an elder in the Presbyterian Church, came to Little Crist and Rosanna. "What does the church owe you for taking care of one of our members?"

Rosanna spoke up. "We would not think of taking anything for caring for Mary Ann. She's been our constant friend for many years and was like one of the family. Lydia Esh told me at the funeral that just a few days before Mary Ann came here this last time, she told Lydia that she hoped, when it came time for her to die, she could die at Rosanna Yoder's house. She got her wish.

"Mary Ann seemed so happy and satisfied, and during her sickness, she tried so hard to tell me something. But all I could really understand was 'So glad.' No, Robert, it would be wrong to take anything for caring for an old, old friend."

"Well," responded Robert thoughtfully, "I thank you for your great kindness. I'm glad you told me about her wish to die at your house. I shall report her dying wish and your kindness to the church."

CHAPTER 19

The Tannery

ONE EVENING DAVID Byler, who was married to Little Crist's sister Franey, came over to spend the evening. Probably there was no man whose friendship and comradeship Little Crist valued more highly than that of David Byler, usually called Davy Byler. He was a big, rugged man. Often when he was not farming a place for someone else, he would work for Little Crist by the day.

While Davy had opinions of his own, he was slow to express them. No one ever saw him angry or heard him say an unkind word about anybody. Davy and Little Crist were good friends, perhaps as close as David and Jonathan in the Bible. Each of Rosanna's boys looked upon Uncle Davy as about the finest man in the world.

In the course of the evening, Davy expressed some regret that he did not have a real job or work of his own but had to do day labor for most of his living. Then he casually remarked, "I heard the other day that the tannery is to be sold. I was thinking that, if I could arrange some way to buy it, I believe I would. But I can't buy it without some help."

"Well, how would you like if I would go into partnership with you, and we'd buy it together?" Little Crist offered. "I wouldn't like to see a stranger take it over, anyway. The creek that furnishes waterpower for the tannery runs right beside my farm. If some careless person bought it, he might raise the water level of the dam and make trouble for me by flooding my fields."

"Nothing in the world would suit me better than for you and me to buy it in partnership," Davy responded. "I'll be glad to do the work and pay you good interest on your money."

"There's only one trouble about you two buying it as partners," Rosanna commented. "Davy, if you work so near, I'll never be able to keep Cristli at home. He'll be over there helping you all the time."

The men both laughed and agreed that working together might not be such a bad idea at that.

When the tannery came up for sale, Little Crist and Davy were there to try to buy it. Besides the tannery building, there were the bark sheds and the mill to grind bark, run by waterpower. The property also included two dwelling houses.

When the bid reached $2450, Little Crist and Davy delayed their next bid to make the competitor feel that they would not bid much more. Then just before the auctioneer declared it sold, Davy bid $2500. That was the last bid, and the tannery belonged to Davy Byler and Little Crist Yoder, his backer. They were both delighted, not only because it was a good investment, but also because it gave them a new chance to work together in a common interest.

Rosanna's prophecy came true. When Davy began working in the tannery, there were things that he could not do well alone. So Little Crist just naturally went over to assist him. The more he helped, the more he saw the advantage of two men working there together. And the more tanning he did, the better he liked it.

Finally Crist told Rosanna, "Davy needs me so much at the tannery, and I like the work there so well that I believe I'll hire a boy to help Joseph. If I manage the farming, I believe they can easily do the work."

"Do you remember my prophecy?" Rosanna teased him. "I told you that if Davy worked at the tannery, you couldn't stay away."

Crist smiled. "Mother, I wish I could see into the future like you can."

Little Crist thoroughly enjoyed working in the tannery with Davy Byler. There were more business dealings connected with it than with farmwork. Every day several men would come to the tannery to buy leather or to sell hides. The social interaction was a pleasure.

Besides, the hours were shorter, and it gave him

more time for Scripture study. As with other Amish ministers, Little Crist received no remuneration from the church in any way. He felt that he had not yet reached a financial level that would allow him to retire. Anyhow, it was Amish custom for people to work as long as health allowed. So he wanted to do something that would bring in a reasonable income.

Crist thought back over his horse-dealing career. He was astonished to see how easy it was for him to give it all up without a struggle when the responsibilities of the ministry were made clear to him. Once he was so interested in the horse business that he thought he could never let go. Little Crist still liked nice horses, but he had no desire to buy and sell and trade them.

His great desire now was to lay something by each year from the farm and tannery. Thus when he was not able to work, he would have enough for living expenses and not be a burden to the state. But right now, Crist wanted to serve the church and inspire men and women and boys and girls to live daily as true disciples of Christ.

☙ ☙ ☙

Levi was teaching his third term of school. Besides being good in arithmetic, he was quite an athlete. He played baseball well and excelled in skating. Like his father, he was good at wrestling. Skating in Jakey Hartzler's meadow attracted many boys from school. When it came to a real race for speed, Levi could pass the best of them.

One day while he was teaching the Maclay school, Jim McCormick was having a public sale nearby. Levi gave his pupils an extra-long noon recess so they could attend some of the sale and learn the auction method of buying and selling. It was a beautiful day in early spring. Jim's place was situated at the foot of Stone Mountain. Many people were there from Stone Valley. Because of outdoor work in the woods, the Stone Valley people were rather rugged.

A husky young wrestler from Stone Valley came to Jim McCormick's sale and was downing everyone whom he wrestled. When Levi's students saw that, they ran to the schoolhouse not far away with a challenge. "Teacher, there's a fellow from Stone Valley up here at the sale, and he's throwing everybody who wrestles with him. Come up and wrestle him. You can throw him. We know you can."

"Oh, I don't want to wrestle him," responded Levi.

However, the boys insisted that he come. Levi had thought of going to the sale anyway, since all his pupils were there. So he walked up to look this wrestler over. Levi soon saw that the Stone Valley champion was well built for wrestling: short, heavy, and strong as a horse.

When Levi appeared, several men called to him, "We've been waiting for you. We want you to wrestle this young fellow."

"Oh, I don't care to wrestle," replied Levi.

Nevertheless, the Stone Valley champion was so eager for a match that Levi either had to wrestle or appear cowardly. Finally Levi agreed to a contest, and the heavy champion smiled with a sneer that filled Levi with determination. They wrestled sideholds. Levi chose the underhold, which made him use his left hand. But the underhold held a decided advantage in "hipping" an opponent.

From the beginning, the champion threw all his strength into the match, breathing heavily, like a straining horse. Since the opponent was so eager, Levi wrestled defensively until the champion was somewhat winded. Then, catching the champion by surprise, Levi sprang forward, gave a quick turn to the right, got the champion on his left hip, lifted him from the ground, and laid him neatly on his back. Interest was so great that it almost stopped the sale. The crowd sent up a roaring cheer.

"I demand a rematch," shouted the champion as he jumped up.

This time Levi had to take the upper hold, but he got to use his right hand. When they were ready, the champion lifted Levi off his feet and whirled him, but when Levi came down, he landed on his feet. The champion repeated this tactic three times, but Levi was still on his feet. When he saw the champion was getting winded again, Levi swung him backwards, tripped him with his right foot, let him go, and down he went. The crowd gave a second uproarious cheer.

The deposed champion jumped up enraged and yelled, "If I can't throw you, I can lick you."

Levi faced him calmly and stated, "I wouldn't try it if I were you."

Several big men promptly stepped forward and told the former champion, "You bantered this young man to wrestle. He threw you fair. Now you keep quiet and behave yourself, or we'll take care of you."

At once, the champion saw that he was in the wrong crowd for starting a fight.

꙰ ꙰ ꙰

One day Simeon Riehl came to the tannery, called Little Crist aside, and confided, "Brother Cristli, I have fallen into sin! I have spoken falsely about Brother John Kanagy, and I feel that I am not worthy to belong to church. I wish you would see the bishop and have me put out of church. I feel that excommunication is my just punishment."

"Couldn't you go to Brother Kanagy and make the matter right with him?" asked Crist.

"Well, I apologized to him, but I feel I've gone so far that not even his forgiveness makes it right. My bad words about John have gone out in the community, and I can't pull them all back."

"Very well, if that is your wish, I will see Bishop Peachey and tell him how you feel and what your earnest desire is."

On the following Sunday when the ministers had gone upstairs to the room for counseling, Little Crist brought up the matter. He told the bishop and the ministers what Simeon Riehl had told him and that his earnest desire was excommunication.

"Did you counsel him to make the matter right between himself and Brother Kanagy?" asked the bishop.

"I did," replied Little Crist, "but he thinks it has gone so far that even the forgiveness of Brother Kanagy doesn't make him free."

At the end of the service, the benediction was pronounced and all were seated. Just before the last hymn, the bishop announced, "After the singing of the hymn, members will please remain for a few minutes."

After the hymn, those who did not belong to church went out, and the bishop said, "It becomes my solemn duty today to make known to you that one of our brethren, Simeon Riehl, has committed sin, has fallen from grace, and has asked to be placed in the *Bann* (excommunicated). The ministers have agreed that we should do this, if the congregation consents."

There was some discussion to clarify the situation and to report warnings repeatedly given to Simeon about the slander he was committing. Then the members voted to take the action requested.

The bishop declared, "I therefore place Simeon Riehl into the *Bann*. Until he repents and is taken into the church again, let no member eat with him or drink with him or have any fellowship with him whatsoever, in accord with Paul's instructions [in 1 Cor. 5:11]. We will speak to him only to bring him to repentance."

For the next eight weeks, Simeon Riehl experienced the life of an outcast as the Amish applied the *Meidung* to him (social avoidance, shunning). No member of any Amish church would eat at the same table with him or drink out of the same cup. Members were allowed to give him something but were not allowed to take anything from his hand.

If Simeon had to eat where church members were present, his food was placed on a small table in another room, and there he ate alone. Even at home he was not allowed to sit at his own table with his wife and family. He took his meals at a separate table or waited till the other members of the family were through.

After almost four weeks of this separation from fellowship, Simeon Riehl decided that his sins had been atoned for and that he now would ask to be reinstated into full fellowship and church standing. He was greatly encouraged in this belief by the bishop, who called to see him.

The bishop assured Simeon that if he felt truly sorry for his sins and would earnestly implore God's forgiveness, God would hear his prayer and would forgive. Consequently, Simeon made it known to the bishop that he believed he had fully repented of his sins and had been forgiven. He was now ready to mend his relationship with Brother John Kanagy and to be restored to full standing and fellowship in the church.

Early in the services on the next three preaching Sundays, Simeon was required to go upstairs to receive the ministers' counsel and instruction on repentance, forgiveness, and godly living. On the third Sunday, he was thoroughly questioned by the bishop. The bishop and the ministers were satisfied that his repentance was sincere. So they excused him and asked him to go downstairs and take a seat near the ministers' bench. Then he would be received into the church at the close of the services.

When the last prayer was over and the benediction was pronounced, the bishop asked, "Will all the members of the church please remain seated a few minutes after the singing of the hymn?" According to tradition, the ministers would not transact church business in the presence of persons, old or young, who were not members of the church.

When the hymn was ended and the nonmembers had withdrawn, including Simeon Riehl, the bishop stated, "We rejoice today that one who had fallen has repented and wishes to be taken into full and active membership again. In the *Abrot* this morning, we interviewed Brother Simeon Riehl, who has been in the *Bann* for eight weeks.

"We find that he has repented thoroughly, and we believe that God has forgiven his sins. So the ministers agree that he should be reinstated into full fellowship again. We will do this only with the consent of the church. If any of you have a good cause to think that Simeon should not be taken in now, please give your reason."

The church consented, and the vote was unanimous, as customary if a church decision is to be valid. All agreed that Simeon Riehl be reinstated to full and active membership.

The deacon went to the door and invited Simeon back in. The bishop reported, "Brother Riehl, the church has heard your request to be reinstated to full membership again. The vote was unanimous to receive you. Come forward and be received."

At this request, Simeon walked forward to where the bishop was standing, and kneeled. The bishop then asked, "Simeon, do you confess that you sinned and that you have done wrong in the sight of God, and do you ask forgiveness for your sins?"

Simeon answered, "I do."

"Do you promise in the sight of God and in the presence of these many witnesses that you will try with the help of God to keep the commandments, obey the rules of the church, and let the Holy Scriptures be the rule and guide of your life, to the best of your ability?"

Again Simeon responded, "I do."

The bishop extended the right hand of fellowship to him and said, "Simeon, arise." The bishop then greeted him with the holy kiss and declared, "I extend to you the right hand of fellowship and thereby receive you into full and regular standing in the church. May God bless and guide you in all truth by his Holy Spirit."

Simeon took his seat, and the bishop, addressing the congregation, exhorted, "Brother Riehl has seen the error of his way and has repented. I believe that God has forgiven him. Let us all pray for him and for ourselves that we, too, may not be overtaken in sin. From now on, let no member despise Simeon, but let us all extend to him the right hand of fellowship and hold his sins against him no more."

After a moment's pause, the bishop added, "We will detain you no longer."

The congregation arose and slowly left the house. Many men—who for the last eight weeks would not under any circumstances have sat down to the same table and eaten with Simeon Riehl—now shook hands with him and encouraged him: "Glad you have taken the step which sets you right with God and the church."

In things religious, the Amish speak few words; so some of the men merely shook hands, which meant, "I approve, and you have my best wishes." John Kanagy gave him an especially hearty handshake, showing that he was ready to let the past be past.

That Sunday evening Simeon Riehl, for the first time in eight weeks, sat down to eat with his wife and family at the table. When the simple meal was ended, Simeon's little daughter, Mary, came around the table to where he sat at the head and lisped, "*Daadi, mir sin so froh des du widder mit uns escht* (Daddy, we're so glad that you're eating with us again)."

In response to her greeting, he put his strong arm around her and kissed her. But his own gratitude was too deep for words when his own child welcomed him back into fellowship.

🙠 🙠 🙠

Summer had been unusually hot. Every few days great black thunderclouds filled the sky, and oncoming thunder grew more and more ominous until its tremendous reverberations filled the valley from end to end. Sometimes the storm was so violent that trees were uprooted, fences leveled, and crops destroyed.

During one of these terrific storms, lightning struck Mike Yoder's barn, filled to the roof with hay and grain. So intense was the heat of the lightning stroke that before help of any kind could come, the barn burned to the ground, with the hay, grain, implements, and all. The only things saved from the flames were the cows in the field and the horses, which Mike and the boys hurried from the stables.

When the smoke from the smoldering embers finally subsided, it was a pitiful sight. There stood crumbling foundations, skeletons of farm machinery lying in the ashes, and the bleak, disconnected barn bank and bridge standing out like a mocking monster. Mike was a prosperous farmer, but he was not prepared for such a catastrophe.

The day after the fire occurred, Bishop Peachey came to see just how great the damage was. When Mike told him that the cost of the barn and the machinery was nearly three thousand dollars, he merely said, "*Jah well* (I think we can take care of you)."

Everyone knew that Jonas Peachey, the deacon of the church, was the proper person to look after a loss like this, by calling on members and receiving their contributions. The bishop went over to see Jonas and tell him what the loss was. "We must do something now to help Mike build a new barn. I'll start the donations with fifty dollars, and on Sunday I'll mention it at church."

At the next preaching service, after the last hymn was sung, the bishop stated, "We are sorry that one of our members, Mike Yoder, lost his barn from a stroke of lightning. He tells me that the loss of barn and machinery is about three thousand dollars. We humbly submit to the will of God, but it is our duty to share this loss and help bear this burden. Remember that the Lord loves a cheerful giver [2 Cor. 9:7]. Brother Jonas Peachey will visit you this week on behalf of Brother Mike, and I hope your gifts will be both cheerful and generous."

When Deacon Jonas came to the tannery next day, Little Crist and Davy Byler each gave twenty-five dollars. There was no paper on which names and gifts were recorded. When it comes to giving alms, the Amish have a biblical philosophy: "Let not your left hand know what your right hand does" (Matt. 6:3). By the time Jonas had seen all the members of the church, he had collected a little more than three thousand dollars. Sol Peachy and Nancy John and a few other members owned three or four farms apiece; they each gave one hundred dollars, promising to give more if needed.

When Robert Maclay, the Presbyterian elder, happened to see Jonas Peachey in town one day, he remarked, "Jonas, I understand that you're receiving contributions toward rebuilding Mike Yoder's barn. Mike is my neighbor and friend. Would you mind if I gave something toward it?"

"We never ask anybody outside our church to help any of our members in need, and we do not patronize fire insurance companies," Jonas responded. "But if you feel prompted through goodwill and charity to give something, we will accept it gladly, in the same spirit of goodwill that you give it."

"I wonder, Jonas, why you people don't insure your buildings with regular fire insurance companies."

Jonas accepted the sincere query and looked him in the eye. "Well, Robert, the apostle Paul says, 'Don't be unequally yoked together with unbelievers' [2 Cor. 6:14]. If we join outside organizations, we don't know whether they are believers or unbelievers. To be sure that we do not violate that Scripture, we refrain from joining outside organizations of all kinds. That is why we help each other in times of accident or need.

"For the same reason, we take care of our own poor so we don't burden the state in any way. We try to order our lives so that no Amish person ever goes to jail unless put there for conscience' sake. Likewise, some of our people do not even vote at election time, carrying out the idea of being a separate people, as Paul exhorts us [2 Cor. 6:17].

"Along the same line, we don't go to war, for the Bible says plainly, 'You shall not kill' [Exod. 20:13]. The New Testament even goes so far as to say that whoever hates a brother or sister is a murderer [1 John 3:15]. We pay our taxes gladly, uphold the government, and obey the laws, if the civil law does not conflict with the Bible [Acts 5:29]. We try to make the Bible our rule of action and conduct in religion, in business, in our social life, and in our political life."

After a pause, Jonas added, "I hope I have not wearied you."

"No, not at all," responded Robert. "I'm glad to know the reasons for some of your practices which differ from our Presbyterian customs. Now I'm more eager than ever to contribute to the building of Michael's barn. If you'll accept it, Jonas, I want to give twenty-five dollars."

"Thank you. I'll tell Mike that you've given and how kindly you feel toward him."

❧   ❧   ❧

One day Rosanna had a quilting party, and her sisters-in-law, Sarah and Franey, and Barbara Sharp, Lydia Kauffman, and Mary Riehl came to help. They quilted in the forenoon, and at dinnertime Rosanna had a fine meal for them.

When dinner was over and old Mary Riehl helped Rosanna wash the dishes, she remarked, "My goodness, Rosanna, it must be nice to have plenty and set a nice table like you do. Since Lewis died, I sometimes have hardly enough to eat."

"Well," suggested Rosanna, "there is plenty of alms money to help widows. Why don't you speak to the bishop about it?"

"Oh, I'm ashamed to say anything to him about my problem."

"All right, I'll tell Cristli," offered Rosanna, "and he'll gladly speak to the bishop for you."

When the bishop was informed about Widow Riehl's need, he brought it before the church in the regular way. The church gave unanimous consent to help her. Thus it was not long until Deacon Jonas Peachey, assigned to look after the poor, came with money, provisions, and encouragement.

"Mary, I'm sure you'll be careful and make this go as far as possible. Help yourself as much as you can, but when you need wood or coal or food or money, just tell me. As you know, we give aid to our people who cannot provide for themselves, and we never let any go to the poorhouse. We take care of our own. So don't worry, Mary; we'll look out for you."

Mary thanked him and added, "I am so ashamed that I have to take help. But Lewis was sick a long time before he died, and it took just about all we had for doctor bills. I'm ashamed to let people know that I'm so poor. But one day I was up at Rosanna Yoder's at a quilting. She had such a good dinner that I just couldn't help mentioning it to her. I guess she told Little Crist right away, and he told the bishop. I'm so thankful that I'll never need to go to the poorhouse. I thank the good Lord every day."

When Mary saw Rosanna again, she inquired, "Did you tell Cristli about how poor I am, and did he tell the bishop?"

"Yes, I told Cristli, and he told the bishop. That's why it was brought before the church. Have they done anything for you?"

"Oh, my, yes. The deacon came the very next day after it was voted on in church and brought me a ham, a bushel of potatoes, a bag of flour, some apples, and ten dollars. Jonas said, 'Make this go as far as you can, but when you need more, we'll get it for you. We'll never let any member of our church go to the poorhouse. We'll look out for you.'

"I'll make that aid go as far as I can. I don't want to be a burden to the church, but just now I couldn't help it. I pray every day that the Lord will show me a way to make my own living, because I don't want to live off the church."

"Don't worry, Mary. There is plenty of alms money. Why, I don't believe anybody needed help in the past ten years. We might as well use the money. And, Mary, I would just as soon see you get some of that money as anybody I know. I'm sure you'll make it go as far as you can. But don't worry about it."

ᨠ ᨠ ᨠ

Joseph was now about fifteen years old and quite interested in school. Physiology had just been introduced. As he studied this subject, he took some delight in poking fun at his mother's powwowing. Educators did not believe in powwowing. Why should he?

When he said something disparaging about powwowing, Rosanna would smile. "Never you mind, Laddy. You'll need me someday."

It was Joseph's duty each Saturday to clean the stables. One Saturday, as he was hurrying to finish his work before dinner, he ran a dung fork into his foot. To save time, he did nothing about his wound till the work was finished and he could go into the house for dinner. Then he casually remarked, "Mother, I ran a dung fork into my foot."

"Well," warned his mother, "you'd better take care of it, or it might get sore."

"Oh, I'll just wait till after dinner."

By the time he had eaten his dinner, the pain in his foot was becoming almost unbearable. He went into the living room and lay on the sofa, hoping the pain would stop, but it didn't. Finally, Rosanna came and asked, "How's your foot?"

"It's hurting terribly."

Joseph knew his mother could powwow and stop that pain in a minute, but he had sided with educators who did not believe in powwowing. Now he was ashamed to ask her to powwow for his foot—until the pain became so severe that he could hardly stand it. With pride overcome by hurt, he begged, "Mother, could you powwow for this pain and take it away?"

"Yes, I can, if you want me to."

"Well, I wish you would."

Rosanna stroked her hand across the wound three times and repeated the prescribed words that allay pain. In about two minutes the pain was gone and Joseph fell asleep.

He never pooh-poohed powwowing again.

CHAPTER 20

The New House

B Y T H I S T I M E all the boys were married but Joseph. Being a great admirer of Levi, Joseph too decided to be a teacher. When he was twenty years old, he took the county examination, passed, and was assigned a school. Since Little Crist was now working at the tannery full time, no one would be left on the farm to do the work.

When this situation became apparent, Little Crist proposed, "Mother, what would you think of building a new house at the tannery, moving into it, and renting our place to some good farmer?"

Rosanna commented, "Work doesn't go so well

with me any more. I'd be in favor of it. With Joseph beginning to teach school, we'd have nothing but trouble here on the farm if we had to depend on hired help."

Davy Byler was agreed to this, too. The dampness in the tannery was giving him trouble with rheumatism. Crist bought him out, and Davy was free to do what he wished.

After planning the new house, the old house at the tannery was torn down and the new one begun. To avoid caring for stock in the winter, Little Crist held a sale of his farming implements and livestock in the fall of the year. By pushing the work on the new house, they were able to move into it in December.

The new house was a joy to Rosanna. There was still much work to be done—grading the yard, locating the garden, adding another coat of paint to the house, and planting flowers and shrubbery. Yet it was much more convenient. Little Crist now ate dinner at home instead of carrying his lunch, as before.

The house was as modern as an Amish house dared be. But Rosanna was sorry she could not have a bathroom, hot-water heat, a telephone, and electric lights. These things were forbidden by the church as "worldly devices" and were not tolerated. However, the new house was on the edge of the village, and its nearness to the stores and the post office made living seem much more pleasant and desirable.

The new house was not built with removable partitions to accommodate preaching. Cristli arranged with another farmer belonging to the Peachey Church to accommodate preaching services when it was their turn. Rosanna felt that she had done enough of that work during all her life, and now someone else could do the work of "taking preaching."

Joseph's school was only two miles away from home. He boarded with his pap and mother, helping in the evenings to get the new home in order. His first winter of teaching went well. But he soon saw that to have any hope for the best positions, he would have to obtain more education. At the end of the first winter, he went off to college to take a teacher's course. When he went away to school, many good Amish people were truly sorry.

Deacon Jonas Peachey, who felt that he was a special friend of the family, came to see Joseph and tried to persuade him not to go. "Joseph, I hear you're going away to college. I'm sorry to hear it. Don't you know that colleges are nothing but worldly organizations, and they'll destroy your faith? Paul plainly says, 'The wisdom of this world is foolishness with God' [1 Cor. 3:19]. So why offend God? At present you're leading a fine Christian life. But if you go to college, I'm afraid you'll lose your own soul."

Joseph heard all these words of kind advice. Yet in his heart, he felt he must go to college. When he went away to school, he decided that if he would observe several fundamental principles, he could prove to the Amish people that he was not losing his soul. Joseph resolved to live as fine a Christian life as possible, to retain his ability to speak the Pennsylvania German language fluently, and to maintain his physical strength and ability to do manual labor of the heaviest kind rapidly and well.

At the college he took part in all Christian activities. To prove his German-speaking ability, he wrote a poem in Pennsylvania German, "*Noch Denke* (Reminiscing)," and had it published in the home paper. During vacations he spoke Pennsylvania German to all the Amish people he met.

In order to keep physically fit in college, Joseph took an active part in athletics. When he came home for summer vacation, he would manage to take the team into the hayfield on his father's farm and set the pace. Little Crist had rented the farm, but he had agreed to make hay with the aid of Sam Kinkle's big six-horse team.

Joseph had learned that white clothing reflects the heat of the sun. So while pitching hay, he wore a white shirt, white duck trousers, and tennis shoes. This gave him sure footing and kept him cooler. He always put a good-sized Amishman on the other side of the wagon to pitch hay against him. Then he would work so fast that by evening, the husky fellow pitching against him would be exhausted.

His plan was to make his Amish co-worker say, "I don't see how that Joseph Yoder can pitch hay like he does. Why, he goes to college, and you'd think he'd get soft. But when he comes home, it takes a mighty good man to keep up with him in the hayfield."

That report soon spread the length of the valley, much to the student's credit.

If any farmer had some especially heavy work to do, Joseph let it be known that he would be glad to help. One day David R. Zook asked, "Joseph, do you know where I could get a good man to help load manure this week?"

"Yes, I'll help you," Joseph volunteered.

"You wouldn't help load manure, would you?"

"Sure, I will. I'll try to do a good day's work, too."

"Well, I'm surprised," said David, "but I'll be awful glad if you help me."

David's son, Milton, who loaded with Joseph, thought he would either show Joseph a fine pace in loading or at least keep up to him. The weather was hot. Joseph had the advantage in height and weight. At the end of the third day, the manure was all hauled out into the field. Milton decided that for the good of his health, he'd better take a few days' vacation.

For a long time after that, David Zook enjoyed telling how fast Joseph Yoder and Milton loaded manure for him. "Why, I hauled the manure into the field just outside the barnyard while they began another load, but I could never catch them. I hurried, too, but every time when I got to the barnyard with one load off, the new load stood ready to hitch to. It was the fastest manure loading ever done for me. I think these boys tried to play each other out."

Each time David retold the story, it was water on Joseph's wheel. These reports of efficient work went over the valley. People commented interestedly on his German poems. They also noticed Joseph's freedom in speaking Pennsylvania German to the Amish folks, old and young. With the good comments, Joseph felt that he was winning his point—holding the respect and friendship of the Amish people.

He was assured more fully of this one day when Crist Hooley of Ohio, a former valley boy, now an old man, was sitting on the Hill Store porch, visiting with

Preacher Nancy John Yoder. Joseph happened to walk by. He was fairly well dressed, and this attracted Crist Hooley's attention, so he asked, "Who is that young man, John?"

"Oh, that's Cristli Yoder's son Joseph."

"So tell me about him. He doesn't look quite like the other young Amishmen around here."

"Well, he goes to college, but Joseph is not like other young men who go to college. It does not spoil him at all. He's just as common as he ever was, and he's one of the best workers in the valley."

When Crist Hooley visited Little Crist a few days later, he mentioned to Joseph what Nancy John had said about him. Joseph was gratified to learn that his plan was working, that the Amish people looked upon him with respect and confidence.

At college, Joseph studied music and learned to write it. No one had ever put down notes for the tunes of the German chorales as sung by the Amish people in America. He wrote three hymns from hearing them sung by his father, Brother Yost, and Reuben Kauffman. Joseph jotted down the notes on a musical staff. Then he surprised the three men by singing these difficult chorales back to them at once—songs that had taken these singers years to learn by memory.

🙠 🙠 🙠

When Joseph finished his first term in school and came home, he found his mother troubled with shortness of breath and discomfort around the heart. Because Dr. Hudson had moved away, Dr. Bigelow was called. The doctor did not consider the trouble serious.

The family thought everything would soon be all right and were not overly concerned about her condition.

After the new house was completed, Rosanna had a great desire to have her sister and niece visit her once more from Philadelphia. She wrote, asking them to come up to Big Valley in July. Margaret, who had been married to William Reese and lived in Arizona for some years, had returned to the city. Her daughter, Mary, was now grown to young womanhood.

They wrote that they would come in July, and Rosanna was very happy. How different this visit would be from her other visits! Margaret had traveled up through the mountains to see Rosanna quite a number of times. On her first visit, she came from Reedsville by stage; now a railroad took its place. Then Rosanna lived on the farm amid the buzz of farmwork; now she lived in the quiet village setting.

Yet Margaret was filled with the same loving interest and concern that was evident when she first came. Now she felt that Rosanna's in-laws were her relatives, too, and the in-laws looked upon Margaret in the same way.

Margaret loved to go to see Sarah Byler, Crist's oldest sister, married to Yonie (Jonathan) Byler. Sarah always had beautiful flowers in the yard, in the garden, and in the house. Her rooms were immaculate, and the dinners she served were a joy to any city appetite.

Frequently Margaret also went to see Franey Byler, Crist's second sister, married to the beloved Uncle Davy. Franey, too, was a fine housekeeper, but she was not quite so interested in flowers as Sarah, nor did she keep her house quite so clean. It was remarkable how Margaret Reese, the well-dressed, sophisticated woman of the city, could sit and visit with these plain Amish women of the country, sharing mutual interest and enjoyment.

Margaret was somewhat alarmed at Rosanna's failing health, the attacks of shortness of breath, and her distress about the heart. They talked a good deal about the probable cause. Rosanna was aware that her condition was serious. When Margaret and Mary were about to return to the city, Rosanna asked, "If I should die soon, will you come to my funeral?"

"No," replied Margaret. "We've had a fine visit again, and I would rather remember you as you are now. But you will not die soon. I'm sure this heart and breathing condition will improve when you rest a while." The last statement was made to give Rosanna courage, for Margaret really was afraid that the end was not far off.

Joseph applied to be principal of the Milroy High School and was selected. The school had become rather disorderly through improper discipline, and Joseph, among other qualifications, was admired as a champion hay pitcher. But Joseph did not use his haying accomplishments to bring them to order.

Some wise professors had taught him that self-control, fairness in discipline, and firmness in decisions were the big factors in discipline. Joseph was determined to try these out to the limit. In a short time, pupils with whom former teachers had trouble voluntarily came to him and expressed appreciation for his methods. They pledged cooperation. That seemed like victory to him.

One Friday evening he came home, delighted with his success as a teacher, only to be met in the barnyard by his little niece, Lena, who reported, "Gramma very sick, Uncle Joseph."

Those childish words struck terror to his soul. Joseph put his horse away quickly, ran to the house, and found Rosanna quite ill, indeed. The doctor had given her strong medicine, and for two days she had been vomiting frequently.

Joseph ran to the corncrib, got an ear of corn, and shelled it. He asked the maid to roast the corn, put it through the coffee grinder, and make a tea of it as quickly as possible. She did so. When the tea was ready, Rosanna drank it, and in fifteen minutes the vomiting stopped almost entirely.

Seeing that, Joseph told his father, "Let's not give mother any more of that strong medicine that upsets her stomach so."

Little Crist agreed. Joseph sat by his mother's bedside all night to see that she lacked nothing that would contribute to her rest and comfort. When the doctor called next day, Joseph and Little Crist told him how the strong medicine had affected Rosanna. They asked if the doctor would mind if they called a homeopath.

"That's your privilege," stated the doctor.

The homeopathic doctor examined her carefully before he made his diagnosis. "Cristli, she's in the last stages of tuberculosis. All we can do is make her as comfortable as possible during her last days. She has not long to live."

Joseph marveled that his mother could not find a way to cure herself. After all, she had relieved so many people in pain and distress. The four sons took turns helping. Two at a time stayed by her bedside night and day so she would not want for anything. But she grew weaker and weaker until Saturday noon.

While her sister-in-law, Lizzie Hostetler, was at her bedside alone for a few minutes, Rosanna whispered, "If I get another attack of shortness of breath like I had this forenoon, it'll be the last. But don't tell the boys till I'm gone."

At two o'clock that afternoon, her breathing became difficult, then quite irregular, and finally stopped. In the presence of her husband and her four sons, her spirit left her body.

Rosanna was gone!

Little Crist and the boys were overwhelmed with grief. At first they could not bring themselves to believe that Mother, who had meant so much to them all their lives, could possibly leave them now. But it was true, and they tried to bear up under the sorrow.

Word quickly spread that Rosanna had passed away, and in a short time men and women of the church came in and took charge of everything. Two of the women washed and dressed the body. Four others looked after the cooking and baking for the dinner the day of the funeral.

Crist chose four men of the church as gravediggers and pallbearers. Levi Hartzler was asked to transport Rosanna's body to the cemetery on the day of the funeral. Other men provided preaching benches to fill the whole lower part of the house on the day of the funeral.

They asked Preacher Nancy John Yoder to preach

the funeral sermon and Sam Peachey to make the beginning *Anfang* (opening sermon). Still others went to see the undertaker about making the coffin and taking care of the legal matters relating to the death. They arranged that in the evening certain persons would come and sit up all night with the body.

Because it was not considered proper to make preparations for the funeral on Sunday, they decided that Rosanna's funeral services should be held on Tuesday at ten o'clock. That way all final preparations could be made by Monday.

On Sunday and Monday, many persons came to view the body. Crist and Joseph were somewhat surprised when three or four young girls from the village came to view Rosanna. One with tear-stained eyes commented, "She was so kind to me one time when I needed help that I just had to come and see her once more."

By Monday afternoon all preparations for the funeral were completed. The bread and pies were baked, the meat was dressed, and the fruits and vegetables were assembled and cleaned. Late in the evening, Crist Peachey (not the bishop), who lived on the farm, brought the preaching benches and placed most of them so that there would not be much to do in the morning.

Another group agreed to stay up all night with the body as others had done on Saturday and Sunday nights. So everything was attended to and made ready through the willing services of friends and neighbors, mostly members of Rosanna's church.

The funeral took place on October twelve. It was a

beautiful sunny day, but already autumn had touched the green of the foliage and turned it to flaming red or somber brown. A slight autumn haze dimmed the mountaintops, and the lazy tinkle of a distant sheep bell lulled the landscape into rest.

The sky was cloudless, and the haze-dimmed sunshine filled the valley with beauty and peace. Only the lowing of cattle grazing on the hillside or the muffled bark of a distant dog now and then broke the solemn stillness that hung over Rosanna's house that day.

At nine o'clock all those who were helping in any way were already present to see that nothing was overlooked. By nine-thirty many people had gathered in the yard and were coming into the house to find seats in the various rooms.

A few minutes before ten, the family and the closest relatives took seats near the coffin, which was placed in the downstairs bedroom. There were Little Crist and Joseph, the older three sons with their wives and children, along with uncles, aunts, cousins, and some unrelated friends. By that time all the other available benches and chairs in the house were occupied. Doors were left open between rooms so all could hear the service.

The men all sat with their hats on, according to custom. When Sam Peachey arose, all hats were removed. He spoke in a general way for about fifteen or twenty minutes, and then everyone except the family knelt in silent prayer. After the prayer, all stood while the deacon read a suitable Scripture. Then all were seated.

Nancy John Yoder stood up to preach the funeral

sermon. He had lived on an adjoining farm during Rosanna's entire married life. The Amish rarely indulge in eulogy, but he did say some fine things about her unselfish generosity, her faithfulness in the church, and her consistent Christian life.

Only Yost had joined his mother's church. The other three boys had joined the Church Amish (later called Amish Mennonites), which was more ready for change and met in church buildings instead of homes. To some extent, this departure was held against them.

Thus the younger boys, Levi, John, and Joseph, wondered whether Preacher John would count them as a captive audience. He might give them a tongue-lashing for their disobedience in not joining the church of their parents. But Preacher John had been present many times during Rosanna's sickness. He had seen how her sons had taken care of her day and night.

Instead of chiding them for not joining the House Amish (Old Order Amish), he made an unequivocal statement: "Some of these sons may be open to criticism for their church affiliations. But I want to say that I was here almost every day during Rosanna's last sickness. With all candor, I can say that I never saw sons anywhere take care of their mother like these four young men did.

"They were by her bedside every minute, and I am glad to bear testimony to their faithfulness and dedication. One of these sons has gone away to college. But it is a high credit to him and his family when we notice him come home with increased loyalty and devotion to his parents."

In order to impress the bereaved ones with the

necessity of righteous living, the preacher as usual gave some rather personal admonitions. He called attention to the vacant chair, the voice gone forever, the broken tie of love and friendship, and the preparation necessary to meet the departed loved one in the hereafter. This personal admonition was filled with sadness, and it was rather hard for the bereaved to bear up under it.

According to Amish tradition, there was no singing at the funeral; singing would have increased the emotional intensity. At the close of the main sermon, the audience knelt while the minister read the prayer from the prayerbook, since the House Amish never offer original prayers. When the prayer was over, all arose, stood for the benediction, and then quietly passed out of the house.

Delegated men removed the benches from the house, and the pallbearers placed the coffin in the kitchen between the front and back doors for final viewing. The men came in the front door and went out the back door. When they had all passed through, the women came in the back door and passed out the front door.

During all this time, the relatives stood opposite the coffin while one of the ministers read a hymn in German (high German, as usual for services, not Pennsylvania German). The title of the hymn frequently used on this occasion is *"Gute Nacht, mein liebe Kinder* (good night, my beloved children)," and it is probably the saddest hymn in the German language.

When the family and the relatives had looked upon Rosanna's face for the last time, the pallbearers closed the coffin. Men of the church did all this as a loving service since the Amish never have a paid undertaker officiating at their funerals. Then the pallbearers placed the coffin on Levi Hartzler's spring wagon, to which Levi had hitched his gentlest horse.

The men who had charge of the teams brought up Little Crist's carriage for him and Joseph, and Aunt Katie and Uncle Jacob. Yost's and Levi's and John's carriages followed in the order of their age. Then came Uncle Eli, Uncle Yonie, Uncle Davy, and Uncle Joe with their families. After them trailed close friends, until a string of carriages a half mile long followed Rosanna to her last resting place.

This was a loving tribute of respect and admiration. The Amish typically do not express much emotion. But when those many friends and recipients of her favors and talents looked upon her face for the last time that day, many eyes shed tears of profound sorrow.

When the funeral procession reached the cemetery, the pallbearers carried the coffin to the burial spot. The relatives and friends gathered around the grave, the coffin was lowered, another German hymn was read, and the minister said, "Let us all pray the Lord's Prayer in silence." All hats were removed.

When the prayer was finished, the pallbearers filled the grave, shaping the dirt into a mound on top, and placing temporary head and foot stones. The people slowly went back to their carriages. Relatives and many friends returned to the house, where dinner awaited them.

When dinner was over and the house set in order

again, the people returned to their homes. Little Crist and Joseph were vividly impressed with the truth of the preacher's words—the empty chair and the voice that was silent.

In a few days Joseph returned to his school duties, and Little Crist gradually resumed his work in the tannery. With the aid of a housekeeper, they maintained for many years the home which Rosanna loved so dearly but was unable to enjoy for long.

Rosanna had taken a special interest in the beautiful plants and flowers in the house and the yard. The garden rose arbors and flower beds and potted plants bore eloquent testimony to her loving attention. In time, these began to fade somewhat for lack of proper care. Little Crist, who had never been interested in flowers before, could not endure the thought of Rosanna's flowers dying. He began to water them and care for them as best he could.

As they revived and became luxurious again, his interest in flowers grew, and he determined that Rosanna's flowers should never die. Little Crist began pruning and fertilizing and propagating her flowers until he was as much interested in them as any gardener. To his credit, for many years, until Little Crist's own passing, Rosanna's original flowers bloomed to tell the beautiful story of this couple's love and devotion.

When Little Crist's hand became too feeble to care for Rosanna's flowers, others followed his instructions. Eventually the final caravan carried Little Crist away to rest beside Rosanna in the Locust Grove Cemetery. Folks shed tears for his charity and consideration. The flowers seemed to join the quiet mourners and mutely beckon, "Good-bye, Cristli, and God bless you."

Thus closed the last chapter in the life of Rosanna of the Amish, and Little Crist, her faithful husband. But the memory of their devotion to each other and to the church, and the stories of their untiring kindness to all who were in need—these will linger in the beautiful Kishacoquillas Valley for many years to come.

Supplement

THE AMISH described in this volume are a conservative people. They still hold to the belief that most new things and innovations are worldly and wrong. That is why they have kept their manner of dress and mode of worship almost without change for three centuries. Accordingly, most do not use automobiles, telephones, electric lights, centralized heating, bathrooms, or any such modern conveniences.

However, in the Kishacoquillas Valley are four or five distinct groups of Amish having the same articles of faith (Dordrecht, 1632). The Rennos and Bylers will commune together, but some of these groups have no church fellowship with each other. Their practices vary somewhat. The most progressive group (the Beachy Amish) allows some conveniences. Members of the various groups mingle rather freely at weddings and funerals and in business affairs, but in church affairs only two have intergroup dealings.

The Beachy Amish worship in a church building, but the more traditional groups still hold their services in their houses, or in barns if the house is not large enough. Only this most progressive group holds evening services and Sunday schools in addition to morning worship. Alongside the Amish groups in Big Valley are Old Order Mennonites and other Mennonites, who have church buildings. Mennonites hold to the same basic Anabaptist confession of faith as the Amish, but most have accepted modern conveniences.

To the credit of the Amish people, they are independent of government social-assistance programs. They pay their taxes, obey the law, and see to it that none of their people go on relief or become a burden to society. A fine example of this took place some years ago when officials from Washington came to Lancaster County, where many Old Order Amish live. The government agents asked the Amish farmers to sign contracts, thus promising to curtail their crop acreage.

The Amish farmers replied, "No, we don't sign government contracts. We obey the law. Tell us what you want us to do, and we'll do it."

The officials were perplexed when the Amish agreed to obey the law but refused to sign contracts. They returned to Washington, not knowing just what to do about it. In the autumn they returned to Lancaster County to see whether these Amish farmers had obeyed the law. They found the crops restricted to exactly the acreage required.

Then the federal agents offered, "We'll pay you for the crops you didn't raise."

The Amish farmers, however, responded, "No, we don't take money for what we don't do." They were immovable in refusing to take money from the government.

Among the more change-oriented Amish in the last nineteenth century and the early twentieth, some young men and a few young women went to college to teach or go into business. There now are no college students among the Old Order Amish groups.

The Amish are often considered clannish because they live in tight-knit communities and do not associate freely with other people. They plan to live within easy buggy-driving range of each other when possible.

As of 1940, there were approximately 35,000 baptized members of the Old Order Amish Church in the United States and Canada. By 1995, counting unbaptized children, their number increased to about 150,000 and is set to double every twenty years. The largest groups live in Pennsylvania, Ohio, and Indiana. More recently the Amish established many congregations (districts) in Wisconsin, Michigan, Kentucky, Missouri, Illinois, New York, and Ontario.

They believe in nonconformity, nonresistance, nonswearing of oaths, and separation from sins of the world. Most of them are in farming or related small businesses, sometimes not making much money. But since their wants are few, they are seldom poor.

The Amish are law-abiding, quiet, and sober. If everybody would live as they do, there would be no need for standing armies or police courts.

Books on the Amish

(From Herald Press, unless otherwise noted)

Beiler, Edna. *Mattie Mae*. 1967.

Bender, Carrie. Miriam's Journal Series: *A Fruitful Vine*, 1993; *A Winding Path*, 1994; *A Joyous Heart*, 1994.

_____, *Whispering Brook Farm*. 1995.

Bender, Esther. *Katie and the Lemon Tree*. 1994.

Borntrager, Mary Christner. Ellie's People Series: *Ellie,* 1988; *Rebecca,* 1989; *Rachel,* 1990; *Daniel,* 1991; *Reuben,* 1992; *Andy,* 1993; *Polly,* 1994; *Sarah,* 1995.

Committee of Amish Women. *Amish Cooking*. 1980.

Denlinger, A. Martha. *Real People: Amish and Mennonites in Lancaster County, Pennsylvania*. Rev. ed. 1993.

Granick, Eve Wheatcroft. *The Amish Quilt*. Good Books, 1989.

Hostetler, John A. *Amish Children: Their Education in Family, School, and Community*. Holt, Rinehart, Winston, 1992.

_____. *Amish Life*. 1983.

_____. *Amish Society*. 4th ed. Johns Hopkins, 1993.

Kauffman, S. Duane. *Mifflin County Amish and Mennonite Story, 1791-1991.* Belleville: Mifflin County Mennonite Historical Society, 1991.

Kline, David. *Great Possessions: An Amish Farmer's Journal.* North Point Press, 1990.

Kraybill, Donald B. *The Puzzles of Amish Life.* Good Books, 1990.

_____. *The Riddle of Amish Culture.* Johns Hopkins, 1989.

Längin, Bernd G. *Plain and Amish: An Alternative to Modern Pessimism.* 1994.

Miller, Jewel. *Whisper of Love.* 1991.

Miller, Levi. *Our People: The Amish and Mennonites of Ohio.* Rev. ed. 1992.

Nolt, Steven M. *A History of the Amish.* Good Books, 1992.

Raber, Ben J. *The New American Almanac.* Baltic, Ohio: Raber's Book Store, annual. Lists Amish congregations.

Scott, Stephen. *Plain Buggies.* Good Books, 1981.

_____. *The Amish Wedding.* Good Books, 1988.

_____. *Why Do They Dress That Way?* Good Books, 1986.

Scott, Stephen and Kenneth Pellman. *Living Without Electricity.* Good Books, 1990.

Smucker, Barbara. *Amish Adventure.* 1983.

Yoder, Joseph W. *Rosanna of the Amish.* Yoder Publishing Co., 1940; 3rd ed., Herald Press, 1995.

_____. *Rosanna's Boys.* Yoder Publishing Co., 1948. Reprinted by Choice Books, 1995.

Yoder, Paton. *Tradition and Transition: Amish Mennonites and Old Order Amish, 1800-1900.* 1991.

Yoder, Paul M., et al. *Four Hundred Years with the Ausbund.* 1964.

The Author

JOSEPH WARREN YODER was born to Christian Z. Yoder and Rosanna McGonegal Yoder on September 22, 1872, at Belleville, Pennsylvania. He was married to Emily A. Lane of Pittsburgh on February 18, 1932. In the story of this book, he is Joseph, the youngest son of Rosanna and Little Crist.

From 1899 to 1900, Yoder attended Northwestern University and won the freshman oratorical contest. While taking further work at Juniata College, he was the first appointed athletic director, a member of the first varsity quartet, and on the first debating team. In 1904 he received his A.B. degree from Juniata College, and his quartet gave a concert at commencement time.

His teaching career started in 1895 near Reeds-ville, Pennsylvania, where he served as principal of the Milroy High School for two years. In Indiana at the Elkhart Institute (now Goshen College), he taught English and music in 1897-1898, and Greek and English in 1900-1901.

From 1904 on, Yoder engaged in teacher institute work and became one of the best-known music directors among the schoolteachers of Pennsylvania, Indiana, Illinois, and Virginia. From 1906 to 1919, he taught music and logic at Lock Haven Teachers College.

Because of Yoder's musical ability, he was frequently sought to lead evangelistic singing for the Church of the Brethren, Methodists, and Mennonites. He also taught many music classes for these denominations, as well as for the River Brethren and the Amish Mennonites.

"J. W." expressed his creativity by writing poetry, adding music to poems, and publishing them in songbooks he compiled. He kept himself physically fit and often slept outside. According to the 1942 *Belleville Times*, "Singer Joe" advised others to "be careful what you eat, get plenty of rest, sufficient exercise, and breathe all the fresh air you can."

In 1948 Yoder received a citation of honor from the Pennsylvania German Society for his books on Amish life. His works include *Amische Lieder, Rosanna's Boys, Amish Traditions,* and this fascinating true story, *Rosanna of the Amish.* The author himself was born into an Old Order Amish home, knew Amish customs intimately, and was well qualified to write this volume.

Amish typically do not give permission for others to photograph them. Once J. W. managed to snap a photo of his elderly Amish father, Cristli, by telling him he wanted to take a picture of the cat—which just happened to be beside his dad.

In his later years, J. W. tried unsuccessfully to get the Amish to use his *Amische Leider*. It recorded tune notations for selected German hymns and was intended to preserve the Amish musical tradition. In *Amish Traditions* (1950), he set out to convince the Old Order Amish of the unscriptural nature of shunning, but they rejected that message.

Joseph W. Yoder died on November 13, 1956, survived by his wife. His funeral services were held at the Maple Grove Mennonite Church near Belleville, of which he was a member.

Information on Yoder and Big Valley churches is available in S. Duane Kauffman's *Mifflin County Amish and Mennonite Story, 1791-1991* (Belleville, Pa.: Mifflin County Mennonite Historical Society, 1991). Kauffman's book (pages 245-257) supplied some details of this description, including the "Singer Joe" quotation. A few of his poems and songs are reprinted on pages 396-401 of the same volume.

As Kauffman says (245), truly Joseph W. Yoder was "an extraordinary literary genius, . . . author, musician, educator, and lecturer."